PSYCHO

Victim

For a moment it seemed to Sister Cupertine that the blurred, bending figure beside her resembled some sort of bird—a bird of prey. But only for a moment.

Then the figure straightened and turned, just as the lightning came.

In its glare Sister Cupertine saw the contorted face beneath the coif and the upraised hand holding the gleaming tire iron as it swung forward.

She never heard the thunder. . . .

Also by Robert Bloch

Psycho

Published by
WARNER BOOKS

PSYCHO II

ROBERT BLOCH

WARNER BOOKS

A Warner Communications Company

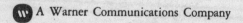

This book
is for

Stella Loeb Bloch

with
life-long love.

PSYCHO II

One

Norman Bates stared out of the library window, trying hard to avoid seeing the bars.

Just ignore them, that was the trick. Ignorance is bliss. But there was no bliss, and tricks didn't work here behind the bars of the State Hospital. Once it was the State Hospital for the Criminally Insane; now we live in a more enlightened age and they don't call it that anymore. But there were still bars on the windows and he was still inside, looking out.

Stone walls do not a prison make, nor iron bars a cage. The poet Richard Lovelace said that, way back in the seventeenth century, a long time ago. And Norman had been sitting here a long time—not three hundred years, but it felt like centuries.

Still, if he had to sit, the library was probably the

best place, and serving as the librarian was an easy chore. Very few of the patients bothered with books and he had plenty of time to read on his own. That was how he'd encountered Richard Lovelace and all the others: sitting here undisturbed in the cool semi-darkness of the library, day after day. They'd even given him a desk of his own to show that they trusted him, knew he was responsible.

Norman was grateful for that. But at times like this, with the sun shining and birds singing in the streets outside his window, he realized that Lovelace was a liar. The birds were free, but Norman was in a cage.

He'd never told Dr. Claiborne because he didn't want to upset him, but he couldn't help feeling this way. It was so unjust, so unfair.

Whatever had occurred to bring him here—whatever he was *told* had occurred, if it was true—happened a long time ago. Long ago in another country, and the wench was dead. He knew now that he was Norman Bates, not his mother. He wasn't crazy anymore.

Of course, no one was crazy nowadays. No one, whatever he may have done, was a maniac; just mentally disturbed. But who wouldn't be disturbed, shut away in a cage with a bunch of lunatics? Claiborne didn't call them that, but Norman knew a madman when he saw one, and through the years he'd seen many. Screwballs, they used to call them. But now television had the last word—wackos, weirdos, freakos who've gone bananas. What was it the standup comics said on the talk shows about not playing with a full deck?

Well, his deck was full, even though the cards were stacked against him. And he wasn't buying this humorous terminology they used to describe a serious illness. Strange how everyone tried to disguise truth with nonsense. Like the slang for death: kicking the bucket, wiped out, snuffed, wasted, blown away. The light touch to dispel the heavy fear.

What's in a name? *Sticks and stones will break my bones, but names will never hurt me.* Another quotation, but not from Richard Lovelace. Mother was the one who used to say that, when Norman was just a little boy. But Mother was dead now and he was still alive. Alive and in a cage. Knowing this, facing up to the truth, proved he was sane.

If they'd only realized it, they'd have tried him for murder, found him guilty, sentenced him to a term in prison. Then he'd have been out in a few years, seven or eight at the most. Instead they said he was psychotic, but he wasn't; *they* were the crazy ones, locking up a sick man for life and letting murderers run free.

Norman stood up and walked over to the window. When he pressed close, his range of vision was no longer limited by the bars. Now he could look down on the grounds, sparkling in the bright sunshine of a Sunday afternoon in spring. The birdsongs were clearer now, soothing, more melodious. Sun and song in harmony, the music of the spheres.

When he'd first come here, there'd been no sunlight and no song—only the blackness and the shrieking. The blackness was inside him, a place where he could hide from reality, and the shrieking was the voice of demons searching him out to threat-en and accuse. But Dr. Claiborne found a way to reach him in the darkness, and he'd exorcised the demons. His voice—the voice of sanity—had stilled the shrieking. It had taken a long time for Norman to come out of his hiding place and listen to the voice of reason, the voice that told him he was not his own mother, that he was—how did they say it?—his own person. A person who had done harm to others, but never knowingly. So there could be no guilt, no blame. To understand this was to be healed, accepting it was the cure.

And cured he was. No restraint jacket, no padded cell, no sedation. As librarian he had access to the books he'd always loved, and television opened another window on the world, a window without bars. Life was comfortable here. And he was used to being a loner.

But on days like this he found himself missing the contact with other people. Real flesh-and-blood people, not characters in books or images on a tube. Aside from Claiborne, doctors and nurses and orderlies were transient presences. And now that he'd completed his task, Dr. Claiborne spent most of his time with other patients.

Norman couldn't do that. Now that he was himself again, he couldn't relate to the crazies. Their mumbling, grimacing, gesturing antics disturbed him, and he preferred solitude to their society. That was the one thing Claiborne couldn't change, though he'd certainly tried hard enough. It was Dr. Claiborne who'd urged Norman to participate in the amateur theatrical program here, and for a while it was an interesting challenge. At least he'd felt safe onstage,

12

with the footlights separating him from his audience. Up there he was in control, making them laugh or cry at will. The greatest thrill of all came when he took the lead in *Charley's Aunt*—playing the role in drag, playing so well that they cheered and applauded his performance—but all the while knowing that it *was* just a performance, pretense, make-believe.

That was what Dr. Claiborne said afterward, and only then did Norman realize this had all been arranged, a deliberate test of his ability to function. *You should be proud of yourself*, Claiborne told him.

But there was something Claiborne didn't realize, something Norman didn't tell him. The moment of fear that came toward the end, just before the hero's disguise was discovered. The moment when, simpering and swishing and coquetting with tossing curls, Norman lost himself in the part. The moment when he *was* Charley's Aunt—except that the fan in his hand was no longer a fan but a knife. And Charley's Aunt became a real live woman, an older woman, like Mother.

The moment of fear—or the moment of truth?

Norman didn't know. He didn't want to know. He just wanted to give up amateur theatricals for good.

Now, staring out through the window, he noted that the sunshine was fading rapidly into an overcast; thunderheads hovered on the horizon, and the trees bordering the parking lot shivered in the chill of rising wind. Warbling gave way to the discord of fluttering wings as the birds rose from bobbing branches to swoop and scatter against the darkening sky.

It wasn't the coming of the clouds that disturbed them. They left because the cars were arriving,

13

pulling into the parking spaces on the lot below. And their occupants emerged, moving toward the entrance of the hospital, just as they did during visiting hours every Sunday afternoon.

Oh, Mommy, look at the funny man!

Now, Junior, you mustn't say such things! Remember what I told you—don't feed the crazies.

Norman shook his head. It wasn't right to be thinking like that. These visitors were friends, family, coming here because they cared.

But not for him.

Years ago the reporters had come, but Dr. Claiborne hadn't let him see them, not even after he'd snapped out of it. And now nobody came.

Most of the people he'd known were dead. Mother, the Crane girl, and that detective, Arbogast. He was alone now, and all he could do was watch the strangers arrive. A few men, a few children, but mostly women. Wives, sweethearts, sisters, mothers, bringing their gifts and their love.

Norman scowled down at them. These people meant nothing to him, brought nothing to him. All they did was scare away the birds. And that was cruel, because he'd always liked having birds around, even the ones he'd stuffed and mounted years ago when he was interested in taxidermy. It wasn't just a hobby with him; he'd had a real feeling for them. *Saint Francis of Assisi*.

Odd. What made him think of that?

Glacing down again, he encountered the answer. The big birds below, moving away from the van in the parking lot, close to the outer gates. Squinting,

14

he could even make out the lettering on the side of the van: *Sacred Order of the Little Sisters of Charity.*

Now the birds were almost directly beneath him. Two big black-and-white penguins, waddling up the walk toward the entrance. Suppose they'd come all the way from the South Pole just to see him.

But that was a crazy idea.

And Norman wasn't crazy anymore.

Two

The penguins entered the hospital and approached the lobby reception desk. The short, bespectacled one leading the way was Sister Cupertine and the tall, younger one was Sister Barbara.

Sister Barbara didn't think of herself as a penguin. Right now she didn't think of herself at all. Her thoughts were centered on the people here, these poor unfortunate people.

That's what they were, she must remember: not inmates, but basically people very much like herself. This had been one of the things they'd stressed in psychology class, and it certainly was a fundamental precept in religious training. *There but for the grace of God go I*. And if the grace of God had brought her here to them, then she must bear His word and His comfort.

But Sister Barbara had to admit that at the moment she wasn't entirely comfortable. After all, she was new to the Order and she'd never been on a mission of charity before, let alone one that would take her to an asylum.

It had been Sister Cupertine who suggested their journey together, and for an obvious reason; she needed someone to drive her. Sister Cupertine had been coming here once a month for years with Sister Loretta, but Sister Loretta was ill now with influenza. Such a tiny woman, and so frail—God grant her a speedy recovery.

Sister Barbara fingered her rosary, giving thanks for her own stamina. A big, healthy girl like you, Mama always said. *A big, healthy girl like you shouldn't have any trouble finding a decent husband after I'm gone.* But Mama had been too kind. The big, healthy girl was just a klutz, lacking the face and figure or even the basic femininity necessary to attract any man, be his intentions decent or indecent. So, after Mama passed away, she was left alone until the call came. Then, suddenly, the way opened; she answered the call, made her novitiate, found her vocation. Thank God for that.

And thank God for Sister Cupertine now, greeting the little receptionist at the desk with such confidence, introducing her while they waited for the superintendant to come out of his office down the hall. Presently she saw him as he emerged from the corridor beyond, wearing a light topcoat and carrying an overnight bag in his left hand.

Dr. Steiner was a short, bald-headed man who cultivated a fringe of bushy sideburns to compensate for his cranial alopecia, and a bulging paunch to distract attention from his lack of height. But who was Sister Barbara to pass judgment on him or guess at his motivations? She wasn't a psych major anymore; she'd dropped out of school in her last year, when Mama died, and now all those head-games must be put aside forever.

Actually, Dr. Steiner proved to be quite pleasant And as a professional, he had obviously recognized her shyness and was doing his best to put her at her ease.

But it was the second man, the other doctor who followed Steiner out of his office to join them, who really succeeded in that task. The moment Sister Barbara saw him, she consciously relaxed.

"You know Dr. Claiborne, don't you?" Steiner was addressing Sister Cupertine, who nodded her acknowledgment.

"And this is Sister Barbara." Steiner turned to her, gesturing toward the tall, curly-haired younger man. "Sister, I'd like you to meet Dr. Claiborne, my associate."

The tall man extended his hand. His grip was warm and so was his smile.

"Dr. Claiborne is something you don't encounter very often," Steiner said. "A genuine non-Jewish psychiatrist."

Claiborne grinned. "You're forgetting Jung," he said.

"I'm forgetting a lot of things." Steiner glanced at the clock on the wall behind the reception desk, his expression sobering. "I should be halfway to the airport by now."

He turned, shifting the overnight bag to his right hand. "You're going to have to excuse me," he said. "I've got a meeting scheduled with the state board first thing in the morning, and the four-thirty flight is the only one out of here until tomorrow noon. So, with your permission, I'll leave you with Dr. Claiborne here. As of now, he's in charge."

"Of course." Sister Cupertine bobbed her head quickly. "You go right ahead."

Glancing at the younger man, Steiner started toward the entranceway. Dr. Claiborne went with him, and for a moment the two halted before the door. Steiner spoke rapidly to his companion in low tones, then nodded and made his exit.

Dr. Claiborne turned and walked back to the sisters. "Sorry to keep you waiting," he said.

"Don't apologize." Sister Cupertine's voice was cordial, but Sister Barbara noted the sudden furrowing of the forehead behind the masking frames of her thick glasses. "Perhaps we'd better postpone our visit until next time. You must have enough to look after here without worrying about us."

"No problem." Dr. Claiborne reached into his jacket pocket and pulled out a small notepad. "Here's the list of those patients you asked for on the phone." Tearing off the top sheet, he extended it to the older woman.

The furrow vanished as she studied the names scrawled upon the white rectangle. "Tucker, Hoffman, and Shaw I know," she said. "But who's Zander?"

"A recent arrival. Tentative diagnosis, involutional melancholia."

"Whatever that means." There was a slight edge to Sister Cupertine's voice now as the furrow returned, and before she quite realized it, Sister Barbara found herself speaking.

"Severe depression," she said. "Guilt feelings, anxiety, somatic preoccupations—"

Conscious of Dr. Claiborne's sudden stare, she faltered. Her companion gave him an apologetic smile. "Sister Barbara studied psychology in college."

"And did quite well at it, I'd say."

Sister Barbara found herself blushing. "Not really— it's just that I've always been interested in what happens to people—so many problems—"

"But so few solutions." Claiborne nodded. "That's why I'm here."

Sister Cupertine's mouth tightened, and the younger woman wished she had kept her own mouth tight instead. It had been wrong to upstage her that way.

She wondered if Dr. Claiborne could read body language. No matter, because Sister Cupertine was verbalizing now.

"And that's why *I'm* here," she said. "Maybe I don't know very much about psychology, but sometimes I think that a few kind words can do more good than all this fancy talk."

"Exactly." Dr. Claiborne's smile stroked her furrow away. "I appreciate that, and I know our patients appreciate it even more. Sometimes a visitor from outside can do more for their morale in a few hours than we're able to accomplish in months of analysis. That's why I'd like you to see Mr. Zander after you look in on your regulars today. As far as we can learn he has no living relatives. I can get you a copy of his case history if you like."

"That won't be necessary." Sister Cupertine was smiling again, very much her usual take-charge self. "We'll just talk, and he can tell me all about himself. Where can I find him?"

"Four-eighteen, right across from Tucker's room," Dr. Claiborne said. "Ask the floor nurse to take you in."

"Thank you." The cowled head turned. "Come along, Sister."

Sister Barbara hesitated. She knew what she wanted to say; she'd been rehearsing it in her mind all during the drive here. But should she risk offending Sister Cupertine again?

Well, now or never.

"I wonder if you'd mind if I stayed here with Dr. Claiborne? There are a few things I'd like to ask him about the therapy program—"

There it was, the warning furrow. Sister Cupertine cut in quickly. "We really mustn't impose anymore. Perhaps later, when he's not so busy."

"Please." Dr. Claiborne shook his head. "We always clear our schedule during visiting hours. With your permission, I'd be happy to answer the sister's questions."

"That's very kind of you," said Sister Cupertine. "But are you sure—"

"My pleasure," Dr. Claiborne told her. "Now don't worry. If she doesn't find you upstairs, you can meet her again here in the lobby at five."

"Very well." Sister Cupertine turned away, but not

before the eyes behind the thick lenses flashed a message to her companion. *The five o'clock meeting will be followed by a lecture period on the subject of duty and obedience to superiors.*

For a moment Sister Barbara's resolution wavered; then Dr. Claiborne's voice put an end to indecision.

"All right, Sister. Would you like me to show you around for a while? Or would you prefer to get down to business immediately?"

"Business?"

"You're breaking the rules." Dr. Claiborne grinned. "Only a qualified psychiatrist is permitted to answer a question with another question."

"Sorry." Sister Barbara watched the older woman enter an elevator down the hall, then turned to him with a smile of relief.

"Don't be. Just ask what you've been meaning to ask me all along."

"How did you know?"

"Merely an educated guess." The grin broadened. "Another privilege we qualified psychiatrists enjoy." He gestured. "Go ahead."

Again, a moment of hesitation. Should she? Could she? Sister Barbara took a deep breath.

"You have a patient here named Norman Bates?"

"You know about him?" The grin faded. "Most people don't, I'm happy to say."

"Happy?"

"Figure of speech." Dr. Claiborne shrugged. "No, to be honest, Norman's rather special in my book. And that's not a figure of speech."

"You've written a book about him?"

"I plan to, someday. I've been accumulating material ever since I took over his treatment from Dr. Steiner."

They had left the lobby now, and Dr. Claiborne was leading her down the right-hand corridor as they spoke. Passing a glass-walled visiting area, she noted a family group—mother, father, and teenaged boy, probably a brother—clustered around a fair-haired young girl in a wheelchair. The girl, who sat quietly, her pale face smiling up at her visitors as they chattered away, might very well have passed for a convalescent patient in any ordinary hospital. But this was not an ordinary hospital, Sister Barbara reminded herself, and that pale, smiling face concealed a dark, unsmiling secret.

She turned her attention to Dr. Claiborne as they moved on. "What sort of treatment—electroconvulsive therapy?"

Dr. Claiborne shook his head. "That was Steiner's recommendation when I came on the case. I disagreed. What's the necessity, when the patient is already passive to the point of catatonia? The problem was to bring Norman out of amnesic fugue, not increase his withdrawal."

"Then you found other ways to cure him."

"Norman isn't cured. Not in the clinical or even the legal sense of the term. But we did get rid of the symptoms. Good old-fashioned hypnotic-regression techniques, without narcosynthesis or any shortcuts. Just plain slugging away, questions and answers. Of course, we've learned a lot more about multiple-personality disorders and the disassociative reaction in recent years."

"'I take it you're saying Norman doesn't think he's his mother anymore.'"

"Norman is Norman. And I think he accepts himself as such. If you recall, when the mother-personality took over, he committed murders as a transvestite. He's aware of that now, even though he still has no conscious memory of such episodes. The material surfaced under hypnosis and we discussed content after the sessions, but he'll never truly remember. It's just that he no longer denies reality. He's experienced catharsis."

"But without abreaction."

"Exactly." Dr. Claiborne glanced at her sharply. "You really studied your texts, didn't you?"

Sister Barbara nodded. "What's the prognosis?"

"I've already told you. We've discontinued intensive analysis—no point in expecting any further major breakthroughs. But he's functioning now without restraint or sedation. Of course, we don't risk letting him wander outside on the grounds. I put him in charge of the library here; that way he has at least some degree of freedom combined with responsibility. He spends most of his time reading."

"It sounds like a lonely life."

"Yes, I'm aware of that. But there's not much more we can do for him. He has no relatives, no personal friends. And lately, with our patient overload here, I haven't been able to spend much time with him in just casual visiting."

Sister Barbara's hand strayed to her rosary beads and she took another deep breath.

"Could I see him?"

Dr. Claiborne halted, staring at her.

"Why?"

She forced herself to meet his gaze. "You say he's lonely. Isn't that reason enough?"

He shook his head. "Believe me, I can understand your empathy—"

"It's more than that. This is our vocation, the reason Sister Cupertine and I are here. To help the helpless, befriend the friendless."

"And perhaps convert them to your faith?"

"Don't you approve of religion?" Sister Barbara said.

Dr. Claiborne shrugged. "My beliefs are irrelevant. But I can't run the risk of upsetting my patients."

"Patients?" The words came in a rush now, unbidden. "If you had any empathy yourself, you wouldn't think of Norman Bates as a patient! He's a human being—a poor, lonely, confused human being who doesn't even understand the reason why he's shut away here. All he knows is that nobody cares about him."

"*I* care."

"Do you? Then give him a chance to realize that others care too."

Dr. Clairborne sighed softly. "All right. I'll take you to him."

"Thank you." As he led her along the hall and into a side corridor, her voice softened. "Doctor—"

"Yes?"

"I'm sorry for coming on so strong."

"Don't be." Dr. Claiborne's voice had softened in turn as he replied, and here in the dimness of the corridor he looked suddenly drained and spent. "Sometimes it helps to get chewed out a little. Starts the adrenaline flowing again."

He smiled, pausing as they reached the double door at the far end of the hall. "Here we are. The library."

Sister Barbara took her third deep breath for the day, or tried to. The air was moist, muggy, absolutely still, and yet there was movement somewhere—a throbbing, pulsing rhythm so intense that for a moment she felt quite giddy. Involuntarily her hand went in search of the rosary beads, and it was then that she discovered the source of the sensation. Her heart was pounding.

"You all right?" Dr. Claiborne glanced at her quickly.

"Of course."

Inwardly, Sister Barbara was none too certain. Why had she insisted? Was it really compassion that moved her, or just foolish pride—the pride that goeth before a fall?

"Nothing to worry about," Dr. Claiborne said. "I'm coming with you."

The throbbing ebbed.

Dr. Claiborne turned and the door swung open.

And then they were in the web.

That's what it was, she told herself—the shelves radiating from the center of the room were like the strands of a spiderweb.

They moved along one of the shadowed rows bordered by shelving on both sides, and emerged into the open area beyond. Here, under the sickly fluorescence of a single lamp on the desk, was the center of the web.

And from it rose the figure of the spider.

Her heart was pounding again. Over it, faintly, came the sound of Dr. Claiborne's voice.

"Sister Barbara—this is Norman Bates."

27

Three

For a moment, when he saw the penguin walk into the room, Norman thought maybe he *was* crazy after all.

But the moment passed. Sister Barbara wasn't a bird, and Dr. Claiborne hadn't come here to hassle him about his sanity or lack thereof. It was purely a social visit.

Social visit. How does one play host to his visitors in an asylum?

"Please sit down."

That seemed to be the obvious thing to say. But once they'd seated themselves at the table, there was a moment of awkward silence. Suddenly and surprisingly, Norman realized that his visitors were

29

embarrassed; they didn't know how to start a conversation any more than he did.

Well, there was always the weather.

Norman glanced over toward the window. "What happened to all that sunshine? It feels like there's rain in the air."

"Typical spring day—you know how it is," Dr. Claiborne told him. And the nun was silent.

End of weather report. Maybe she is a penguin, after all. What do you say to your fine feathered friends?

Sister Barbara was glancing down at the open book on the table before him. "I hope we didn't interrupt anything."

"Not at all. Just passing the time." Norman closed the book and pushed it aside.

"Can I ask what you were reading?"

"A biography of Moreno."

"The Romanian psychologist?" Sister Barbara's question caused Norman to look up quickly.

"You know about him?"

"Why, yes. Isn't he the man who came up with the psychodrama technique?"

She really isn't a penguin, then. He smiled at her and nodded. "That's correct. Of course, it's just ancient history now."

"Norman's right." Dr. Claiborne cut in quickly. "We've more or less abandoned that approach in group therapy. Though we still encourage acting out one's fantasies on the verbal level."

"Even to the point of letting patients get up on the stage and make fools of themselves," Norman said.

"Now that's ancient history too." Dr. Claiborne

was smiling, but Norman sensed his concern. "But I still think you gave an excellent performance, and I wish you'd stayed with the group."

Sister Barbara looked puzzled. "I'm afraid I'm not following this."

"We're talking about the amateur dramatic program here," Norman said. "I suspect it's Dr. Claiborne's improvement on Moreno's theories. Anyway, he coaxed me into taking a part and it didn't work out." He leaned forward. "How did—?"

"Excuse me."

The interruption came suddenly, and Norman frowned. A male nurse—Otis, the new one from the third floor—had entered the room. He approached Dr. Claiborne, who looked up.

"Yes, Otis?"

"There's a long-distance call for Dr. Steiner."

"Dr. Steiner's out of town. He won't be back until Tuesday morning."

"That's what I told them. But the man wants to talk to you. It's very important, he says."

"It always is." Dr. Claiborne sighed. "Did he give you his name?"

"A Mr. Driscoll."

"Never heard of him."

"He says he's a producer with some studio out in Hollywood. That's where he's calling from."

Dr. Claiborne pushed his chair back. "All right, I'll take it." Rising, he smiled at Sister Barbara. "Maybe he wants us to put on a psychodrama for him." He moved to the seated nun, ready to assist her from her seat. "Sorry I have to break this up."

"Must you?" Sister Barbara said. "Why don't I wait here until you come back?"

Norman felt his tension returning. Something told him not to say anything, but he concentrated on the thought. *Let her stay, I want to talk to her.*

"If you like."

Dr. Claiborne followed Otis through the stacks to the doorway beyond. He paused there, glancing back. "I won't be long," he said.

Sister Barbara smiled, and Norman sat watching the two men out of the corner of his eye. Dr. Claiborne was whispering something to Otis, who nodded and followed him out into the hall. For a moment Norman saw their silhouetted shadows on the far wall of the corridor beyond; then one shadow moved off while the other remained. Otis was standing guard outside the door.

A faint clicking claimed Norman's attention. The nun was fingering her rosary beads. *Security blanket,* he told himself. *But she wanted to stay. Why?*

He leaned forward. "How did you know about psychodrama, Sister?"

"A college course." Her voice sounded softly over the clicking.

"I see." Norman spoke softly too. "And is that where you learned about me?"

The clicking ceased. He had her full attention now. He'd taken over. For the first time in years he was in charge, controlling the situation. What a wonderful feeling, to be able to sit back and let someone else do the squirming for a change! Big, rawboned, ungainly woman, hiding behind her penguin disguise.

Quite suddenly he found himself wondering exactly what was underneath that habit, what kind of body it concealed. Warm, pulsing flesh. His mind's eye traced its contours, moving from thrusting, thirsty breasts to rounded belly and the triangulation below. Nuns shaved their heads—but what about their pubic hair? Had that been shaved too?

"Yes," said Sister Barbara.

Norman blinked. Could she read his mind? Then he realized she was merely replying to his spoken question.

"What did they say about me?"

Sister Barbara shifted uncomfortably in her chair. "Actually, it was a footnote, just a few lines in one of our texts."

"I'm a textbook case, is that it?"

"Please, I didn't mean to embarrass you—"

"Then what did you mean?" *Strange, watching someone else trying to wriggle out of a spot. All these years he'd been the one who wriggled, and he still wasn't out, never would be. Out, damned spot!* Norman hid behind a smile. "Why did you come here? Is the zoo closed on Sundays?"

There she was, clicking away at those damned beads again. Damned beads, damned spot. Was the damned spot really shaved?

Sister Barbara looked up. "I thought we might talk. You see, after I came across your name in that book, I went through some newspaper files. What I read interested me—"

"Interested?" Norman's voice didn't match his smile. "You were shocked, weren't you? Shocked, horrified, revolted—which was it?"

Sister Barbara's voice was scarcely more than a

whisper. "At the time, all of those things. I thought of you as a monster, some sort of bogeyman, creeping around in the dark with a knife. For months afterward I couldn't get you out of my mind, out of my dreams. But not anymore. It's all changed."

"How?"

"It's hard to explain. But something happened to me after I took the veil. The novitiate—meditation—examining one's secret thoughts, secret sins. In a way it's like analysis, I suppose."

"Psychiatry doesn't believe in sin."

"But it believes in responsibility. And so does my faith. Gradually I came to acknowledge the truth. You weren't aware of what you did, so how could anyone hold you responsible? It was I who had sinned by passing judgment without trying to understand. And when I learned we'd be coming here today, I knew I must see you, if only as an act of contrition."

"You're asking me to forgive you?" Norman shook his head. "Be honest. Curiosity brought you here. You came to see the monster, didn't you? Well, take a good look and tell me what I am."

Sister Barbara raised her eyes and stared at him for a long moment in the glare of the fluorescence.

"I see graying hair, lines in the forehead, the marks of suffering. Not the suffering you caused others, but that which you brought upon yourself. You're not a monster," she said "only a man."

"That's very flattering."

"What do you mean?"

"No one's ever told me I was a man," Norman said. "Not even my own mother. She thought I was weak, effeminate. And all the kids, calling me a sissy—the ballgames—" His voice choked.

"Ballgames?" Sister Barbara was staring at him again. "Please, tell me. I want to know."

She does. She really does!

Norman found his voice again. "I was a sickly child. Wore glasses for reading, right up until a few years ago. And I never was any good at sports. After school, on the playground we played baseball, the oldest boys were the captains. They took turn choosing up kids for their sides. I was always the last one chosen—" He broke off. "But you wouldn't understand."

Sister Barbara's eyes never left his face, but she wasn't staring now. She nodded, her expression softening.

"The same thing happened to me," she said.

"To you?"

"Yes." Her left hand strayed to her beads and now she glanced down at it, smiling. "You see? I'm what you call a southpaw. Girls play baseball too, you know. I was a good pitcher. They'd choose me first."

"But that's the direct opposite of what happened to me."

"Opposite, but the same." Sister Barbara sighed. "You were treated like a sissy. I was treated like a tomboy. Being first hurt me just as much as being last hurt you."

The air was close, sticky; shadows crept through the window, detaching from the dusk beyond to cluster around the circle of lamplight.

"Maybe that was part of my problem," Norman said. "You know what happened to me—the transvestite thing. You were lucky. At least you escaped loss of identity, loss of gender."

"Did I?" Sister Barbara let the rosary fall. "A nun is neuter. There is no gender. And no true identity. They even take away your given name." She smiled. "I don't regret that. But if you stop and think, you and I are very much the same underneath. We're kindred spirits."

For a moment Norman almost believed her. He wanted to believe, wanted to accept their similarity. But in the pool of fluorescence on the floor he saw the shadow that separated—the shadow of the bars on the window.

"One difference," he said. "You came here because you wanted to. And when you wish, you'll go of your own free will."

"There is no free will." Sister Barbara shook her head. "Only God's. He sent me here. I come and go only at His choosing. And you remain only to serve the same divine purpose."

She halted as a livid light lanced through the room. Norman sought its souce in the sudden darkening beyond the window. Then thunder shook the bars.

"Looks like we're in for a storm." Norman frowned, glancing at Sister Barbara. "What's the matter?"

The answer to his question was all too evident. In the lamplight the nun's face was deathly pale, and her eyes closed as she clutched at her rosary. There was no hint of spiritual security here, not even a trace of tomboyish bravado. The harsh, almost masculine features had melted to reveal the fear beneath.

Norman rose quickly, striding to the window. Peering out, he caught a glimpse of sullen sky over the grounds beyond. Now another streak of lightning razored across the parking area; for an instant it shimmered nimbuslike above the cars and the nuns' van. He drew the drapes against the greenish glow, then turned away as, once more, thunder hurled its threat.

"Better?" he said.

"Thank you." Sister Barbara's hand fell away from the rosary.

Something clicked. *The beads.* He stared at them.

All that mumbo-jumbo about psychological insight, all that nonsense about God's will, had vanished with a thunderclap. She was only a frightened woman, afraid of her own shadow.

Shadows were all around them now. They huddled in the corners, crawled between the looming bookshelves that stretched to the distant doorway. Glancing past it now, Norman realized the corridor beyond was empty; the shadow there had vanished. He knew the reason, of course. Whenever a storm broke, there was trouble with the loonies. God must have sent Otis off to calm his charges upstairs.

Norman turned back to Sister Barbara as the clicking sounded again. "You sure you're all right?" he said.

"Of course." But the beads clicked beneath her fingers and the quaver echoed behind her voice. Afraid of thunder and lightning; just a defenseless female, after all.

Suddenly, surprisingly, Norman felt a stirring in his loins. He fought it the only way he knew, with words that were bitter on his tongue.

"Just remember what you told me. If God sent you here, then He also sent the storm."

Sister Barbara looked up, the rosary beads dangling, jangling. "You mustn't say such things. Don't you believe in God's will?"

Thunder roared again outside the walls, hammering at Norman's skull, beating at his brain. Then the lightning flash flared up behind the drapes, illuminating all. *God's will. He had prayed and his prayers had been answered.*

"Yes," said Norman. "I believe."

The nun rose. "I'd better go now. Sister Cupertine may be worried."

"Nothing to worry about," Norman said. But he was speaking to himself. *There'd been rain that night long ago when it all started. And now it was coming again. Rain from heaven. God's will be done.*

Thunder rumbled, and then the rushing rain thudded against the outer wall of the shadowy room. But Norman didn't hear it.

All he could hear was the jangling of Sister Barbara's beads as he followed her into the shadows between the shelves.

Four

Sister Cupertine didn't get an opportunity to visit the new patient in 418. She was still in Tucker's room when the storm broke, and by the time she left him the rain was already drumming down.

She made her way as quickly as possible through the confusion of the corridor, jostled by excited patients as they returned to the open wards, escorted by friends and family. Orderlies and floor nurses hurried past, responding to the outcries emanating from locked rooms at the end of the hall. When she reached the fourth-floor elevator door, a crowd was already waiting before it, anxious and impatient.

Then the elevator arrived and the visitors crowded in, Sister Cupertine started forward, but by now the car was filled with passengers. The door closed with a clang, leaving her standing with half a dozen other stragglers.

There had been no attempt to make room for her in the elevator, and none of the others left behind paid Sister Cupertine the slightest attention. *No respect anymore, not the slightest. Holy Mary, forgive them—what is the world coming to these days?*

Sister Cupertine's lips pursed as she recited the rosary of indignities she had suffered here. Old Mr. Tucker had been in one of his contrary moods, rejecting her offer to pray with him and meeting her reprimand with foul language. In a way, of course, that was to be expected from someone in his condition. But there had been no excuse for Sister Barbara's behavior; her refusal to come upstairs was outright insubordination. It might be necessary to have a few words about her conduct with Mother Superior when they returned to the convent.

Thunder boomed as the elevator returned again. This time Sister Cupertine was among the first to enter. But the move did nothing to speed her progress; the descent was interrupted on the third floor and again on the second as more passengers shoehorned their way into the car. Little Sister Cupertine was squeezed uncomfortably in the metal corset of the elevator's left rear corner. And when the door slid back at the lobby level, she was forced to wait until the other occupants moved out. Underneath the habit she felt the trickling and tickling of perspiration; her glasses had steamed over in the body heat of the crowded cubicle.

Removing them, she wiped the lenses on her sleeve, and was almost knocked off her feet by a couple blundering past in their rush toward the outer exit. Sliding the bows back beneath the cowl and over her ears, she surveyed the lobby. By this time only a few others remained in the reception area, but Sister Barbara was nowhere to be seen.

Sister Cupertine peered up at the wall clock behind the reception desk. *Five-ten*. Already pitch dark outside, with the rain coming down in buckets. *Holy Mother of God, they'd be soaked just getting to the van. Where was the girl?*

She moved to the desk and the receptionist looked up.

"Can I help you?"

Sister Cupertine managed a smile. "I'm looking for—"

Thunder crashed over her question and part of the little receptionist's answer.

"—saw her going out just a minute ago."

"She left? Are you sure?"

"Yes, Sister." The girl seemed concerned. "Is there something wrong?"

"No, thank you."

Sister Cupertine turned away, starting toward the exit. *Peccavi*. A white lie, to be sure; it was none of the girl's affair and there was no sense in upsetting her. But something was very much wrong when such an outright act of disobedience occurred. Mother Superior would definitely hear about this whole affair before the evening was over.

If only it *was* over! There would still be the ordeal of the long drive back through this awful storm. Sis. r Cupertine paused for a moment and stared through the glass door panel, contemplating the seeth-

41

ing, wind-driven downpour beyond. Swiftly moving headlight beams crisscrossed the darkness as departing cars sped off in the night. Now a slash of lightning momentarily illuminated the outline of the van, still standing near the gate of the parking lot. *Thank heaven for small favors!* And thank heaven, too, for the protection of her habit.

She opened the door and moved out, water sloshing against her heavy shoes and rain pelting her coif. Midway across the lot, the heavy drops clouded her lenses and blurred her vision almost completely.

As she wrenched the glasses off to wipe them clear, her ankle twisted and she felt a stab of pain. Stumbling, she cried out, then recovered her balance as the sensation mercifully ebbed. Only then did she realize the glasses had slipped from her fingers.

Sister Cupertine glanced down helplessly, trying to locate them in the watery expanse of blackness below. No use—they were gone. Thank goodness she had a second pair to replace them back at the convent. Best to stop fretting and get out of this rain.

Now, as she started blindly forward, the wind rose to a howl, tearing at her water-soaked sleeves and flapping skirts.

Suddenly a light burst through the blur, and the snarl of a starting motor echoed over the wind's wail.

Glancing up, she saw that the van ahead was moving. *What on earth*—did Sister Barbara mean to leave without her?

"Wait!" She floundered toward the light source. "Wait for me!"

Sister Cupertine gasped as she reached the side of

the vehicle, groping for the door handle as the van slowed to a halt. The door swung forward and she clambered up into the passenger seat.

The motor roared and the van wheeled out to the gateway. Before it turned onto the road, Sister Cupertine was already launched into a tirade she knew she would later regret.

"Where were you, Sister? Why didn't you wait in the lobby? Haven't you any consideration? If you had to come out alone, the least you might have done was pull up to the entrance and pick me up there."

"I'm sorry—"

Her companion's reply was punctuated by the growling thunder. Not that it mattered, because Sister Cupertine wasn't finished yet.

"Look at me—soaking wet! And I dropped my glasses back there in the parking lot. Really, it's—oh, look out!"

The van skidded across the highway toward a gaping ditch, and Sister Barbara swung the wheel just in time to avoid disaster.

"Please, watch where you're going—"

Sister Cupertine broke off, abruptly aware that this was not the time to voice further complaints. Distraction would be dangerous, driving in this downpour.

She fell silent, peering ahead as the windshield wipers wheezed rhythmically to reveal the blurred expanse of the road beyond. Sister Barbara glanced at her but said nothing; it was impossible to read her reaction in the darkness. After a moment she turned away, concentrating on keeping the van steady on the slick pavement. Rain rattled against the roof.

Sister Cupertine stared forward, dimly discerning

a clump of trees, branches bowing in the wind. Directly past them was a side road leading down through a wooded area. Now the van slowed, turning left into the deeper darkness there.

"Wrong way!" she called above the sound of the storm, but Sister Barbara drove on and the van moved through a tunnel of twisted trees. Sister Cupertine tugged at her sleeve. "Didn't you hear me? You made a wrong turn!"

This time Sister Barbara nodded and pulled to a halt on the shoulder of the narrow roadway, her right hand reaching out to switch off the ignition. Then she leaned forward and her left hand descended to the floor of the van, between her feet.

For a moment it seemed to Sister Cupertine that the blurred, bending figure beside her resembled some sort of bird—a bird of prey. But only for a moment.

Then the figure straightened and turned, just as the lightning came.

In its glare, Sister Cupertine saw the contorted face beneath the coif, and the upraised hand holding the gleaming tire iron as it swung forward.

She never heard the thunder.

Five

Pumping. Pumping. Plenty of room in the back of the van. Room to strip away the concealment of cloth, to spread the lifeless legs. Maybe the other one—Sister Barbara—had shaved the spot, but this one was unshaven. It was the other one he'd really wanted, from the moment he'd followed her back into the stacks, only there wasn't time. Not even time enough to look; it all had to be done so quickly. This one was old, but now he did have time, and if he closed his eyes he couldn't see the face.

The feeling was what mattered. *Pumping. Pumping life into the dead. The Mother Superior position. Mother?*

That was incest. But he knew Sister Cupertine wasn't his mother. *Or was she?* With his eyes closed, he couldn't see the face. *Pumping*. Harder, faster now. *Mother, Oh God, God, God*—

Norman rolled to one side, sat up. Sweaty, still panting, but it was over now, thank God. God sent the nuns to deliver him from evil. *The Bride of Christ was his bride now. Or had been. It was all ancient history—the Norman Conquest.*

He giggled softly in the darkness as he fumbled the unfamiliar contours of his habit back into place. A perfect disguise. He'd fooled Sister Cupertine, he'd fooled them all, walking out this way. But then he'd had experience in the role. *All the world's a stage . . . and one man in his time plays many parts.* He'd played the woman and now he'd played the man. Mother had always called him a sissy; maybe she thought he couldn't get it up. Well, she knows better now, don't you, Mother? *Mother of God*—

His giggle was lost in the sound of thunder, jerking him back into full awareness of the moment. And when lightning flickered again, Norman couldn't escape the sight of the grotesquely sprawling figure beside him. Averting his eyes, he quickly pulled the black skirt down over the naked obscenity of thighs and legs.

No need for that anymore. The thing to do was to get rid of it as soon as possible. But how?

He peered forward over the seat at the rain-streaked windshield. There was a narrow ditch running along between the road and the trees. He could conceal the body there, under a pile of brush, but not for long. Someone was bound to come this way and see. Unless he could dig a grave—

Norman turned, waiting until another lightning

flash gave him a glimpse of what was contained in the back of the van. That was where he'd found the tire iron. But he didn't see a shovel; it was foolish to think they would carry one there. And he certainly couldn't dig in that muck with his bare hands.

With a start, Norman realized he was trembling, and not just from the cold. *There had to be another way; Oh God, there had to—*

He eased forward toward the cab of the van, and as he did so, something clattered beside him. Reaching down, his hand closed around a metal container. Its contents made a sloshing sound as he raised the heavy can to eye level and squinted at the label. But even before he did so, his nose told him what he needed to know.

Gasoline. A gallon can, carried in case of emergency.

Well, it would solve this one. *Burn the body, burn the van too. Cover all traces.*

The perfect solution. *Seek and ye shall find.* Norman's hand groped out across the floorboards, searching for a matchbook.

Suddenly he was trembling again. Because he found no matchbook. No matchbox. No matches anywhere. Why should there be? Under ordinary circumstances, matches were as unnecessary as a shovel. Unless, of course, they kept some in the glove compartment—

He clambered back into the driver's seat and yanked at the little rectangular cover on the dash. It fell forward, revealing the contents of the shelf behind. His hand took groping inventory: an empty box of facial tissues, a road map, a small screwdriver, the

47

car registration framed in a plastic folder, a phalliform flashlight. But no matches.

No matches. You've met your match.

Numbed, Norman sat there listening to the voices stammering, clamoring, yammering.

The stammering voice was his own. *Help me—please, somebody, help me!*

The clamoring was an echo of Dr. Claiborne's voice. *Relax. Just remember, I can't do it all for you. In the long run you've got to learn to help yourself.*

The yammering wasn't a voice at all, just the sound of rain on the roof of the van overhead.

And Dr. Claiborne was right. In the long run he had to help himself. But he couldn't run for long, not in this storm. He'd have to stay in the van. The one way he could help himself now was to stop trembling. What he had to do would need steady nerves, steady hands.

He remembered seeing a blanket in the rear, covering the spare tire in the right-hand corner. Norman turned and forced his way back into the dark recess as he edged past the thing lying there—the Mother-thing, the Sister-thing—staring silently up from the shadows. Strange how he couldn't bear the thought of touching it or even seeing it again.

But for a moment he did see it as the lightning flared, forming a halo around the hideous head. *Holy Mother!*

Closing his eyes, he reached for the blanket, pulling it free and spreading it out with frantic haste. When his eyes opened again, the motionless mound was covered. Carefully he tucked the sides down, then surveyed the results of his effort. You couldn't tell what was underneath now; no one could tell. And if anyone tried—

Norman's hand found the tire iron where he'd tossed it. just behind the seat. He carried it with him as he crawled back into the cab, and dropped the heavy length of metal between his feet. At least he had that much, the means of protection in case of need.

But there would be no need, not if he was careful. His hands weren't trembling now, and he could drive. That's what he had to do now. Drive, get away from here.

He turned the key in the ignition and the motor responded. Carefully he edged the van back onto the road, moving through the trees, then past them to a clear stretch beyond. The mere act of driving was in itself a reassurance. Controlling the van meant that he was controlling himself. And he who controls himself controls the future. All that remained was the need to plan ahead.

Somewhere along the road he'd come to a store or a service station. He'd get matches there.

But there wouldn't be much chance of finding a roadside business place here on this bypass. His best bet was the main highway. Norman found a spot ahead, made his turn, and drove back to the junction.

Once on the wider stretch, he relaxed. Better road, better opportunity ahead. Or so he thought, until the flapping sleeve of his robe brushed against the steering wheel. He glanced down at his habit, frowning.

Back at the hospital it had been his salvation. No

one had given him a second glance during the brief moment of hurrying out through the confusion of the lobby and into the darkness beyond.

But now the robe was damnation. He couldn't hope to enter a country store unnoticed; even Sister Barbara herself would be an object of curiosity there. And driving into a service station was equally dangerous.

The picture formed quickly in his mind. A rainy Sunday evening, with no traffic, no business—some kid attendant sitting inside the office with his old man, reading a comic book and listening to the radio, then scowling in resentment as the sound of a horn summoned him out into the rain. *Jesus Christ, it's a nun! And she doesn't want gas—she's asking for matches. What the hell does a nun need with matches? Something funny going on here. Hey, Pa, maybe you better go see what gives—*

The picture faded and he was staring at the sleeve again. Easy now. Just keep thinking, keep driving. But where? Where could he go in this outfit?

Get thee to a nunnery.

Hamlet said that.

But Hamlet was mad.

This way lies madness. What other way remained? Removing the habit was no solution; the regulation blue hospital uniform underneath would identify him anywhere he appeared. The choice was his: either as escaped patient or a creature of habit. He needed matches, yes, but he needed ordinary clothing even more. *Clothes make the man.*

Thunder rocked, shocked, mocked. The voice of God. But God wouldn't mock him, not now, not after

50

guiding him safely through all this. *The Lord will provide*. God will send a sign.

Then the lightning came. Only for an instant, but long enough for Norman to see the figure huddling under a lone tree at the side of the highway ahead, holding up the square of cardboard with the word scrawled on it in crude capital letters.

God had sent a sign, and it said *Fairvale*.

Six

Dr. Adam Claiborne didn't realize how tired he was until he reached Steiner's office and lowered himself into the chair behind the desk. It was an executive chair with leather-covered arms and back, and a well-padded, oversized cushion designed to accommodate well-padded, oversized butts. The seats of the mighty.

Momentarily his exhaustion gave way to irritation as he contrasted this comfort with the hard, confining contours of the cheap plastic and plywood furnishing of his own small office down the hall. No wonder he was exhausted, working double shifts while Steiner sat giving orders in his padded chair or ran off to meetings on his padded expense account.

Claiborne sighed, reaching for the receiver of the waiting phone on the desktop. So much for self-pity.

"Hello, this is Dr. Claiborne. Sorry to keep you waiting."

"That's okay." The voice on the other end of the line was deep, booming loudly enough to be heard over a background of stereo sound. "Marty Driscoll here, Enterprise Productions. I'm calling about the picture."

"Picture?"

"The film. Didn't Steiner tell you?"

"I'm afraid not."

"That's funny. I talked to him Thursday and laid out the whole deal. Did the package get there?"

"What package?"

"I sent it out registered, special delivery, Friday morning." A faint click punctuated Driscoll's sentence, and the stereo music behind the voice faded out. "He should have gotten it by now."

Claiborne nodded, then caught himself. Why did people nod when talking to someone on the telephone? That was the sort of thing you'd expect a patient to do. Maybe psychosis was contagious. *You don't have to be crazy to work here, but it helps*.

"I wouldn't know anything about a package," he said. Then, "Wait a minute."

While speaking, he'd noticed the big brown envelope lying in a wire basket on the far side of the desk. Now he pulled it out, reading the printed return address in the upper left-hand corner. "Your package did arrive. It's here on his desk."

"Did he open it?"

Claiborne examined the slitted flap. "Yes."

54

"So why the hangup? He promised to call back as soon as he read the script."

Thunder competed with conversation, and Claiborne wasn't quite sure of what he'd heard. "Would you mind repeating that? We're having a thunderstorm here—"

"The screenplay." Driscoll's voice boomed louder, emphasizing impatience. "It's gotta be there. Take a look and see."

Claiborne upended the envelope, and its contents cascaded across the desktop: three eight-by-ten glossy photographs, plus a bulky segment of manuscript pages stapled together in a leatherette binder. He glanced at the typewritten title on the card affixed to the center of the cover.

"Crazy Lady," he said.

"That's it. You like that title?"

"Not particularly."

"Neither did Steiner." Driscoll's reply conveyed amused tolerance. "Don't worry, we're not married to it. Maybe you and Ames can get together and come up with something better."

"Ames?"

"Roy Ames. My writer. I'd like to send him out to see you people for a coupla days. Sort of get the feel of things in case he's screwed up on technical details. I know Bates is still flaky, but maybe if he talked to him—"

"I'm not following. Are you referring to Norman Bates?"

"Yeah. The fruitcake."

"But what has he got to do with—"

"Easy, Doc." Driscoll chuckled. "I keep forgetting

55

you didn't read the script. We're doing a film on the Bates case."

Claiborne dropped the leatherette binder on the desk. *Crazy Lady.* He stared at it numbly. What was it he'd said to Sister Barbara about psychodrama? *You don't have to be crazy to work here, but it helps.*

"Doc—are you there?"

"Yes."

"So say something. How does it grab you?"

"You want my professional opinion?"

"Yeah, that's it."

"Then listen carefully. As a practicing psychiatrist, I think you're out of your skull."

Driscoll's laugh boomed louder than his voice until Claiborne cut in, "I mean it. You can't make a picture about Norman Bates."

"Don't worry, the legal department checked it out. The whole *kapoosta* is public record, like the Boston Strangler and Charlie Manson—"

"This is different."

But Driscoll wasn't listening. "Trust me. We'll knock their socks off. Set it for a late-fall release and go right through the roof."

"What you're proposing is cheap sensationalism—"

"Cheap, hell! This is a biggie. We're budgeted at eleven-five, minimum."

"I'm not talking about finances."

"Right. That's my department."

"And mine is the welfare of my patients."

"Stop worrying. We don't want a piece of *schlock* any more than you do. That's why I sent the script— give you people a chance to catch any mistakes—"

"If you ask me, the whole thing is a mistake."

"Come on, Doc, you haven't even read it yet!" The booming voice resounded through the receiver. "Why don't you take a look, do us both a favor? Just remember, if there's any changes, we got to get them set by a week from Monday at the latest, so's we'll have a couple days for run-through and rehearsals. All I want from you is a little cooperation. And if you think Ames should come out to look around for a few days, just say the word."

"Did Dr. Steiner agree to this?"

"He said he'd get back to me as soon as he read the script. So if you'll ask him to call me when he gets in—"

"I'll do that."

"Thanks." Now the stereo surged again, signifying an end to further conversation. "Nice talking to you," Driscoll said. "Have a good day."

Claiborne cradled the receiver and leaned back. *Have a good day.* For a moment he envisioned the good day Marty Driscoll was having, probably calling from a poolside phone in Bel-Air, basking in Technicolor sunshine surrounded by Dolby sound.

There was no sunshine here, only the storm-stirred darkness; no sound except thunder and rain.

He thought of Steiner sitting snugly, smugly, in his first-class seat on the plane. Why hadn't he mentioned the script? Didn't he realize the implications? How could he even consider lending support to such a project, endangering the dignity of his profession, putting indignity upon his patient? But he wasn't concerned about how Norman would feel; all Steiner cared for was that big meeting in St. Louis. What happened back here had no importance. But that was

57

showbiz; the star takes all the bows and the supporting players do all the work.

Claiborne shook his head. *Prejudgment. You're just too damned tired to be logical. You don't really know what Steiner thinks. And you haven't read the script—*

He pushed the leatherette binder aside, glancing at the eight-by-tens beneath. The first was a head-and-shoulders glossy print of a glossy man with a glossy smile, instantly recognizable. Paul Morgan, one of the current crop of stars who were—how did they put it?—bankable. Surely they weren't casting him in the role of Norman?

But that was the only male photo; the other two were head shots of a girl Claiborne didn't know. Or did he? There was no identification beneath the smiling, wide-eyed face, and yet it was somehow vaguely familiar.

Suddenly he realized where he'd seen that face before—staring up at him in smudgy reproductions photocopied from old newspaper clippings which were a part of Norman Bates' case-history file.

She was Mary Crane!

Impossible. Mary Crane had been Norman's victim, the one he'd killed in the shower.

They'd found a lookalike.

Gazing at the girl in the photos, Claiborne had the feeling he'd known only in dreams—dreams where something threatened and pursued, something menacing that he couldn't see or identify. But he knew it was coming after him, so he'd keep running until he was ready to drop, even though there was no escape. Then, just as it closed in, he'd wake up.

He wasn't dreaming now, yet the threat was still there. *Something*—

"Dr. Claiborne!"

Otis was standing in the doorway, breathing hard.

Claiborne looked up, letting the photos fall to the desktop. "Yes?"

"Hurry—the library—something's happened—"

Something.

He hurried, the way he did in the dreams, but this time he wasn't running away. He was running toward the thing. Running down the stairs, not waiting for the elevator, following Otis.

He called to him as they descended. "What's happened?"

"I don't know—I wasn't there—"

"You mean you left them alone?"

"The storm—I had to check Ward C, get those patients back to their rooms—nobody else on duty there." Otis was panting and the stairwell's echo amplified his gasps. "They were just talking when I left. Wasn't away more than five minutes, but when I got back he was gone."

"Norman?"

Otis reached the first level, pushing the door open, and Claiborne followed him into the corridor.

"I told the desk to alert all floors. Allen's on security, he's out searching the grounds."

Claiborne was panting now as they ran towards the library. His footsteps hammered in the hall, and the voice hammered in his head. *Norman's gone. He ran away. And you're running now. Running towards something.*

Running. Through the doorway and into the darkened room, into the shadowy stacks where something waited.

Claiborne halted, staring down.

"Sister Barbara—"

But it wasn't Sister Barbara, not anymore. It was just a thing. A naked thing lying cold and still, staring sightlessly back at him with bulging eyes protruding from behind a mask.

* * *

It had to be a mask, for her body was ghastly white; the face above, hideously purple. *A mask*, Claiborne told himself. What else could it be?

Then bending forward, he saw the answer, imbedded in swollen flesh—the rosary, twisted tightly around Sister Barbara's neck.

Seven

Bo Keeler must of been standing there almost half an hour, standing in the frigging rain.

Only two cars came by the whole time, and both mothers passed him up. Either in too goddam much of a hurry or too scared to stop.

So okay, maybe the hair and the beard and the bushhat turned them off. Maybe they figured him for a freako, maybe the jacket got them uptight, like they thought he was in with a bike club.

Shee-it, if he was, he wouldn't be standing here in the rain without wheels! And he could of been, once. Two years ago he made his move to get it on with the Angels down in Tulsa, but he didn't have his own chopper. Sorry, kid, up yours.

So no sweat, he cased out the Honda dealer's

layout and set the rip for Labor Day, everybody gone for the weekend, dynamite. The lock in back was a mickey-mouse job, and inside he eyeballed the biggest goddam bike in the joint. Super, a two-G ticket, all the extras, lubed and ready to roll. How the hell could he of figured on that silent alarm system? But they came crashing in and did the whole number on him, yelling freeze, and he froze. Lousy mothersuckers busted him, breaking and entering, second offense, take two in the slammer, do not pass go.

Bo shivered and edged back under the tree, trying to keep the sign dry. Fat chance in this storm. If he had any smarts he would've took the bus. When they sprung him yesterday, they popped for the ticket.

Cashing it in was a big mistake, but he got what he craved: six joints and sack time with that jungle bunny he'd flashed on at the bus station. And today, when he split, it looked like it would be easy to thumb his way. First off, he lucked out with the oil rig—trucker said he was routed smack through Fairvale, he could of dropped him off right in front of Jack's pad. But then the frigging storm come up and the guy chickened out on him. *Sorry, buddy, can't take a chance, I'm laying over right here in Rock Center until it clears up.*

So it was over and out. Out on the highway in the rain, up the creek without a paddle, only this goddam cardboard sign on a stick.

But he had to get to Fairvale tonight before old buddy Jack cut out for the coast, like he wrote him last month. Jack owed him some bread, maybe he'd take him along for the ride. He sure to Christ had to, because there was nobody else who gave a diddlydamn what happened to him, no other way to go. Not with half a pack of butts and thirty-seven cents in change.

The wind was blowing so hard now that the rain came down almost sideways, and standing under the tree didn't help much. Bo shivered, holding the sign in front of his face like a shield. You could goddam well drown out here in the middle of nowhere. What he needed was an umbrella.

No way. What he needed was a score. Face it, Fairvale was a crock and so was old buddy Jack. But if he could score, score big enough to get hold of some real bread and his own wheels—

Something flickered off to the right. It wasn't lightning, it kept flashing steady. A car was coming along the road.

Bo stepped out in front of the tree, holding up the sign. As the headlights moved closer he squinted at the outlines of a van.

Stop. Stop, you mother—

It did. The van stopped and Bo moved up to the door.

The driver peered down at him from the far side of the darkened cab.

"Do you need a lift?"

What the hell do you think I'm standing here for, dummy? Only he wasn't about to say so. *Play it cool.*

"You going to Fairvale?"

"That's right."

Bo tossed the cardboard sign into the ditch and climbed in, slamming the door as the van started off. Neat in here with the heater on, warm and dry. He settled back in his seat, then glanced over at the driver.

For a minute he thought he'd flipped out. Who the hell goes around driving a van wearing a big black cloak, the kind you see in one of those Dracula movies?

Then he flashed on the head—the cowl, whatever they called it—and he knew. The driver was a nun.

Bo wasn't one of those born-again Jesus freaks, he didn't go for that crap, but this was like somebody answered his prayers. *A nun, driving a van. His own wheels.* Right away, other wheels began spinning in his head. If he could only figure how to orchestrate. *Play it cool. Go with the flow.*

The van moved on. The cowled figure glanced at him, but only for a second, not long enough for Bo to get a good make on her face in the dark. He laid a smile on her, just in case his gear put her off.

Mostly she watched the road, but he knew she was watching him too, out of the corner of her eye. And all at once she started talking in a kind of a husky voice, like she was coming down with a cold.

"Do you live in Fairvale?"

"No, Sister." *Play it cool.* "Just passing through. I got friends there."

"Then you know the town?"

"Sort of. Is that where you come from?"

She nodded. "I grew up near there. But I haven't been back for years."

"I guess when you're in a convent they don't let you get around very much."

She kind of giggled—funny sound, coming from a nun. "That's true."

"Well, you didn't miss much. I bet Fairvale's just the same as when you left."

The rain was coming on hard, and she kept her eyes on the road ahead. "You say you have friends in town?"

"Yeah."

"I was wondering. You wouldn't happen to know a Mr. Loomis, would you? Sam Loomis?"

"Seems like I heard the name," Bo said. "Is he the one who runs the hardware store?"

"Then he's still there?"

Bo nodded. "It's like I told you. Nothing much changes."

But a lot had changed, right here and now. All the while they talked, he'd been trying to set up the action. And then, when the old bitch came out with that last question, he flashed on the answer.

Sam Loomis. Damned right he'd heard of him. He was the sucker mixed up in that heavy murder case years ago, when they collared some weirdo doing snuff jobs out at the old motel. The Bates Motel, way off in the boondocks on County Trunk A. Place burned down, but the road was still there. Hardly anybody used it on account of the highway going through, and sure as hell nobody'd be using it tonight.

How long had they been driving? If he remembered right, the turn off should be coming up pretty soon. Bo squinted through the windshield, but the rain was so heavy the wipers couldn't clear it and everything was dark. He heard thunder, and then lightning streaked across the stretch of road ahead just long enough for him to spot what he was looking for. *Play it cool.*

"Sister—"

"Yes?"

"See that fork up ahead? If you take a right, it's a shortcut into town."

"Thank you."

Was he hearing things, or did she giggle again? No, it sounded more like coughing.

"You catching cold?"

The sister shook her head. "I'm fine."

You better believe it, she was. Kind of on the heavy side, almost as big as he was, but he knew he could hack it. One good swipe, just enough to put her out and dump her alongside the road. Then take over the wheel and screw Fairvale, cut out for Ravenswood, across the state line. *Go with the flow.*

They were bumping along the county truck now, hitting those big potholes in the dark. For a minute he thought she was going to give him a hard time about it, but she didn't say anything. And the storm was letting up a little; maybe the rain would stop soon.

Trick now was to get *her* to stop. Trees up ahead, nice and dark, super. Time to get his act together now.

When he opened his mouth, he was the one who sounded like he had a cold. His throat went all dry and cottony and he started to tighten up inside. *Go with the flow, goddammit!*

He reached into his jacket pocket and pulled a butt out of the pack. "Mind if I smoke?" he said.

She jerked her head around fast, like he'd just

come out with a dirty remark, but there was just enough light for him to see she was smiling.

"Do you have matches?" she said.

Jesus, what a dumb question! Instead of saying anything, he fished them out for her to see. Then he gave her the nod.

"Maybe if you slowed down for a minute, so's I can get a light—"

"Of course."

And she pulled over and stopped next to the trees. Beautiful!

He stalled for a second, making sure he had his moves figured out. Light the butt first, then quick shove it in her face. She'll jerk away, put up her hands, and that's when to let her have it, whammo, right in the gut. Then, when her hands come down, give her one good chop on the jaw. *Over and out.*

Bo lipped the butt, struck a match, cupped his hands around the flame. When the match flared up, he lost her in the glare, but only for a moment or two.

Just long enough for her to bend forward and pick up something lying between her feet...

Eight

Claiborne had lost track of time.

It seemed to take forever for the highway patrol to arrive, and when they finally drove into the hospital parking lot, the rain had stopped.

There were three men in the car. The driver remained seated behind the wheel while the other two climbed out and started toward the entrance, where Claiborne stood waiting.

Introductions were brief. The big, thick-necked, gray-haired man was Captain Banning and the thin one was a trooper named Novotny. Claiborne found himself wondering about that. Why are the mesomorphs always the chiefs and the ectomorphs always the Indians?

Not that Banning didn't seem capable. He was

firing questions at Claiborne even before they entered the lobby, and he ordered Novotny to stay there and take a statement from Clara at the reception desk.

Banning and Claiborne went straight to the elevator. "Sorry about the delay," Banning told him as the car ascended. "You hear about the accident?"

"What accident?"

"Greyhound bus smacked head-on into a big semi and flipped over, right outside Montrose. Seven dead so far, and around twenty other passengers injured. Damn near every unit in the county's over there right now—sheriff's department, ambulances, and our people. On top of that, we got a problem with power outages on account of the storm. You lucked out, getting through to us at all. Hell of a mess."

Claiborne listened, nodding at the appropriate intervals, but somehow the captain's remarks weren't registering. The thing that mattered to him was the one right here, in the library.

And that was where the questions began again.

On Claiborne's orders, Otis had draped a sheet over the body, but nothing else had been touched. Now Banning was interrogating them both, jotting down their replies on a pad. Halfway through the session he sent Otis away to fetch Allen and when the security guard appeared there was another go-round.

Yes, the grounds had been covered—everything, including storage sheds and the employee's quarters. At Claiborne's direction there'd been a quiet but thorough checkout of the hospital itself: patients' rooms, lavatories, kitchen, laundry, even the broom closets.

"Waste of time," Banning said, flipping the notepad shut. "Your man put on the victim's outfit and walked right out the front door. Chances are he headed straight for that van the sisters came in."

"But Sister Cupertine left, too," Claiborne said. "Wouldn't she have recognized him?"

"Captain—"

Banning turned as another uniformed man came through the doorway. It was the trooper who'd remained in the patrol car, and now Banning started down the aisle to where the newcomer stood waiting. "What's up?" he asked.

The trooper's reply was muffled. But when Banning spoke, his words came loud and clear.

"Jesus H. Christ!" he said.

Claiborne moved toward him between the stacks. "What's the problem?"

"The van." Banning scowled. "Some salesman spotted it just now, when he was coming down County Truck A. Had a phone in his car and he called the fire department right away—"

"Fire department? What happened?"

Banning shoved the notepad into his pocket. "When I find out, I'll let you know."

Fire department. Claiborne's dreamlike feeling returned, the way it had when Otis summoned him here to the library; the nightmare feeling of something waiting. No sense in running now; sooner or later you had to face it. Only then could you wake up.

"Can I come with you?" Claiborne asked. "My car's outside."

"Okay if you want to follow." Banning headed for

71

the doorway. "In case you lose me, it's County Truck A—"

"Don't worry, I won't lose you," Claiborne said.

But he did.

By the time he'd instructed Otis to take over, and cautioned him to keep the staff silent about what was happening, Banning's patrol car was already backing out of the parking lot.

The two troopers had stayed behind to take further statements and call an ambulance for Sister Barbara's body. But Banning didn't need any help driving; his taillights were winking in the distance before Claiborne wheeled onto the road.

He gunned the motor, watching the needle arc over to seventy. No use; the car ahead must be doing ninety or better, and he couldn't hope to match its speed on the wet pavement.

In a moment or so the patrol car rounded a curve and disappeared completely. Claiborne slackened his speed to sixty, but even then it required his full concentration to keep from going into a skid. As a result he overshot the fork in the road and had to head back when he realized his mistake. Then, after turning onto County Truck A, he needed no further guidance.

On the highway the rain-cleansed night air had been cool and fresh. Here there was an acrid odor mingling with a sickly sweet stench, and in the glare ahead, Claiborne found its source.

He'd expected to see fire trucks, but only two cars stood parked on the shoulder of the road, their headlight beams focused on a third vehicle.

Claiborne recognized the van, or what was left of

it. The windshield was gone and there was a gaping hole in the charred roof of the cab; its doors hung open on melted hinges. The back had blown out completely, and the hood was gone up front, exposing a tangle of melted metal from which wisps of smoke still curled upward to mingle with the reek of gasoline fumes. Beneath bubbling tires lay a litter of broken glass and unidentifiable debris.

Leaning against the trunk of his car, the salesman was vomiting noisily into the ditch. The patrol car on the other side of the road was empty, but as Claiborne parked and emerged, he saw Banning turn away from the cab of the van. He glanced up, his face livid in the light.

"Gas tank exploded," he said.

"Accident?"

"Can't tell. Could be arson. Fire department ought to know, if they ever get here." Banning peered up the road, frowning.

The air was poisonous; Claiborne's stomach churned. "What's your theory?" he said.

"Something's wrong somewhere. The van was parked when it happened—the brake's still on. And the fire started up front, from the looks of things. Seems to me like they'd have had time to get out before the tank blew."

Claiborne stiffened. "They?"

He moved up to the open cab, but Banning put a restraining hand on his shoulder. "No point looking." He nodded toward the retching salesman across the road. "Bet he wishes he hadn't."

"I've got to know."

73

"Okay, Doc." Banning's head dropped and he stepped back. "Don't say I didn't warn you."

Claiborne leaned forward, glancing into the cab. The leather was burned away from the seats, and plastic had fused on the dash. The sickly sweet odor was stronger here, almost overpowering. Now he saw its source.

Lying crossways on the floorboard frame below was a charcoal-colored blob with two stumps outthrust on either side. The reeking mass was only vaguely recognizable as a human torso, and the rounded protuberance atop it was just a burnt black ball from which all trace of features had been seared away. Eyeless, noseless, no vestige of skin or hair remained, and what had been a mouth was now just a yawning, tongueless opening, grimacing in a silent scream.

He turned, choking from the smell and the sight of it, and peered down at the interior of the van behind the seats.

Another blob lay in the shadows, its limbless bulk crisped like a barbecued side of beef. There was no head; apparently the gas tank explosion had shattered the skull. Only one anatomical detail identified the remains as female: the charred cavity of the vagina. Here a single sliver of skin had curled away, revealing a fleck of pinkish flesh beneath.

Claiborne backed out of the cab, breathing deeply. Conscious of Banning's scrutiny, he fought to control his features and his voice.

"You're right, it's useless. You'll need a complete autopsy."

"That'll take a while," Banning said. "Coroner's going to have his hands full after that bus crash over

74

at Montrose. But I've got a rough idea of what happened here." He ran two fingers across the grayish stubble on his chin. "Way I figure, Sister Cupertine was either knocked out or killed and shoved out of sight in the back of the van. Next move was to find a spot off the main highway and—"

"Wait a minute." Claiborne frowned. "First you tell me you don't know if it was an accident or not, and now you're saying there was a murder."

"Never had any doubt about that part," Banning told him. "Body in back tells us that much. If she hadn't been dead or at least unconscious, Sister Cupertine would have been up front trying to fight her way out of the cab when the fire started."

"But we still have no way of knowing what caused the van to explode," Claiborne said.

The salesman moved up beside him, silent and shaken, as Banning reached down into the shadows at his feet and picked up a blackened metal cylinder.

"Here's your answer," he said. "Found this gasoline can here in the road while you were looking around inside. It's arson, all right. The idea was to soak the body and van, let the fire take care of the evidence." Banning nodded. "But somewhere along the line something went wrong, and he got himself trapped in the cab."

"He?"

"Your patient. Norman Bates."

Trapped. That thing up front in the van was Norman. Of course, it had to be.

"No!"

"What do you mean?"

Claiborne stared at Banning without answering.

75

Because there was no answer, only the conviction, born of years of professional experience, years of working with his patient.

Ths salesman glanced at him, puzzled, and Banning shook his head. "Makes sense, Doc. We know Bates got away in the van, and Sister Cupertine must have gone with him. Get the picture? She doesn't recognize him in the nun's outfit at first, and when she does it's too late—he clobbers her and comes here, like I said. Then, when he touches off the gasoline, whammo! What else could have happened?"

"I don't know," Claiborne said. "I don't know."

"Take my word for it. Bates is dead—"

The rest of his words were lost in the wailing.

The three men looked up, finding its source as lights flashed and whirled on the roadway ahead. A screech of brakes announced the rumbling arrival of the fire truck. It slammed to a halt and spotlighted the scene.

Turning, Banning started toward it, with the salesman tagging along behind. Claiborne hesitated, watching the uniformed men clamber down and cross to the wreckage of the van. A bareheaded fire captain stood waiting beside the truck, then began talking as Banning and the salesman approached.

From now on there'd be a lot of talking, endless talking, because talking was all anyone could do. An ambulance would come to haul the burned blobs away, but the talk would go on—useless, meaningless talk. It was all meaningless now, and there was no need for Claiborne to hear it again. He'd given his testimony, his presence wasn't required here. *Leave*

*the postmortems to the coroner. You're just an inno-
cent bystander.*

He walked back to his car and slid behind the
wheel. Nobody noticed and nobody tried to stop him
as he drove off, turning back to retrace his route to
the main highway.

Gradually the smell and the sound faded, at least
externally. But the sight remained, looming before
his eyes more vividly than the road ahead—the sight
of the blackened, twisted torsos, the charred crea-
tures at the scene of the crime.

No postmortems. Innocent bystander.

But the postmortems went on, somewhere deep
inside, and the protestations of innocence died.

Because Norman was dead.

Norman was dead, and Claiborne was guilty. Guilty
of misjudgment for allowing Norman and Sister Barbara
to meet. Guilty of negligence in leaving them alone
together. By the same token he was indirectly responsible for Sister Cupertine's death too. But above
all, he was guilty of failing Norman. His professional
errors of diagnosis and prognosis were the real crimes.

Claiborne reached the highway and made his turn
almost automatically. The fresh air helped clear his
lungs and his head.

Now he could face facts. Now he could understand
his resistance to the reality of Norman's death. For in
a way it wasn't Norman who'd died back there in the
flaming van; it was Claiborne himself. It was *his*
self-image that had been burned beyond all recognition; his plans, his hopes, his dreams had exploded,
his life had gone up in smoke.

There would be no book now, no scholarly but

subtly self-congratulatory account of restoring reason to an apparently incurable psychotic without the use of ECT, psychosurgery, or ataractics. That, he knew, had been the goal all along: write the book, make a name and a reputation, get out from under Steiner's shadow, out of the dead-end job, and into a decent post. He'd been as much a prisoner there in the hospital as Norman was, and if only things had gone right, they could both have been free.

And he'd come close, so very close. Close to succeeding, close to Norman himself. They'd worked together so long, he knew the man, or thought he did. How could he have made such a mistake?

Hubris.

Pride, the belief in the superiority of science, the omniscience of intellect. That was the fatal error.

Sometimes it was better to trust to the gut feeling, the way he had when he'd almost blurted out that Norman wasn't dead.

With a start, he realized the feeling was still there. *Suppose it was true?*

Of course that made no sense, but what had happened to the van made no sense either. Banning was jumping to conclusions; he had his hubris too, needed an easy answer. But why would Norman spread gasoline around and ignite it without first getting out of the van? No matter what else might be, Norman was neither suicidal nor stupid.

There had to be another answer. What if someone else was involved—a third party?

But who?

That didn't make sense either. Nothing made sense except the gnawing feeling. Unless it was just wishful thinking, voicing itself over and over again. *Norman is alive, alive, alive—*

Claiborne blinked, forcing himself to focus full attention on the highway ahead. And it was then, at that precise instant, that he saw what was lying in the ditch on the left-hand side of the road. Saw it, slowed, and stopped.

Climbing out, he crossed over for a closer look. Perhaps his eyes had played a trick on him.

But as he picked up the soggy cardboard sign mounted on the makeshift pole, he knew there was no mistake. The lettering was still plainly visible.

Fairvale.

Claiborne stood staring down at the sign, and suddenly everything fell into place. He glanced at the shoulder of the road beside it.

The van could have stopped here and picked up a hitchhiker.

If so, there ought to be tire tracks in the mud. He stooped for a closer look, but all he saw was a puddle of water. Of course; the rain must have washed the marks away. And it didn't matter, nothing mattered but the truth. *Trust your instincts. There was a third party after all.*

And if there was a third party, then everything was possible. The hitchhiker could have been lured to the spot where the van was to be destroyed, knocked over the head there, and left to the flames after being stripped of his clothing. While Norman—

Claiborne picked up the sign and carried it over to the car. He placed it carefully on the back seat, then started the engine racing. His thoughts raced with it.

The car made a U-turn. Fairvale was back up the

79

highway, beyond the fork. And that was where Norman would be heading after leaving the burning van. A man capable of killing innocent strangers in a manic state would certainly not hesitate to kill known enemies.

Sam Loomis and his wife, Lila, lived in Fairvale.

The fork loomed ahead. For an instant Claiborne debated; should he turn off and alert Banning? But that meant talk, more talk, and he already knew what the reaction would be if he told him what he suspected.

Okay, but where's your proof? All you've got is a sign you found lying in a ditch. From this you expect me to believe a whole number about Norman killing a hitchhiker and stashing his body in the van? And even if he did, how do you know he'd go after the Loomises? You may be a shrink, but that doesn't make you a mind reader. Look, Doc, you're tired. Why don't you go on back to the hospital and get some rest, leave the police work to us?

Banning's voice. The voice of *hubris*.

Claiborne shook his head. He did feel tired, completely spent, that much was true. And he wasn't a mind reader. How could he convince Banning that he did know, knew for a certainty, what Norman was thinking?

No way. And no time.

The car moved past the fork, gaining speed as Claiborne's foot pressed down on the gas pedal in sudden decision.

Coming abreast of the roadside marker on the right, he read the legend without slowing down. *Fairvale—12 mi.*

The car zoomed forward.

Now the feeling was stronger than ever—the feeling of moving toward some dreadful destination in a dream.

But this wasn't a dream.

And there was no time.

Nine

Norman walked down the street and it was dead.

The storm had killed it; the storm, and Sunday night. Every small town has its Main Street, and when sundown comes on Sunday, death arrives. The stores close, parking spaces stand empty, and if any life lingers at all, it retreats to the residences beyond, hiding behind drawn blinds.

That was where Sam and Lila would be—hiding in one of the houses. Sam, who ran the hardware store, and Lila, his wife. She was Mary Crane's sister, and she'd come here looking for Mary after she disappeared. She'd gone to Sam, knowing that he and her sister were lovers.

No one would have known what had happened if it wasn't for their meddling. Mary Crane and the detective who'd tried to find her were both dead, and Sam and Lila should have gone to their graves too. Instead they'd come to the Bates Motel and discovered Norman, and he was the one who got buried—buried alive in that asylum all those years.

Shutting him away was a worse punishment than death—punishment for crimes he'd never committed. It was Mother who did it, taking over his mind and body and putting them through the motions of murder. He wasn't responsible, everybody admitted that. If he were, they would have held a trial.

But there was no trial, only the long years of punishment, while Sam and Lila went free. *And so they were married and lived happily ever after.*

Until now.

Tonight it would end. Not because he was crazy; he was sane again and he, not Mother, would be the avenger. Thank God for that.

No, not God. Thank Dr. Claiborne. He was the Savior, the one who had saved him from madness. If it weren't for Dr. Claiborne, Norman wouldn't be here.

And perhaps he shouldn't be, because Dr. Claiborne wouldn't approve. All these years together, talking it out, helping him find himself again, get rid of Mother, get rid of the fear and the hatred—wonderful man, so much kindness and caring, so much empathy. If things had been different, maybe Norman would have become a doctor himself.

But things weren't different. And they couldn't be until justice was done. Justice, not vengeance. Surely Dr. Claiborne must realize that.

There could be no justice as long as Sam and Lila

lived. They were the ones who'd branded and sentenced him with their testimony—but who were they to pass judgment? Lila, giving her warm body to satisfy the lust of her dead sister's lover. And Sam, living on the blood of the innocent, selling guns and knives in his store—hunting rifles to shoot down helpless animals, and knives to cut them up with. He was the killer, the butcher, the dealer in death—why couldn't anyone see that?

Dr. Claiborne would never understand, but Norman did. Those who live by the sword must die by the sword. Tonight.

But Main Street was dead and the side-street homes were dark. Sam and Lila were hiding from him, hiding behind the windowshades. Where—in which house? He couldn't go around knocking on doors. How could he find them?

Norman halted at the corner, frowning. No one saw him standing there under the streetlight, but he wouldn't go unnoticed forever. He was a fugitive, they'd come looking for him. If he meant to act, it must be now. There wasn't time—

Then he noticed the phone booth in the shadows at the side of the darkened filling station. Of course, that was the answer. Look in the telephone directory.

He moved past the deserted gas pumps and entered the glass cubicle. There he stood, eyes fixed on the rusty length of chain dangling empty-ended beside the phone.

The directory was missing. He'd have to call the operator for information.

Norman reached for the receiver, then pulled his hand away. He couldn't call. Nobody asks for addresses;

even if she gave it out, the operator would remember. In a place like this, everybody was curious about strangers. The minute he hung up, she'd probably call Sam and Lila and tell them someone was looking for them. It would be a dead giveaway.

Dead. He wasn't dead and wouldn't be, if only he took care. But he had to act quickly. No time—

Norman left the booth, moved out from under the light, and crossed at the corner, passing the tavern there. Its windows were darkened, thanks to Sunday-closing laws. All the windows on the street were dark, all but one.

One storefront up ahead was lighted. He couldn't see it clearly until he started forward, then peered across the street at the sign.

Loomis Hardware.

A light in the window, but that was just for display. It was the other light that mattered—the one overhead, shining dimly from the back of the store.

Someone was inside.

Norman started across the street, then slowed.

Careful now, stop and think. Be cautious. The thing to do was move on, cross at the corner, and come back along the side of the store, in case anyone might be looking out. Stay in the shadows. *Out of sight, out of mind.*

Norman nodded to himself, then moved quietly. It was only when he reached the shadowed shelter of the narrow walkway between the store and the adjoining building that he began to giggle softly. He had to, because the old saying was wrong. As he came around to the back door and fumbled with the latch, he was out of sight.

But he wasn't out of his mind.

Ten

Lila Loomis was at home when it happened, sitting in the darkened living room and watching some stupid game show on television. The program wasn't her choice; reception was poor because of the storm, and Channel 5 was the only one coming through clearly. At least the show served to distract her attention from what was going on outside.

For the hundredth time she found herself wondering about what she was seeing. The game was silly and the questions offered to its contestants were even sillier. *Here we go now with the Giant Jackpot! For ten thousand dollars in cash, a brand-new Ford Galaxie, and a fun-filled, all-expenses-paid week's vacation for two at the beautiful Acapulco Hilton . . . What was Jackie Onassis' maiden name?*

"Minnie Schwartz," Lila murmured. Then, catching herself, she smiled at her own silliness. Talking back to the tube made no sense at all, but lately she'd fallen into the habit. And she wasn't the only one; other people seemed to be responding to quizmasters, talk-show hosts, and the anonymous idiots who shouted out commercials over a background of some unseen heavenly choir lifting angel voices in praise of a liquid fertilizer. A few more years of this, and everybody would end up talking to themselves.

Lila was just about to get up and go into the kitchen when the evening news came on. She settled back and listened gratefully. The normal voice and features of the commentator offered welcome relief after the phony hysteria of the gameshow's MC and the shrieking responses of the grinning contestants.

Most of the bulletins concerned the recent storm, and the top story dealt with the terrible bus accident over at Montrose. Fortunately for Lila's peace of mind, there was no live coverage of the scene, though the newscaster promised film at eleven. She made a mental note not to tune in; maybe it was childish of her, but she just couldn't stand the sight of death or suffering.

Lila shook her head, dismissing the self-criticism. It wasn't just a childish reaction; she of all people had the right to feel that way, after what had happened. Of course it had been years ago, ancient history, and she hadn't been present when her sister and the detective were murdered by that maniac. But Lila had seen Norman Bates coming at her with a knife in his hand, and the fear remained. Sometimes it returned in dreams; she'd shiver and cry out until Sam took her in his arms and comforted her. *Honey, it's all right*. Then he'd switch on the light beside the bed. *See? No one's there. You had a nightmare.*

Even now, Lila wished Sam were here. Way past seven, and he was still at the store, working on those figures. He had to, of course, with the quarterly tax payment coming up, and Sunday afternoon was the best time to do the books. But it ruined plans for a decent dinner, and there was no point in even thinking about going out later in the evening.

Not that they'd want to anyway, after this storm. Still, it was over now, thank goodness, and reports of local damage and power outages around the country didn't really concern her. Lila was only half listening when the newscaster started to talk about the all-points alert for a patient who'd escaped from the State Hospital this afternoon after murdering a visitor.

"Authorities believe he fled in a van belonging to the murder victim, who was a member of a religious order, the Little Sisters of Charity. The patient, Norman Bates, is still at large."

Norman Bates.

Lila froze.

Murdering. Escaped. Still at large.

She couldn't move, couldn't see, couldn't hear. Everything was frozen now, the way it was in the nightmares. But she was wide awake. And Norman—

Somehow she managed to externalize her perception again, listening closely as the commentator brought her another late bulletin. "Lightning struck the Weiland Nurseries greenhouse in Rock Center late this afternoon, with damages estimated at—"

Was that all? She'd missed the rest of the report

about Norman when she panicked. But damn it, she had a right to panic, every right. And if that ignoramus reading the news had any brains, he'd panic too. *This isn't just another bulletin. Norman's loose!*

And she was talking to the tube again, talking to herself. When the one she should be talking to was Sam.

Lila rose, went to the TV set, shut it off. Then, crossing the room in darkness, she turned to switch on the lamps, but stopped herself in time.

No lights. What if *he* was out there?

But how could he be? Even if Norman knew where she lived, there was no real reason to think he'd come here. Except that people like Norman weren't guided by reason or reality.

Lila was still standing beside the lamp when she heard the sound.

Suddenly alert, she strained to listen, but now there was silence. *Just nerves. Imagining things.*

Then she flinched as it came again—a muffled scraping.

Footsteps?

She couldn't identify the noise, only locate its source. It was coming from outside.

Now, once more, silence. Silence and darkness. Not hearing, not seeing, Lila edged her way to the front window. Her hand trembled as she raised the shade to one side. Slowly, just an inch, enough to look out and see—

Nothing.

The walk, the lawn, the street beyond, stood empty in the night.

And the sound came again as the tree beside the

90

house swayed in the wind, its upper branches brushing against the eaves of the roof.

Norman wasn't here.

Lila didn't realize she'd been holding her breath until she found herself exhaling in sudden relief. *You see, it was your imagination. Why should Norman want to harm you? You're not his enemy. He wouldn't come here.*

Then, as she let the shade swing back into place, the relief faded into realization.

Of course he's not here. In Norman's mind there was another enemy. He'd be coming after Sam.

Lila was trembling again by the time she reached the end table and found the phone. Fumbling in the dark, she forced herself to concentrate, counting off the unseen digits as she dialed the number of the store.

Then she waited for the ring, but it didn't come; all she heard was a buzzing sound. Busy signal? No, the tone was wrong. What had they said on the news about a power outage?

As she replaced the receiver, the scraping noise resumed outside. Now, even though she knew its source, she held her breath once more. Perhaps this time she could hear another sound over it, the sound of a car motor. Sam's car coming down the street, pulling into the driveway—

Silence.

If Sam had been listening to the radio at the store, he'd have heard some kind of news report and come home to her. But there was no car, so he hadn't listened, didn't know.

She glanced at her watch; the luminous hands on the dial told her it was eight o'clock.

Eight o'clock. Even if he hadn't heard anything, he should be home by now. Unless—

There was no need to pursue the thought. The need was to stumble across the room into the kitchen, grope for her purse on the serving counter, carry it to the back door. And then to peer out through the door-window toward the walk beyond, making sure no one was standing there.

The walk was empty. Slowly she opened the kitchen door and stepped outside. Night wind fanned her face as she turned and surveyed the backyard, the side lawn, the stretch of walk leading to the street. All clear.

Gripping her purse, she shut the door and went up the walk, glancing at the darkened outline of the house next door. Maybe she ought to tell the Dempsters, let Ted drive her to the store. Then she remembered that her neighbors were away; they'd said something about visiting their married daughter in Ravenswood over the weekend. And the people across the street had left this morning for a vacation at the lake.

Lila emerged onto the street, slowing to scan the sidewalk leading to the right. Nothing moved there but the shadows under the trees. But in the shadows—

Don't panic. Just keep your eyes open, take your time, only three blocks to go.

She kept telling herself that, over and over again, but in spite of everything, Lila found herself hurrying. The shadows were merely shadows and the night was silent except for the sigh of wind and the quickening clatter of her heels against the wet cement of the sidewalk.

Then, turning onto Main Street, Lila saw the headlights of a car coming from the left.

Sam?

She halted, ready to wave, but it wasn't their station wagon that swept past her, and the face of the driver was unfamiliar. Perhaps she ought to have waved anyway; now it was too late, for the car rounded the corner up the street, making a right turn. Main Street was empty again.

Lila moved forward. One more block. She was approaching the store now, glancing ahead to look through the lighted window.

But the light was out.

She slowed, staring through the glass into the darkened store beyond.

Don't panic. Maybe he's just closed up, gone out the back way to the car.

Lila started along the walk at the side of the building, moving slowly, cautiously. She gone only a few yards when she caught sight of the station wagon parked next to the alley exit in back. Its doors were closed and the driver's seat was empty. Sam hadn't left.

Then why were the lights out?

Perhaps he'd fallen asleep. Or maybe—

Now it came to her, the other thought, the one she'd tried to push out of her mind. Sam's visit to Dr. Rowan last month, and the medical report—the electrocardiogram. *Nothing serious, just a little murmur, don't worry about it.* But doctors didn't know everything, and half the time those reports were wrong. Suppose Sam had had a heart attack? *Don't panic.*

Carefully, Lila made her way down the walk. She moved silently, and only silence greeted her as she rounded the corner to reach the back entrance. The blinds of the windows on either side were drawn, and the door was shut. A touch of the knob told her it was locked.

There was a key in her purse, but she didn't reach for it. That was one lesson she'd learned from that awful experience years ago. Play safe, don't take chances when you're alone. And if something *had* happened to Sam, there was nothing she could do about it unless she got help. *Don't panic.*

Lila turned and walked past the empty station wagon to the alley beyond, pausing to inspect its expanse in both directions. There was no sound, no movement in the night.

Satisfied, she walked along the alley to the right, emerging on the side street at the far end. Across the way, the courthouse stood in the square. She started over to it, moving past the wet, empty benches and the granite shaft of the war memorial. The building beyond was dark, but here on the annex side the door was unlocked, and a light shone out from the corridor behind it.

Entering, Lila climbed the stairs and moved down the hall. As she did so, she had this feeling—what was it called, *dèjá* view, or *vue*, something like that, when you think a thing has happened before?

Then she corrected herself. It was memory, not feeling. This *had* happened before, years ago, when she and Sam were looking for the murderer of her sister. They'd come here on a Sunday morning to see Sheriff Chambers, and the clerk—what was his name? —Peterson, old man Peterson, told them he was at church. Peterson and Chambers were both gone now and she was here alone, but the similarity of her present errand to the former one was unnerving. Lila's pace quickened as she crossed the threshold of the office at the far end of the corridor.

Little old Irene Grovesmith sat at her desk, reading a magazine. She put it aside to peer up owlishly over her reading glasses, then recognized her visitor and nodded.

"Lila—"

"Hello, Irene. Is Sheriff Engstrom busy?"

"You can say that again." Behind the thick lenses, Irene's eyes narrowed in sour disapproval. "Left here more than three hours ago. Going over to Montrose on account of that bus crash, you heard about it? He promised me he'd be back by seven at the latest, and here it is, past eight-thirty. The squawk's out, and the phones don't work either. They're supposed to be fixing the lines now."

"Then there's no way I can get in touch with the sheriff?"

"I just told you—" Irene caught herself, took off the glasses, and cleared her throat self-consciously. "Sorry. What's the trouble?"

It's about time you asked, you old bat. Lila hid the thought behind a token smile and a shake of her head. "I'm a little worried about Sam. He's been down at the store all afternoon and didn't get home for dinner. I was just over there now and the car's still outside, but the door's locked and all the lights are out."

"Don't you have a key?"

"Yes. It's just that I don't like the idea of going in alone." Lila hesitated, wondering how much she ought to reveal. One word to Irene, and it would be all over town by tomorrow morning. But that didn't matter; what mattered now was Sam. If something had happened to him—

"There was a report on the news," she said. "They were talking about a patient escaping from the State Hospital this afternoon."

"Norman Bates?"

Lila caught her breath. "You heard about him?"

Irene nodded. "Chuck Merwin stopped by here looking for the sheriff half an hour ago. He's with the fire department, you know, Dave Merwin's boy? Tall, dark-complected fella with bad teeth—"

"Yes, I know him. What happened?"

"Well, the truck just come from there, and they wanted to let the sheriff know before heading over to Montrose again. Couldn't raise him on the squawk."

"Came from where?"

"I made a note." Irene fished a pad out from under the magazine. "Here it is." She slid the glasses on and glanced down. "Chuck says they found the van that lunatic escaped in. Over on County Trunk A, right outside of town. Looked like there'd been a gasoline explosion—two bodies inside. One was a woman, some nun visiting the hospital, at least that's what they think. The other was this Norman Bates."

"He's dead?"

"Burned to a frazzle. Chuck said he never saw

96

anything so awful, not in five years with the department."

"Thank God."

Irene glanced up quickly. "What's all this got to do with Sam?"

"Nothing." Lila shook her head. "Look, I'll be going over to the store now. But when the sheriff gets back, would you ask him to please stop by? If the station wagon's not there, it means we've gone home and everything's all right. Just ask him to take a look."

"Of course. I'll make a note."

Irene was scribbling on the pad as Lila left. This time she had no need to move slowly; the street outside was still deserted, but the night held no terror.

The only thing to worry about now was Sam himself. That damned electrocardiogram—

Don't panic. He could have fallen asleep.

In spite of the thought, Lila found herself hurrying as she turned back into the alley. She half hoped the station wagon would be gone, but when she saw it still parked before the rear entrance of the store, her pace quickened.

The key was already in her hand as she reached the darkened doorway. Steadying her grip, she fitted it to the elusive lock. Metal met metal and the knob turned.

Lila entered, then halted just inside, trying to recall the location of the light switch. Which wall was it on—the left or the right? Funny, she couldn't remember a simple thing like that.

Her hand groped against the plaster on the right,

found and flipped the toggle, but nothing happened. Had the bulb burned out? *Burned. Norman's burned*, she reminded herself. *Don't panic.*

Perhaps the power outage explained the lack of light here and up front. Lila forced herself to wait while her vision adjusted to the dark. As she did so, her eyes inventoried the contents of the room. File cabinets flanked the far wall, shelving stood on both sides, a desk and chair occupied the center of the floor ahead. The desktop held a litter of ledgers and file cards, but the chair was empty. Sam wouldn't leave things in a mess, so he must have gone up front.

Now she moved past the desk to the doorway leading into the store area. The darkness was deeper there, and she paused on the threshold, scanning the shadows beyond.

"Sam?"

The shadows were silent.

"Sam!"

Oh my God—something's happened—his heart—

She started forward, rounding the corner of the rear counter, and found him there.

He was lying face upwards on the floor, staring at her.

Lila stared back. She'd been right, it *was* his heart.

That was where the knife had struck, leaving the gaping, bubbling hole in his chest.

For a moment she thought he wasn't dead. He couldn't be, because she could hear the sound of breathing.

Then, as the shadow moved out from the counter behind her, Lila turned and the knife came down.

And down.

And down...

Eleven

When Claiborne pulled up before the hardware store, the sheriff's car was already parked in front.

The sight of it caused him to slam on the brakes. He climbed out and headed for the lighted, open entrance.

"Just a moment, please."

Claiborne halted as the tiny man stepped out to intercept him at the doorway.

Almost automatically he made an instant professional appraisal of the stranger: the thin, sallow face, the sparse brown hair matching the color of the eyes, the neatly trimmed mustache. He was dressed in a dark business suit, a white shirt, and a dull gray tie. It was the typical Sunday garb of the typical small-town merchant, and as Claiborne noted it, he smiled in sudden relief.

"Sam Loomis?" he said.

The little man shook his head. "Milt Engstrom," he said. "County sheriff."

Claiborne's relief faded and his gaze dropped. It was then that he caught sight of what he'd overlooked before: the shiny, pointed black boots protruding from beneath the conservatively cuffed trousers.

So much for keen psychological insight. And so much for renewed hope.

Claiborne looked up to meet the sheriff's level stare, knowing what he had to ask and dreading the answer.

"Where's Mr. Loomis? Did something happen to him?"

The expressionless eyes didn't waver. "If you don't mind, I'll ask the questions. For openers, suppose you tell me who you are and what you're doing here."

Claiborne felt a muscle spasm shoot through his legs as he shifted his stance to accommodate the weight of weariness. How long had it been since he'd been given a chance to rest? Driving into town after leaving the highway, he'd found himself dozing off behind the wheel; too much tension had taken its toll. All he wanted right now was to sit down and relax.

"It's a long story," he said. "Couldn't we just go inside and—"

The sheriff frowned. "Start talking," he said. "I haven't got all night."

By the time Claiborne identified himself and told

Engstrom what had happened at the hospital and on the road, he was ready to drop. Unlike Banning, the sheriff wrote nothing down, but there was no doubt that he carefully absorbed everything he was told. Finally he nodded, signifying that his mental notebook was closed.

"Maybe you better step inside now," Engstrom said. "There's been an accident."

Turning abruptly, the sheriff walked into the store without giving Claiborne time to reply. But now, as he followed Engstrom down the aisle, he had a chance to speak.

"Is Loomis dead?"

The sheriff stopped before the rear counter and gestured down toward the floor at his left.

"You're a doctor," he said. "Suppose you tell me."

Claiborne moved forward, following the arc of gesturing fingers with his gaze.

For a long moment he stood silent, conscious of Engstrom's scrutiny, the cold eyes boring into his back. *The little sadist—he's enjoying this! What does he expect me to do, throw up like that salesman at the van? I'm a doctor, I've seen violent death before.*

And he'd seen Sam Loomis before, too. It was that which really disturbed him—the familiarity of the corpse's contorted features. Then realization came to him; there were clippings in the file, newspaper clippings with photos of the people involved in Norman's case.

Norman's case. Claiborne forced himself to look up and meet Engstrom's stare. He couldn't match its impersonal coldness with his own eyes, but he did his best to convey it in his voice.

"The incision is quite large," he said. "Obviously made by a knife with an extremely broad blade. From the amount of hemorrhage, I'd assume that the aorta was punctured, probably severed. Do you want me to make an examination?"

The sheriff shook his head. "My man's on his way over from County General—or will be, when he gets back from the mess over in Montrose. I'm running shorthanded tonight, can't even rouse an extra deputy." Engstrom turned to step behind the rear counter. "While we're waiting, there's something else you might want to take a look at."

Claiborne moved around the corner from the other end, then glanced down.

The sheriff was wrong. He didn't want to look at it—not that hacked and horrid handiwork sprawling supinely beneath the counter's edge, bathed in blood from a dozen wounds gaping like red mouths against the white flesh.

There was no sense of recognition stemming from what he saw here, but even before Engstrom spoke, he knew.

"Lila Loomis," the sheriff said. "Sam's wife."

Claiborne turned away, sickened in spite of himself, like a premed student confronting his first dissection. When speech came, all he could muster was a murmur.

"Then he killed them both."

"He?"

"Norman Bates. The patient I told you about."

"Maybe so."

"But there's no doubt now. I knew I was right—he came straight here after burning the van. Remember what I said about the hitchhiker he must have picked up on the road?"

"Must have? Seems to me you're jumping at a pretty big conclusion."

"I've got his sign out in my car." Claiborne turned. "Come along, let me show you—"

"Later." The sheriff walked to the end of the counter. "I want you to see this first."

As Claiborne joined him, the sheriff pointed down at the open drawer of the cash register on the counter top. "Empty," he said. "Nine hundred and eighty-three dollars there this afternoon and it's all gone."

"How do you know the amount?"

"Found this on the floor." Engstrom pulled a piece of paper from his jacket pocket. "Deposit slip all made out and ready for the bank tomorrow morning."

"Then Norman took the money."

"Somebody did, that's for sure." The sheriff turned. "Come along, there's more."

He reached under the glass-topped counter and brought out a display tray. Its slotted surface held a dozen bone-handled carving knives of varying sizes, their steel blades glittering under the light.

No, not a dozen—Claiborne counted them off quickly and corrected himself. There were eleven knives and one empty slot at the far end.

Watching, Engstrom nodded. "One missing," he said. "The murder weapon." He pivoted and walked into the back room, gesturing up at the overhead light as Claiborne followed.

"When I came here looking for Mrs. Loomis, the back door was unlocked and the light didn't switch on. At first I figured it had burned out, but then I spotted the bulb lying here on the table. I screwed it back in and you can see there's nothing wrong with it."

"Of course." Claiborne noted the desk and chair. "Norman slipped into the store and killed Loomis while he was working at his desk. He dragged the body up front where it would be out of sight—look, you can see blood here on the floor. Then he came back here, unscrewed the bulb, and waited for Mrs. Loomis in the store—"

"How did he know she'd be coming?"

"He must have expected her to show up looking for her husband. Don't you understand? That's what he was here for—he wanted to kill them both."

Engstrom shrugged. "Suppose we try it my way," he said. "Let's take a thief, an ordinary thief. Could be someone who lives around here, or even this hitchhiker you claim got burned up in that van. But whoever he is, he's looking to rip off a store. Maybe he checks out a couple of others first and can't break in. Then he sees a light here. He tries the back door and it isn't locked. I'll buy what you said about sneaking in unnoticed. But that's all."

"What about the rest? What's wrong with it?"

"What's wrong is that you're not much of a detective." Engstrom glanced down at the floor. "Sure, there's blood here, but only a few drops. I'd say it came off the knife when the thief carried it away with him. Sam wasn't stabbed sitting at his desk; the wound's in his chest, not his back. In fact, the thief didn't even have a knife when he came in; he got it from under the counter in the store."

Claiborne frowned. "I still think—"

"Never mind, let me finish." Engstrom gestured toward the doorway. "The way I figure Sam was up front turning off the store lights when the thief got in. He came for money, not murder, and all he wanted to do was keep out of sight until Sam left. There was no place to conceal himself in back, so he went on into the store to hide behind the counter in the dark. But then something goes wrong; Sam either sees him or hears him. That's when the thief reached up, grabs a knife, and lets him have it.

"The thief takes the money from the register. He's ready to run out the back way when Lila shows up in the back alley. He locks the door, thinking she'll try it and go away.

"But he's got a surprise coming; she has a key. There's just time to unscrew the overhead bulb so she can't switch on the light. And when she gets inside, he's waiting up front in the dark with the knife."

Claiborne frowned. "You saw her body," he said. "Perhaps someone who's committed murder in a moment of panic would strike again to avoid discovery. But not like that. She wasn't just killed, she was slashed over and over again, the way Norman slashed her sister in the shower—"

He broke off, conscious that his words weren't registering. No one would believe him, not without proof—solid, incontrovertible proof.

"Don't worry," Engstrom said. "If Bates really is alive, he can't get far."

"But he has money now."

"And we have an ID, photos, his entire record on file. He can't hide out for long; where would he go?"

Claiborne didn't answer. There was no answer.

Then, glancing down at the clutter of ledgers and file folders on the desk, he saw the newspaper lying on the edge. It was partially folded, as though it had been tossed aside ready to discard, but the headline of the two-column story on the uppermost side was plainly visible.

Hollywood Producer Plans Film on Bates Case

And now he knew where Norman would be going.

Twelve

Jan Harper inspected her makeup in the bathroom mirror and decided it was perfect. Then she stuck out her tongue at the image in the glass.

Okay, kid. Let's get the show on the road.

Picking up her purse from the counter, she turned and tiptoed out. The precaution wasn't really necessary; in the second bedroom on the far side of the bath, Connie was still snoring away. Jan's roommate would probably be dead to the world until noon and wish she were dead when she finally awoke, hungover and overhung with remorse for last night's fun and games.

But as she made her way down the hall to the front door, Jan felt a nagging prickle of envy. Connie didn't have to slave away in front of a mirror; a cold shower and a quick comb-through would do the trick when she arose. No point in her worrying about a perfect makeup job, not with that big nose and those tiny tits. When you needed to cut it in this business was a small nose and big tits, and that let Connie out.

Abruptly, Jan felt a sudden surge of shame. Connie wasn't to blame for the way she looked; at least she was honest and didn't try to fake it with a nose job above and styrofoam below. She did the best she could with what she had, and that deserved praise, not a putdown.

Jan shrugged as she let herself out and locked the door behind her. Connie would manage; right now it was time to consider her own goals. That's why she'd spent an hour on makeup, that's why the neat little Toyota stood waiting for her in the carport. Every time she thought of the monthly payments, she shuddered, but when she opened the door and got a whiff of that wonderful new-car smell, her good vibes returned.

The Toyota wasn't a luxury; it was part of her outfit, her image. And the new-leather smell was as necessary as the Chanel she sprayed on after a shower, even though gas was begining to cost more than perfume. If you want to get to the top, don't take the bus.

Starting the motor, she backed out carefully, then climbed the road and turned east on Mulholland Drive. Clusters of homes huddled at intervals along the winding way, but most of the stretch was given over to cliffside and brush. In the Monday-morning mist it was still possible to catch a glimpse of gophers, coyotes, joggers, and other forms of wildlife.

Ignoring them, Jan stared down into the San Fernando Valley at her left. Rising out of the yellowish smudge of smog, she could see the sound stages of Coronet Studios, midway between CBS Studio Center and Universal's black tower.

Now the Toyota turned left again and began its descent. Jan took a deep breath, just as she always did before spiraling down into the smog. The damned stuff ate right into the Toyota's chrome; God only knew what it did to human lungs. But when you're headed for the top, sometimes you've got to go down into the pits.

Crossing Ventura Boulevard, she drove north to the studio gate on her right. A shiny Rolls preceded her, then halted at the guard's cubicle ahead, but only for a moment. The striped crossbar blocking the entrance swung up quickly as the uniformed man at the gate grinned and waved the driver forward. The Rolls moved onto the lot.

Now, as Jan came abreast of the cubicle, the crossbar dropped back into place. The guard stared at her.

She gave him a smile. "Jan Harper," she said.

There was no change in his expression—or lack of it. "Who did you wish to see?"

"I'm on the lot. With the Driscoll unit."

"One moment, please."

Turning, the guard entered the cubicle and checked the listings stacked on a shelf beside the doorway. Then he peered out and nodded. "Okay. Better tell them to give you a sticker."

"Thanks. I'll do that."

The crossbar lifted and Jan drove on, hoping her

smile hadn't cracked. That wimp in the Rolls got the big hello, but after all these weeks the guard didn't even remember her name.

Cool it, kid. Someday when you drive through that gate, they'll lay out a red carpet for you all the way to Driscoll's office.

Jan was passing that office now, in the Administration Building at her right, but she didn't stop there. All the parking slots were posted with neatly lettered signs reserving them for executive personnel. That was the way the system operated: execs had the spaces nearest the offices; working stars and directors got choice spots next to the sound stages; top production people owned the openings before their headquarters.

But signs can be rubbed out and new names lettered in. And the way things were going in the industry, the sign painters had the only steady jobs in town.

Jan shrugged and headed for the parking area at the rear of the lot, moving past mailboys on bicycles, elderly producers with motorcarts, drivers of vans and trucks filled with props and camera equipment. The Toyota edged through narrow openings between portable dressing rooms and trailers, then halted before a stage as a red light flashed and whirled, signaling a take in progress, which could be ruined by traffic noises.

The industry was turning out its product.

Once upon a time these studio streets had been glutted with glimpses of glamour: bit players in oriental robes conceived in Arabian nightmares; pirate outfits; French Empire ballroom gowns; Confederate cavalry uniforms. Dress extras had sauntered along in top hats and tails, chorus girls had paraded like walking rainbows. Indian chiefs, wearing full warpaint, and cowboy stars with white suits and matching Stetsons had mingled with leading ladies resplendent in creations designed in the cerebral salon of Edith Head's head.

But the costume picture had been swept away in a tide of red ink. Today, Valentino's Sheik would be a squat little oil profiteer in a business suit, sunglasses, and a soiled *kayyifeh*. The pirate ships were sunk, discos had replaced ballrooms, the Confederate army was gone with the wind. Fred and Ginger had hung up their dancing shoes forever, Indians carried briefcases when they went on the warpath at Senate hearings, cowboys looked like any bearded university student, and most leading ladies performed in bedroom scenes, wearing nothing at all. When you go to a studio now, don't look for glamour—look for a parking place.

Jan drove into the rear area, glancing at her watch. Quarter to ten; she still had fifteen minutes. But the lot was already full, or almost so.

Circling, she found an opening at the far end and started to angle in, then braked quickly as the door of a car on her right swung open and a figure backed into her path.

She leaned on the horn. "Hey, watch it—"

The figure turned, and Jan recognized Roy Ames.

He waved and moved to her left as she parked. "Sorry, I didn't see you coming." Opening the door, he took her arm as she slid across the seat.

Jan suppressed her frown, but she couldn't suppress her thoughts. What was with this character? Even after all these weeks of contact, she still couldn't get used to his here-let-me-help-you routine. Common courtesy wasn't very common nowadays; most men let a girl emerge from a car unaided, and a fairly high percentage would goose her as she backed out.

Roy Ames was a problem case. He didn't even look like most of the other screenwriters she knew. To begin with, he was well groomed—not exactly handsome, but far removed from the specimens who were heavily into hair and horn-rims. His wardrobe lacked Levi's, and apparently he'd learned to ride a typewriter without wearing boots. She'd never seen him stoned or strung out, and if he had other hangups, he did a good job of hiding them.

Hiding. These straight-arrow types were usually hiding something. So where was he coming from, behind his old-fashioned manners and the open grin?

And where are you coming from? Jan caught herself wondering what was wrong with her. Why did she automatically suspect instead of respect a man like Roy? There was no reason for it; he was probably as upfront as she was.

They crossed the lot and started down the street, dodging agents and clients en route to Monday-morning meetings, carpenters scurrying onto sets, memo-bearing messengers racing their rounds—the usual organized confusion.

"I called you earlier," Roy said. "Connie told me you'd left."

"How'd she sound?"

"Bitchy. Guess I woke her up."

"Don't worry, she'll survive the shock. I did."

Roy glanced at her. "Then you know about it."

"Know about what?"

"Didn't you listen to the news? Norman Bates escaped."

"Oh my God."

"Report says he went on another murder rampage. Five victims. They're not sure, but he could still be on the loose."

Jan halted. "So that's why Driscoll wanted us to come in! You think they're going to shut down the picture?"

"Maybe."

"But they can't—" Jan put her hand on Roy's arm. "We've got to stop them. Please, promise me you'll help."

He was staring at her. Why didn't he say something?

Taking a deep breath, Jan gave him her best shot. "It's not just my part I'm worried about. You need this picture too, that screen credit is your future. Don't throw it away."

Roy's eyes were ice. Suddenly his face contorted and his voice rose. "What the hell's the matter with you? A maniac breaks out and kills five innocent people, and all you're worried about is killing a goddam movie!"

He jerked his arm free so quickly that for a moment Jan thought he intended to hit her. Instead he turned and strode away, leaving her stunned and shaken.

She'd guessed right, after all. There had been something hidden behind the good manners and the friendly smile, and now she knew what it was.

Violence.

Oddly, she felt no fear of him. But after the initial shock faded, the emotion that remained surprised her. It was disappointment.

Damn it, Roy must have been turning her on more than she'd realized. Even now it wasn't possible to reject him completely. Maybe she wasn't as hard-nosed as she pretended, because a part of her had really responded to that Mr. Nice Guy image.

Perhaps his anger was justified; his concern about those murders might be genuine. And if it was—

Jan shook her head. What he believed was his own business, but she couldn't go along with him. She'd worked too long and too hard to settle for that.

All her life, ever since she was a little girl, staring into the mirror at her acne-riddled face and wondering if she'd ever grow up and find someone who thought she was pretty, someone who'd love her, she'd been working—working to become the kind of person who would deserve attention, the kind she saw in the movies and on TV.

And now she *had* grown up, she'd been on TV, she was going to be in the movies, and they'd all love her—not just a single someone, but everybody. She was going to make it. Not just for herself; it was a debt she owed to that pimply-faced girl in the mirror, the little girl with the big dream.

Watching Roy enter the Administration Building, Jan started forward with renewed determination. All the violence in the world couldn't hang a guilt-trip on her now. Feeling sorry for the victims, whoever they were, wasn't going to help them. They were dead and she was alive and what you called "a goddam movie" was the break she'd worked and waited for. She and the little girl.

No matter what happened, Jan wouldn't let them stop the picture.

Thirteen

Anita Kedzie was ambidextrous.

Seated in Driscoll's outer office, with copies of *Variety* and *Hollywood Reporter* resting on her desk, she turned their pages simultaneously in search of items that might interest her employer and circled them in red with a felt-tipped pen.

Jan had observed this ritual before, and she'd never been able to figure out just how Miss Kedzie managed to read both trade papers at the same time. But one had to remember that the woman was a little strange; anyone who would take a job as a producer's secretary *had* to be strange. Part insect, perhaps. Weren't there some insects whose eyes functioned independently, so that they could see in two directions at once?

Correction: *three* directions. For, without shifting her gaze from the pages before her, Miss Kedzie said, "Please go right in. Mr. Driscoll will be with you in a moment. He's running a little late this morning."

Jan nodded and moved past the desk and through the doorway behind it.

He's running a little late this morning.

So what else was new? According to their secretaries, producers were always running a little late, like cheap watches. An apt comparison, really, because you always had to keep an eye on their hands, and some of them wouldn't give you the time of day.

Of course, there were exceptions to the rule, men whose talent and good taste were indisputable and indispensable. The industry couldn't survive without them.

But nowadays anyone could call himself a producer. All he had to do was plant a few items in the trades announcing the purchase of properties for future filming, rent office space, put his name on the door, and wait for the chicks to walk in and lie down.

Marty Driscoll didn't seem to fit into this category, thank God; he'd never tried to come on to her, and he certainly had an impressive layout.

Jan glanced around the private office as she entered, taking inventory of the Daumier prints on the walls, the oversize couches right-angled before the huge glass coffee table, the massive fruitwood desk with its intercom system and the silver-framed portrait photographs of the most recent wife and two smiling children.

Impressive, that was for sure, but not entirely

convincing. Something about the office disturbed her.

From what she'd seen of Driscoll, he wouldn't know a French print from a French postcard. The contemporary decor, however elaborate and expensive, reflected no particular style except Early Executive—running a little late, of course. And the family portraits in their expensive frames were standard equipment; the whole spread might have come straight out of the studio's prop department, just moved in and set up overnight. Which meant it could be moved out just as quickly when Driscoll lost his parking space. And that was what bothered her. The decor wasn't contemporary—just a temporary con.

Jan dismissed the thought quickly. Driscoll wasn't a phony; he had a long track record as a producer of top-grossers. At least he'd taken credit for them, and that was what counted. He knew the business, knew where the money was, knew where the bodies were buried.

Bodies. Five victims, Roy said. *Don't think about it.*

She glanced across the room and saw Roy, already seated in the corner with his back to the doorway. Oblivious to her quiet entrance, he was leaning forward and talking to Paul Morgan, her co-star in the picture.

Come off it, she told herself. *You're no co-star—he gets the billing.*

And why not? Paul Morgan was almost an institution. Standing there silhouetted in profile against the light from the window, he looked like a miniature model of his oversize screen image. It still puzzled her to think he'd take an offbeat role like Norman Bates.

But then, he was probably just as puzzled to have her as his female lead instead of a name star. Maybe that was why he ignored her now as she came in; come to think of it, Paul Morgan hadn't said a dozen words to her directly since the day she was set for the part.

Whatever his reason, she'd better do something about it, and fast. Chat him up, stroke him, make it plain that this was his ego trip and she was only along for the ride.

Jan started toward the two men, then halted at the touch of a hand curling around her waist. A wave of sickly scent accompanied the movement.

A good thing she already had a smile on her face, intended for Morgan; now she could give it to Santo Vizzini. Not that he didn't deserve a smile for his own sake; after all, he'd been responsible for her getting the role. But it wasn't easy to register pleasurable emotion at the sight of the man with the caterpillar moustache. The odor of his perfumed presence was overpowering, and his fingers probing and moving downward toward her thigh gave Jan the creeps.

She turned quickly, preserving the smile and hoping it would atone for her evading his touch. "Mr. Vizzini—"

"Santo." The caterpillar was crawling now as the thick lips parted beneath it. "Please, there is no need to stand on ceremony."

Jan nodded. *I get the message, buster. You don't want me to stand on anything—just lie down.*

But she didn't say it. Luckily she didn't have to say anything, for now all conversation broke off as Marty Driscoll's voice echoed from the outer office.

"Hold my calls," he said.

It was part of the ritual, the classic invocation signifying that the conference, the meeting, the ceremony was about to begin.

The next step was Marty Driscoll's own, as he moved into the room. The fat, balding producer had a tall thin shadow; it glided behind him, closing the door as Driscoll hunkered down into the overstuffed chair behind the big desk. The shadow's name was George Ward, and its hair and face had gone gray in long years of service as Driscoll's *eminence grise*. Now the shadow slithered to a halt at the end of the desk, poised for a signal.

It came as Marty Driscoll hunched forward, broad shoulders bowed under the weight of the thick neck and heavy head. "Sit down, everybody," he said.

Roy Ames and Paul Morgan took the sofa facing the desk. Vizzini lowered himself on a lounger at the right, near George Ward, while Jan settled into a chair on the left.

Now she waited for Driscoll to utter the prescribed opening: "Anyone want coffee?" Instead he sat silently, a tonsured Buddha, staring down at the desk top through heavy-lidded eyes. He might have been meditating on Infinity or contemplating his navel, but Jan doubted it. From what she knew of Driscoll, he was neither a mystic nor a navel-observer. All he did was make her nervous, and perhaps that was his intention. A quick glimpse of the others grouped before the desk told her that they were equally uncomfortable as they waited for him to break the silence.

Then, abruptly, the head arched upward and the eyes widened.

"You all know what happened yesterday," Driscoll said. "Since then, I've had some second thoughts about the picture."

Second thoughts. The phrase echoed and Jan stiffened in response. *He's going to shut down. Roy was right.*

And Roy was speaking now. "You're not the only one. I was just telling Paul the same thing. We're in trouble."

"I don't see it." Paul Morgan broke in quickly. "Norman Bates's escape has nothing to do with our story. As long as the script sticks to the facts—"

Roy shook his head. "The facts have changed now."

"So we change the script." Vizzini spoke rapidly. "A little fix, perhaps, a few pages. We've still got a week. And since I'm shooting the scenes with the Loomis characters in sequence, we won't be using Steve Hill and the Gordon girl until next month, when they come out from New York."

"What is this, a story conference?" Roy gestured impatiently. "Forget the script! As long as Bates was in the asylum we had no problem. Our story was only a fairy tale, something that happened a long time ago. Audiences wouldn't give a damn if it was fact or fiction. But now we're up against reality."

"Right."

Driscoll nodded and Jan felt a knot forming in the pit of her stomach.

He was running scared. That meant the picture was dead, she was dead, and all her talk about not letting them stop was dead too.

"But you can't!" Her voice rose and she was rising with it, ignoring their sudden stares, ignoring everything except the inner urgency. "You can't quit now."

"Jan, please—" Roy was moving toward her, his eyes troubled, his hand reaching out to grasp her arm. "This is no time for hysteria—"

"Then stop being hysterical!" She shook herself free, ignoring him, concentrating on the bald man behind the desk. "What's the matter with you people? You're behaving like a bunch of old women! It would be crazy to stop. Don't you see what you've got here? You're sitting right on top of a gold mine and you're afraid to dig!"

Jan hesitated as Driscoll's hands came up from the desktop, palms moving inward. For an instant she thought he was assuming an attitude of prayer; then, as the sound came, she realized he was applauding.

"Bravo!" he said. "Cut and print."

"That isn't funny, dammit!" Jan felt her face redden as the anger burned outwards. "I'm not doing a performance, I'm telling you the truth. If you'd only stop and think for a minute, you'd realize the publicity—"

Driscoll gestured, halting her. "You stop," he said. "Give me a chance to say what I've been thinking." He turned and poked a pudgy finger at George Ward. "Here, you tell her."

The Gray Eminence nodded. "As Mr. Driscoll told

you, he had second thoughts about the production. At first we were upset by the reports; like Mr. Ames here, we wondered about having problems. Then we got into what you're talking about. The news value, the publicity. And we came up with the same answer. Norman Bates's breakout could be the best thing that ever happened to *Crazy Lady*. It ties us right into front-page headlines, top-of-the-show exposure on every TV and radio newscast in the country. Sure, Bates is dead, but the story will stay alive; they'll be investigating those murders for months now. A media event like this is something money couldn't buy. Every mention of the case is a free plug for our film."

The knot in Jan's stomach began to loosen. "Does that mean you're going ahead?"

"Full speed," Driscoll said. "Make it fast, get it shipped, and laugh all the way to the bank."

Jan felt the knot unwind.

"Great!" Paul Morgan grinned at Roy. "I told you there was nothing to worry about."

"The hell there isn't." Roy stood up, ignoring Morgan, and stood before the desk, facing Driscoll. "You're forgetting the script. What happened yesterday shoots down our ending."

"I'm not forgetting." Driscoll's index finger jabbed forward. "Like Santo says, you've got a week for changes. If you don't finish by next Monday, you'll stay on after the start-date. We'll follow the production schedule as is and shoot the new scenes last."

"Now wait a minute, I haven't made any commitment—"

"Your agent has. I called him this morning and set the deal."

Jan listened, smiling. The knot in her stomach was gone.

"Don't worry." Santo Vizzini moved up beside Roy. "It's only a few pages. I've got some ideas. Think of the material we can work with now—the new murders, and Norman's death."

Roy scowled, but when he spoke his voice was soft. "Just one thing," he said. "What makes you so sure Norman is dead?"

Fourteen

"Of course he's dead."

Dr. Steiner stubbed his cigarette against the side of the ashtray on Claiborne's desk. "Look, Adam. I know how you feel—"

"Do you?"

"For God's sake, stop being defensive! Nobody's blaming you for what happened. So why are you blaming yourself?"

Claiborne shrugged. "It's not a question of blame," he said. "What it comes down to is responsibility."

"Word games." Steiner took out another cigarette. "Blame, responsibility, what difference does it make? You want to go that route, then Otis was responsible for leaving Bates alone with the nun. And what about

129

Clara? She was on the desk when Bates slipped out. If anyone's to blame for his escape, it's those two."

"But I was in charge."

"And I'm the guy who put you there." Steiner reached into his pocket for matches. "If you're looking for the ultimate responsibility, the buck stops here." He lit his cigarette, dropped the match into the ashtray, and blew a spiral of smoke toward the ceiling. "When I say I know how you feel, it's not just a figure of speech. Why do you think I skipped my meeting and scooted back here the minute I got word? I had the same reaction you did—first shock, then guilt. Thank God there was a little time to think things over during the flight. I admit I'm still traumatized by what happened, we all are, and it's only natural under the circumstances. But the guilt is gone."

"Not for me."

Dr. Steiner gestured with his cigarette. "Look, nobody's perfect. We all make mistakes. Isn't that what you and I tell our analysands? We can't go through life blaming ourselves for honest errors. And yesterday was a comedy of errors—a tragedy, if you prefer. But the point is that none of us—Otis, Clara, you, or myself—could foresee what was going to happen. The only thing we can be faulted for, individually and collectively, is lack of infallibility."

"Now you're into word games," Claiborne said. "Whether or not I'm infallible doesn't matter. I had a job to do and I fell down."

"Fell down." Steiner puffed reflectively. "Fell down and tore your stockings and what will Daddy say

130

when he gets home? Come off it, Adam, you're not a child! And I'm not your father."

"Jesus, Nick, if you're going to play doctor with me—"

"Let me finish." Steiner leaned forward, peering through a gray halo of smoke. "Okay, so you're guilty. But of what? All you did was instruct Otis to watch the library while you took a phone call. That's the extent of it.

"You had no way of knowing Otis would leave, no way of knowing Norman was planning a break. And from then on, we're dealing with hard facts. It was Norman who killed Sister Barbara and took over the van. He was in the van when it exploded, his actions resulted in Sister Cupertine's death and his own—"

"But that's just it." Claiborne rose. "Norman wasn't killed in the van. They picked up a hitchhiker. I know because I found the sign, back on the other road. Norman got rid of him and Sister Cupertine, set fire to the van, then went after Sam and Lila Loomis in Fairvale. Didn't Engstrom tell you?"

Steiner nodded. "Yes, I heard all about your theory when I spoke with him this morning. But let's stay with facts. He's convinced the Loomises were killed by another party—a sneak thief, maybe even the hitchhiker you're talking about—"

"Convinced?" Claiborne said. "By what? Where are *his* facts? All he's got is another theory. A nice, convenient theory that wraps up everything. That is, if you're willing to accept the Loomises' deaths as just coincidence.

"Well, I'm not. I think they were deliberately murdered by the one man in the world who had a

131

motive." He paced the narrow opening between the wall and his desk. "If it's hard evidence you're looking for, consider this: Sam and Lila Loomis weren't just struck down. They were butchered. Put motive and method together and you get a clear picture of Norman Bates at work."

Dr. Steiner extinguished his second cigarette. "Nothing's going to be clear until we have the complete autopsy report," he said. "Engstrom talked to Rigsby at the coroner's office. He expects to give us his findings by the end of the week—"

"End of the week?" Claiborne halted and turned, frowning. "What's the matter with those people? Nick, I don't know a damned thing about forensic procedure, I haven't even sat in on a PM since medical school, but give me three hours with that corpse and I'll bet we'll come up with a firm ID."

Steiner nodded. "So will Rigsby, when he has the time. But Engstrom tells me it's like a madhouse over there." He smiled self-consciously. "If you'll pardon the Freudian slip."

"You mean because of that bus crash?"

Dr. Steiner sighed. "Seven victims yesterday. Two of the injured died during the night. That makes nine. Total of fourteen, when you add the five we're concerned with."

"I'm only concerned with one," Claiborne said. "Couldn't Engstrom lean on Rigsby to give us priority?"

"He tried. But don't forget, county coroner's an elective office."

"Meaning what?"

"Meaning that Engstrom is one man, and the families of the victims run into several dozen people.

They're leaning too, and all of them are voters. So much for Rigsby's priorities." Dr. Steiner produced another cigarette. "I'd hate to be in his shoes right now. He's going to be working night and day, and until he gets around to us, we'll just have to sweat it out."

"Because politics is more important than murder?" Claiborne shook his head. "Maybe Engstrom and Rigsby can believe that, but not me. And I never thought you would, either."

"I don't." Dr. Steiner held up his hand. "Look at this—third one in fifteen minutes!" He scowled ruefully and tossed the unlit cigarette into the ashtray, then settled back in his chair. "Believe me, I'm just as uptight as you are. But we have no options. We've got to make up our minds to be patient until the word comes down."

"While Norman is running loose?"

Dr. Steiner shrugged. "All right. I still don't buy it, but let's say he's still alive. Engstrom tells me his department is cooperating with Captain Banning. They've put out an all-points, they're making appeals asking possible witnesses to come forward, they're going over the available evidence. But until they come up with something concrete, you can't stop them from having their own opinions, any more than you can stop those people out in Hollywood from making their picture—"

Claiborne looked up, a question in his eyes, and Dr. Steiner nodded.

"Forgot to mention it. I had a call from that producer, the one you talked to yesterday."

"Marty Driscoll?"

"He phoned this morning, right after I got back. Said he'd heard the news and wanted more details on what happened yesterday."

"And you gave them to him?"

"Of course not." Steiner frowned. "I've no intention of helping him, never did. I haven't read his script, don't want to talk to his writer. And in view of the circumstances, my advice to him was to cancel the picture entirely."

"Did he agree?"

"He as much as told me to go to hell. He thinks all this is great publicity. They're going to start shooting next Monday."

"But they can't!" Claiborne shook his head. "Nick, we have to do something."

"Of course." Dr. Steiner pushed his chair back, rising. "I'm going to work. And you're going to take a few days off, get some rest."

"I don't want—"

"Never mind what you want, it's what you need. I'll take over your case load this week. You're overtired and you're overreacting."

"Overreacting?"

"This business about the picture. When you come right down to it, what's the difference whether they go ahead or not? We can't stop them."

"Maybe not," said Claiborne. "But if we don't, Norman will."

Fifteen

It had been a mistake to tell Steiner anything.

Claiborne should have known the minute Nick started talking about overreacting. But he hadn't caught the implication then; he'd gone on explaining about the newspaper item in the hardware store, how Norman must have seen it, where he guessed Norman would be going and what he'd do. He should have realized that Steiner wouldn't understand, but it was too late now.

Now they had him in the hospital.

God knew what the diagnosis was—they wouldn't tell him, weren't going to tell him. The nurses and orderlies never forgot to call him "Doctor" when they addressed him; they were all very courteous, but they were also very firm.

Claiborne understood the need for firmness. It was a necessary measure, a professional procedure that he himself had followed, something he'd accepted as part of the job he had to do. But now they were doing a job on him. And he couldn't take it.

He couldn't get used to being a patient, being ordered around, treated like a child. Getting examined, inspected, searched as though he were some kind of criminal. Told to stand there, sit here, served his meals on a tray.

And then there were the noises. The syrupy, supposedly soothing sound of canned music, interrupted by buzzing voices issuing commands. And always the droning that music couldn't disguise, the droning that set up a vibration inside his head, a pressure that made his ears ring. Even with his eyes closed, Claiborne couldn't escape; there was no escape.

Because he was strapped down.

That was when it really hit him, when he knew he couldn't move. *They had him in restraint!*

Claiborne began to tremble. He forced himself forward, his body arching up against the confinement of the unyielding straps. But the straps held, they were firm, everyone was firm, no escape, no way. *Got to get out of here, out of here—*

His eyes opened and he stared down.

At the seat belt.

Relax. You're on the plane.

He sank back, conscious that he was smiling, relieved and ashamed at the same time. Steiner had been right; he was overtired, and that's why he'd fallen asleep during the flight. And overreaction had emerged in his nightmare.

Its elements seemed obvious. The nurses and orderlies were the airline personnel. In his dream, going through the airport security check became a physical examination. The directions—being told to wait for boarding, to remain seated and fasten his belt—were self-explanatory. And of course they'd served him a meal on a tray.

The canned music and the pilot's messages had come over the cabin intercom. Now there was only the drone of the engines as the plane began its long, gliding descent. But the vibration was real enough, and he did feel pressure in his ears.

He felt pressure, period. But now was not the time to think about it. Now was the time to *please remain seated until the aircraft reaches the terminal*—although all around him, Claiborne noted, passengers were rifling the overhead storage compartments for their hand luggage and crowding down the aisle, propelled by competitive compulsion to be first in line.

Now was the time to pick up his own briefcase and move through the exit, running the gauntlet of mechanical smiles and automated goodbyes from the perspiring stewardesses stationed there.

Welcome to Los Angeles International.

In the airport's upper lobby, friends and family greeted his fellow passengers. For a moment Claiborne caught himself scanning faces in the crowds clustering around the semicircle of arrival and departure gates, then smiled self-consciously. Who the hell was he looking for? Norman wasn't waiting at the terminal to say hello—if, indeed, he was waiting anywhere at all.

Suppose Steiner had been right and all this was a fool's errand?

Only one way to find out. Claiborne started forward, shouldering through the throng and escalating down—neat contradiction in terms, that!—to the lower level. Now he began to plod the interminable tunnel leading to the outer lobby.

The symbolism of these movements didn't go unnoticed; it was like reenacting one's birth. Once in the tunnel, everyone became impatient, anxious to reach the exit, emerge reborn into the new world beyond.

But actual birth was a simple phenomenon compared to what still had to be endured. Making the car-rental arrangements, buying the street guide, locating his baggage and snatching it from the conveyor—everything took time, taxed patience, enhanced irritation.

How long had it been since travel had transformed itself from pleasure to an endless ordeal? Perhaps he had a low pain threshold, or maybe he was just too damned tired; whatever the reason, he resented the regimentation and the herding, the hordes jabbering and jostling at the luggage stations. No amount of soporific sound could disguise the discomfort, whether it came from the speaker system or rose in recollection of the television commercials chorusing the delights of flight.

Flight, escape—all he wanted was to get out of here. And even after he'd reached the rented car, stowed his bag, consulted the map for guidance, appraised the instrument panel on the dash, and started moving, there was still the problem of leaving the airport. Inching along in bumper-to-bumper traffic, interpreting the constantly confusing overhead signs, fighting to change lanes, Claiborne finally reached Century Boulevard and crawled east to the San Diego Freeway. Here, exhausted by exhaust, he located the northbound entrance ramp and moved up, swerving left between a thundering semi and a lurching camper. Life in the fast lane wasn't all that great, either, but at least now he was headed in the right direction.

Or so he hoped.

The mere mechanics of driving at a regular speed, of functioning as a comparatively free agent once again, had a relaxing effect. Now he was calm enough to review the situation objectively.

No point in faulting Steiner; actually, Nick had been extremely supportive. Once he'd realized Claiborne's mind was made up, he'd put his skepticism aside and cooperated fully. Maybe he didn't give the trip his unqualified blessing, but he helped get plane reservations, ordered Otis to drive Claiborne to the airport, promised to stay in touch and pass on a report of autopsy findings or any other developments as soon as possible.

Best of all, he'd called a halt to that cheap-shot analysis of motivations, perhaps because Steiner knew Claiborne would be doing the job for him.

And he was, now.

The nightmare on the plane—sorting out its elements had been easy enough, but unimportant. The meaning behind those elements was what counted.

His dream of incarceration was a dream of punishment. Nobody had punished him for letting Norman escape, so he was punishing himself.

The actual trip was another expression of guilt feelings. He'd taken a flight, and flight was *fugue*, running away. But he couldn't run away from his responsibility.

And that was where he parted company with Steiner. He *was* responsible. If Norman had come out here, he must find him, and quickly. Maybe he had no solid proof to support his position, but Steiner and Engstrom had none to support theirs. Not yet, anyway. And until proof was forthcoming, he must go with his instincts, his convictions, his training.

So much for the professional reaction, but there was more to it than that. Norman wasn't just another patient. When you saw someone every day for years, shared his confidence, learned his innermost secrets, counseled and guided him in moments of stress, there was only one word to describe the relationship. Norman was his friend.

A friend in need. To hell with the professional reaction. He was here because Norman needed help.

Claiborne angled right and took the eastbound interchange onto the Ventura Freeway. Checking the overhead signs, he got off at Laurel Canyon, headed south for a half-mile, turned left onto Ventura Boulevard.

Coronet Studios would be another mile or so down the street, and a block north. But there was no need to locate it precisely at the moment. Right now he had to find a place to stay.

He drove slowly, noting a number of motels along the boulevard route, most of them standing flush against the sidewalks, aligned with the pet hospitals, cocktail lounges, and car lots. What he saw didn't attract him; never mind the heated pools, the color TV. He wanted a place set back from the busy arterial, away from the traffic noise.

Then he spotted it, on his right.

Dawn Motel.

The sign was weathered, and so was the modest L-shaped structure behind it, but both stood well to the rear of the combination patio and parking area. He didn't see a pool, and only one car stood slanted in a slot near the office entrance—an indication, he hoped, of peace and quiet.

Claiborne pulled in, killed the motor, clambered out. His legs ached, signaling fatigue, as he moved to the office door, blinking against the rays of the late afternoon sun. Pulling the door open, he stepped into the welcome coolness of the dim domain beyond.

His vision blurred, then adjusted to inventory the small, makeshift lobby area. Plastic-backed chairs huddled behind a battered coffee table supporting a metal ashtray amid a litter of old magazines. The right wall held the usual trio of vending machines offering the weary traveler a choice of carbonated citric acid, stale candy bars, or overpriced cigarettes. At his left was the reception desk, unoccupied. Behind it, surrounded by a cluster of framed and faded photographs, was a wall clock, its insistent ticking commanding his attention.

He stared at the face and hands. *Why do we personify Time? Is it because we're afraid to admit that our lives are measured by an abstract force that neither knows nor cares about our entry into existence or our departure into death? Time is our mysterious master; giving it a face and hands, we attempt to transform it into our servant.*

Claiborne shrugged. Enough of that; it was only a clock and he was just tired. The hour hand stood at six, though his wristwatch insisted it was eight. He adjusted the latter to local time, but his own internal chronometer was still functioning unchanged, and he'd need a good night's rest to compensate for jet lag and fatigue.

So where was the proprietor?

Walking over to the desk, he caught sight of the metal bell and clanged it with his forefinger.

Then he stepped back, waiting, and as he did so, his eyes moved to the pictures on the wall. The clock was ticking away, but in the photographs surrounding it, Time had stopped.

Sun-fading had bleached the backgrounds and blurred the inked inscriptions, but the faces in the portrait frames smiled forth bravely and unchanged from the security of a darkened, distant past. Poses and garments suggested their subjects' affinity with showbiz, though Claiborne recognized only one: the sole unsmiling countenance staring down from the shadows.

Now the door leading onto the patio was opening and the clerk entered, moving behind the desk.

He was tall, thin, cotton-haired, his deeply tanned face seamed and cracked with wrinkles like a dry riverbed. But age hadn't erased his smile, and his gray-green eyes were inquisitively alert.

Claiborne's appraisal was automatic; he dismissed

it quickly now and concentrated on the routine of room rental.

Yes, forty dollars a night would be okay, and he expected to stay until Sunday. Stove and refrigerator? Good enough, though he didn't intend to do much cooking; he'd probably be out most of the time. If Number Six was a rear unit, it sounded fine to him.

Signing the register, Claiborne checked the impulse to put down a fake name. No need for any cloak-and-dagger stuff; after all, he expected to be getting his calls here. But he did refrain from initialing *M.D.* after his signature. As he glanced up at the wall photos, once again the single somber face caught his attention.

"Isn't that Karl Druse?" he said.

The elderly man nodded.

"I thought I recognized him." Claiborne studied the portrait. "Remarkable actor. Next to Chaney Senior, probably the best of the early horror stars."

"Right." The inquisitive eyes brightened. "But that was back in the silent days. How'd you know about him—are you in the industry?"

Claiborne shook his head. "No. Are you?"

"A long time ago." The clerk gestured toward the cluster of photographs. "I knew them when they owned this town. Now they're hanging on the wall and I'm still moving around down here. Funny how things work out."

"You were an actor?"

One of the cracks in the riverbed widened to produce a smile. "If I was, you can bet my picture would be up there, bigger than any of the others." The clerk chuckled. "No, I never acted. Just a writer—

143

what they used to call a scenarist—down the street here at Coronet Studios."

"Coronet?" Claiborne glanced at him quickly. "That's interesting, Mr—"

"Post. Tom Post."

"You must know quite a bit about the business, Mr. Post."

"Not anymore. When the talkies came in, I got out. Got pushed out, if you want the truth." Tom Post chuckled again.

"You don't sound unhappy about being retired."

"Who said I was?" Post's smile faded. "I ran a used-car lot in Encino before I built this place down here. No big deal, but at least it keeps me busy. I'll never quit working, not now." He gestured with a bony finger. "You know what retirement is today? An old man with diseased lungs, catching poisoned fish in a polluted stream."

Claiborne grinned. "I see you're still a writer."

"Just an old fart with a leaky mouth, if you'll pardon the mixed metaphor." Tom Post reached into the desk drawer and selected a key attached to a wooden paddle. "Here you are. Want some help with your luggage?"

"Don't bother—I can manage."

"Number Six is down at the end, next to the alley."

Claiborne nodded. "Before I go, I'd like to make a few calls."

"There's a phone in your room."

"Good."

"If you need anything else, feel free."

"Thanks."

Claiborne went out to the car for his bag and

144

briefcase, then carried them down the patio walk to Number Six.

The room was like an oversize microwave oven, but he located the thermostat on the window air-conditioning unit and turned it on high. The ancient appliance rasped in senile response. He shed his jacket, sprawled out on the double bed, and picked up the telephone.

It was after six-thirty now, probably too late to reach anyone at Coronet, but he took a chance and dialed the operator for the number. Then he called the studio, and a girl on the switchboard put him through to Driscoll's office. Much to his surprise, he heard the click of the phone being picked up.

"Yeah?" Marty Driscoll's deep voice was instantly identifiable.

"This is Adam Claiborne, Mr. Driscoll."

"Who?" The question conveyed casual irritation rather than actual interest.

"Dr. Claiborne. We spoke on Sunday, when you called the hospital."

"Oh sure Doc, I remember." Annoyance vanished from Driscoll's voice. "Glad to hear from you. Maybe you can set me straight on what's coming down."

"I'd be happy to, if you'll give me an appointment."

"Appointment?" A brief pause. "You here in town?"

"Just arrived. I was hoping we might be able to get together sometime tomorrow—"

"Whenever you say. I'll be in all day."

"Nine o'clock?"

"Make it nine-thirty. There'll be a pass waiting for you at the gate."

"Good enough," Claiborne said. "Nine-thirty."

"Wait," Driscoll cut in quickly. "That boss of yours, Dr. Steiner—I called him yesterday and all I got was a brush. What's the real poop on Norman Bates?"

"That's what I want to talk to you about." Claiborne started to lower the receiver as he spoke. "See you tomorrow."

He hung up, leaving Driscoll hanging. A cheap ploy but an effective one, or so he hoped. It was good to find that the producer worried. So far, nobody else seemed to give a damn.

Twilight invaded the room as the air conditioner whined in feeble protest. Claiborne debated before switching on the bedlamp. What he really wanted to do was stretch out and sleep around the clock. Seven o'clock here now—that meant it would be nine back home. And he'd promised to give Steiner a call when he got in.

Picking up the receiver again, he dialed the private number. A hollow ringing echoed in response. *For whom Ma Bell tolls.* On the tenth ring he hung up. Wearily he tried again, this time on the regular hospital line, and Clara answered from the reception desk.

Steiner was out, she said. Something about a dinner meeting with the Fairvale Rotary.

Good public relations, business as usual. Don't you understand, Nick? The bell tolls for thee.

Controlling his voice with an effort, Claiborne gave Clara his motel address and the phone number, telling her he'd call Dr. Steiner sometime tomorrow. No point in asking what was happening back there; she'd be the last to know. And very probably nothing had happened, if Steiner was free to go off and eat rubber chicken with the Rotary.

By the time he set the phone down again, his annoyance had faded with the last rays of sunset. For a moment he debated going out for some food, then rejected the notion. Let Steiner chase the canned peas around his plate. Right now, for Claiborne, rest was more important.

He kicked off his shoes and hung his clothing in the narrow closet. He opened his bag, unpacked, stowed garments in the bureau drawers, put his second suit on a hanger, carried the shaver and toiletries to the bathroom. If traveling salesmen had to go through this boring routine every night, no wonder they got drunk and picked up hookers.

He used the toilet and considered a shower, then decided it could wait until morning. After donning his pajamas, he returned to the bedroom and pulled down the shade, then the bedcovers.

As he did so, he noticed his briefcase resting on top of the bureau and remembered its contents. The script of *Crazy Lady* had remained untouched on the plane. He could read it now, but what would be the point? He wasn't seeing Driscoll to discuss the script; tomorrow's meeting had another purpose.

Claiborne silenced the air conditioner, lowered himself onto the bed, and flicked off the lamp on the nightstand. *Tomorrow's meeting*. How was he going to handle Marty Driscoll? What was the case entry here?

Case entry. Of course, that was it. Lead from strength, establish a doctor-patient relationship. Dr. Claiborne, the authority figure. Stripped of all the

Latin and Greek buzzwords, that was what therapeutic technique amounted to: let the patient talk. Break through the reaction formation.

Let Driscoll argue himself hoarse about the spectacular potential of the picture, the money it would make. Listen to him the way you'd listen to a man standing on the window ledge of a tall building, ready to jump.

Then and only then, explain his position to him. Certainly the picture would be spectacular and attract attention—just like jumping out of that high window. And it would probably make a lot of money. But if the man who jumped out of the window was insured, that could mean a lot of money too. The trouble was he wouldn't be alive to enjoy it.

So look before you leap, look down into the darkness below and you'll see what I see. Norman Bates, waiting for you. Mark my words, he's waiting for you to jump into this thing. I'd stake my life on it. And that's why I'm warning you not to stake yours—

Stake my life.

The phrase echoed. He still thought of Norman as a friend, but what did Norman think? To him, Claiborne might be an enemy.

And perhaps it was true, in a way. In his dream he'd come here to punish himself. But in reality maybe he'd come to punish Norman for running away, ruining his plans.

The book, that was it. The book had been the key to the whole thing. He'd hoped to write it as a record, a report, on five years of successful therapy. Reputations had been made with less.

To hell with reputations! It didn't matter now.

What mattered was what had happened to those innocent people back in Fairvale and to those who survived them.

Claiborne frowned up into the darkness. It was time to stop worrying about himself, stop worrying about whether Norman was his friend, his patient, his enemy. The important thing was the trauma, the suffering of the victims' families. They were the ones who deserved concern, needed help. And it was his duty to give it to them. Not because he was a psychiatrist—to hell with that, too!—but because he was a decent, caring human being.

He couldn't change the past, but at least he could try to alleviate some of their anguish and anxiety in the future, save them from exploitation and exacerbation, relieve their fears of further danger. That's why he had to stop this picture, find Norman and bring him back, even if his own life was on the line—

The sound was so faint that Claiborne scarcely heard it. Only the fact that his eyes had become accustomed to the darkness gave him a clue. Lying on his side, facing the door, and seeing the doorknob turning—

Click.

And the thump of Claiborne's bare feet hitting the floor as he bounded off the bed. Impulse impelled him; there was no time to think until it was too late, he'd already unlocked the door, flung it open—

A shadow stood in the doorway.

"Sorry. I didn't mean to disturb you," said Tom Post.

"What's the idea? You could have knocked."

"Thought you were asleep." Turning, half-profiled

149

in the outside patio light, the leathery lizard face wrinkled into a grin. "Just a security check. I always make sure the doors are locked before I turn in for the night." Post peered into the darkened room. "Everything all right?"

Claiborne nodded, his tension draining.

"Then I won't bother you. Have a good night's rest."

"I intend to." Claiborne started to close the door.

As he did so, Post chuckled. "Don't worry, you're safe here. Remember, this isn't the Bates Motel."

The door closed.

The lock clicked.

The footsteps moved away along the walk.

And Claiborne stood enshrouded amidst the darkness, hearing nothing but the echo of the old man's chuckle in the night.

Sixteen

The caterpillar was gone.

Jan stared at Santo Vizzini as he rose from behind his desk.

"Something wrong?" he asked.

"Your mustache—you shaved it off."

Vizzini nodded as he moved toward her in a swirl of scent, running a pudgy forefinger over the bare spot between his nose and upper lip.

"You approve?"

"I'll have to get used to it. You look so different."

Which was true, of course. Without the mustache, the director seemed to have shed his ethnic stereotype. But he was still gesticulating nervously, still smelled as if he mainlined cologne. And there was nothing different about his approach.

Jan managed to drop the copy of the script she was holding and stooped to retrieve it just in time to avoid the touch of his hand on her arm.

"Clumsy," she said, stepping back.

"Relax," Vizzini told her. "I won't bite you." He grinned, exhibiting a serration of yellow molars and incisors that seemed to belie the statement. *What big teeth you have, Grandma.*

Jan smoothed the crumpled cover of the script. "About the reading—"

"Reading?" Vizzini's grin faded into a puzzled pout. His lips seemed thicker without the protection of a mustache.

Jan nodded. "Tuesday afternoon, three o'clock," she said. "Here I am, right on the button."

Vizzini struck his forehead with the flat of his palm, an exaggeratedly melodramatic gesture he would never have permitted in an actor under his direction. "Of course! That stupid cow, Linda—I told her to call you this morning—"

"Problems?"

"Paul Morgan. He's coming in for a rehearsal. I promised to walk him through the scene on the parlor set."

"But I'm in that scene too. Couldn't we do it together?"

"That's what I suggested. He says he prefers to work alone."

"I get it," Jan said. "The star treatment."

"Star, no. Treatment, yes. Just between us, he is very unsure of himself. Playing a transvestite, he has to go against his image. It is important that I help him."

152

"What about me?" Jan did her best to conceal her irritation. "I've got some questions about my own part—"

"They will be answered, I promise you." Vizzini perfumed the air with his gesture. "We will schedule another reading later in the week. I'll have Linda check and let you know when to set it up. Perhaps by that time you will have a better grasp of the character." He led her to the door, patting her shoulder, and this time she didn't flinch away from his touch. "Believe me, if you get up in your lines there will be nothing to worry about. I trust my instinct. When I selected you for the part, I knew you would come through."

Not for you, buster, Jan told herself. *Stuff yourself.*

But when she drove back up the hillside to the apartment in the humid heat of late afternoon, she did decide to have another go at the script.

Connie was gone, out on a casting call for a commercial, so there were no distractions. Once she'd changed into slacks and settled down on the living room sofa, Jan opened the pages of *Crazy Lady* and addressed herself to the sides of dialogue she'd carefully underscored in vivid green.

The trouble was that she couldn't stick to her own lines; before long she was reading the entire script straight through. And once again she was disturbed by the impact and import of the subject matter. This was no whodunnit, it wasn't structured like a routine suspense film, and it didn't rely on what they called "pop-ups" for its shocks. The thing read almost like a documentary; its fright was factual. And what disturbed her most was that Roy Ames had written it.

Once again she recalled his outburst the other day. That was disturbing too—not just what he'd said or the way he'd said it, but the realization of how completely it had caught her off guard. Up until then she'd had a thing about Roy, and it wouldn't have taken much more to turn her on. But now—

Now the phone rang.

"Hello?"

"That's a great line. Mind if I steal it?" said Roy Ames.

Speak of the devil.

But she didn't hang up. She listened to his apology and accepted it. And when he came out with an invitation to dinner at Sportsman's Lodge, she accepted that too.

"No, don't pick me up—I'll meet you there," she told him. "Eight o'clock's fine. See you."

Jan put the phone down, but the burden of doubt remained. Had she made the right move? The words of an old proverb emerged from memory. *He who sups with the devil must have a long spoon*

Maybe so. But whoever had invented that one-liner was speaking of men, not women. And she'd made sure the spoon was long enough, by not inviting him here to pick her up.

Besides, he wasn't a devil, but merely an opponent in this hassle about the film. So the right thing had been to accept, to try to win him over.

Jan shelved the script on the bookcase. No more time to rehearse it now; this evening she had another part to play.

She dressed for it carefully and considered her role. Roy had handed her the right cues. His apology amounted to an admission that he was the heavy, and the dinner invitation indicated he'd be doing his best to make amends for past behavior. All she had to do was remember to play the injured party and steal the scene.

By the time she arrived at Sportsman's Lodge, Jan had her act together.

She came into the lobby a few minutes before eight, but Roy was already waiting for her; a good sign. He had two martinis before ordering dinner, and that was good too. Meanwhile he kept chatting her up with a lot of small talk, indicating that while the drinks had loosened his tongue, he wasn't really relaxed. And he never said one word about the picture; obviously he intended to avoid the subject entirely.

But it had to be discussed if she meant to end his opposition. Jan half listened to him over her fruit cocktail, and by the time their steaks arrived, she'd found the lead-in.

"I hate to admit it, but I'm glad I canceled my other date," she said.

Roy put down his salad fork and looked up. Jan met the question in his eyes with a smile.

"Vizzini wanted me to have dinner with him and discuss the picture."

"That creep." Roy's reaction was even better than she'd hoped for. Or worse. "Don't get yourself involved. I know it's none of my business, but—"

"Right. It's mine." Jan retained the smile as she interrupted. "I agree he's a creep, but he also happens to be my director. And it could be important, having him on my side."

"He'll be on something more than just your side if you aren't careful," Roy said. "You know how he operates. The stuff that went on at his place in Nichols Canyon, the dog-and-pony act with the rock groupies. Sure, it was all hushed up, he was right in the middle of shooting that twenty-million-dollar turkey, and the money people couldn't afford to see him indicted. But you don't need trouble. Not with a kink who's that far into S-and-M and violence."

Roy slashed at his steak as he spoke, then paused as Jan caught his eye.

"Look who's talking," she said.

"Sorry." His motion slowed, his knife and voice lowered self-consciously. "Maybe it's contagious."

"I know," Jan murmured. "I caught some of it today, going over your script. Scary."

"Guess I was in shock when I wrote it. But you wouldn't understand."

"Try me."

"Stop and think." Roy pushed his plate back. "I've done spooky stuff before, mostly teleplays, but that's why Driscoll handed me the assignment. Writing about vampires and werewolves is like writing fairy tales. It never got to me because I knew the monsters were just make-believe.

"But this time was different. What I wrote about was based on something that actually happened, and Norman Bates was for real." Roy nodded. "He got to me."

"How?"

"You're an actress. You know what's needed when you play a part, the way you try to get a handle on the character's motivations?" Roy gulped coffee. "A

156

writer does that upfront, too—his job is to find that handle. Dong the script, I had to somehow get inside Norman, figure out how he thought, how he felt, what made him tick until he exploded.

"It wasn't easy, but somehow I managed, and it worked. But when I finally managed to get into that sick head of his, all I wanted was to get out again, finish the script so I'd be finished with Norman.

"What I forgot is that Norman wasn't finished with me. At least when I was writing the character, I could control him, just like the real Norman was controlled back there in the asylum. But now—"

Jan put down her fork. "I know how you feel. He freaks me out too. But scrubbing the picture won't change anything. Besides, Norman's dead. You saw the paper this morning; they're almost positive now he died in that van explosion."

"Almost positive." Roy leaned forward. "Suppose they're wrong?"

"You said the same thing yesterday at the studio." Jan spoke softly. "Why? Do you know something we don't?"

"It's not what I know." Roy paused and Jan had the feeling his usual glibness had deserted him; he was fumbling for something deep inside that couldn't be captured by a phrase. "All I've got is a gut instinct that Norman is still alive. Alive and waiting.

"For what?"

"I don't know." Roy grimaced. "How can I expect you to understand when I can't even understand it myself?"

He's hurting. Really hurting. Jan's resentment vanished with the realization. This was no adversary, merely a deeply troubled man tormented by something he couldn't exorcise or express.

She'd forgotten about her role-playing, but now she needed its help if she wanted to come to his rescue. Perhaps the best way was to laugh it off.

And so Jan smiled her I'm-putting-you-on smile and said, "Sounds bad. Maybe you ought to see a shrink."

Roy nodded. "I will."

"What?"

"Didn't you know?" Roy leaned forward. "Driscoll called me tonight just before I left. He's set up a meeting for tomorrow morning with Norman Bates's psychiatrist."

Seventeen

Jan lucked out at the studio gate on Wednesday morning.

She arrived early, her Toyota wedged into a queue of cars conveying regular employees, and when the guard saw the new sticker pasted on the windshield, he waved her forward.

No one asked her if she had an appointment, and that was a break because she wasn't expected.

Certainly, Anita Kedzie was surprised when Jan showed up in Driscoll's outer office. The moment she appeared, the insectoid eyes behind the bulging lenses began a quick scan of the ruled notepad resting on the desktop between the intercom and the telephone.

"I don't seem to have you down here," said Miss

Kedzie. "What time did Mr. Driscoll say for you to come in?"

"He didn't." Jan's smile was casual. "I just happened to be on the lot and thought I'd stop by for a moment."

Miss Kedzie's pursed lips revealed her reaction. *Stop by? But nobody sees a producer without an appointment. It's like dropping in at the Vatican to have a surprise quickie with the Pope.*

"I'm afraid he's tied up," the secretary said. Her brisk tone didn't indicate whether Driscoll was bound and gagged or merely suffering from constipation. "If you like, I can tell him you're here."

"Don't bother," Jan told her. "It's really not important."

But it *was* important. She glanced at her watch. Nine-forty-five. Roy hadn't mentioned a specific time for the meeting and she hadn't risked arousing his suspicions by asking. She'd guessed it would probably be scheduled for ten and had made her plans accordingly. Barge in early, give Driscoll some excuse about coming on the lot for wardrobe fittings, and just happen to be on hand when this Dr. Claiborne arrived.

She didn't expect an invitation to stick around, but at least she might have a chance to say hello and size him up, maybe even get some clue as to why he was here. Of course, Roy would be furious, but after last night Jan had decided it was no use trying to turn him around. What she needed to know right now was whether Dr. Claiborne was on her team or the enemy list.

Too late now—she'd blown it.

Jan was already turning away when Anita Kedzie called after her.

"Miss Harper—"

"Yes?"

"Would you do me a favor? I want to go down the hall, just for a minute. Mr. Driscoll doesn't like for me to leave the office unless someone's here to take calls."

"No problem. I'll stick around."

"Thank you."

The secretary rose and scurried into the corridor, closing the door behind her.

Jan smiled. She wasn't into entomology, but apparently insects had bladders too. *Let's hear it for Miss Kedzie's kidneys.*

Now, if there was only some way to take advantage of her security leak—

The desk intercom offered the obvious solution. Keeping a wary eye on the outer door, Jan stepped over and flipped the unit's audio switch.

Driscoll's voice. "Okay, Doc, let's put it this way. I'm already committed. The deals are made, the contracts are signed, the sets are going up. You got any idea what the interest charges are on even one day's delay? I'm talking facts and figures now. All you've got is this hunch—"

"But it's not just a hunch." *Roy Ames.* "It's a professional evaluation."

"What about Dr. Steiner? He doesn't go along with it, he told me so himself. Neither do the police."

"This man was Norman Bates's therapist. He's the only one in a position to know. He came out here at his own expense."

"Believe me, I appreciate it! But there's no point arguing now. Look, Doc, I'm sorry you had to waste your time—"

"Maybe it isn't wasted." George Ward's soft murmur. "Remember your idea about sending Roy to Fairvale before he did a final polish on the script?"

"Yeah. But Steiner turned me down."

"Dr. Claiborne is the man Roy should talk to. And you've got him right here. If you put him on as technical advisor for a few days—"

"Now you're talking!" *Driscoll, cutting in.* "Make a good story—"

"But I'm not interested in promoting your film." *The firm, resonant voice had to be Dr. Claiborne's.* "I'm warning you—the only publicity the press will get from me is a statement that this picture should not be made."

And there goes the ballgame. Jan snapped off the intercom. *Smug bastard sounds like he means it, too. If he goes public he could raise enough stink to get the PTA and all the other pressure groups into the act.*

Behind her, Jan could hear footsteps approaching in the other hall. Probably Miss Kedzie, returning.

Jan didn't wait to find out. She moved to the door of the private office and flung it open.

The occupants of the room stared up in surprise as she entered. Presumably the big smile on her face was for all of them, but Jan zeroed in on the tall man standing directly before Driscoll's desk. That would be Dr. Claiborne.

"Hi," she said. "Hope I'm not interrupting anything."

Driscoll scowled. "What do you want? We're in a meeting—"

"So I heard."

"Heard?"

Jan gave him her no-big-deal look. "Somebody must have left the intercom on accidentally."

"Where the hell is Kedzie?"

"She went down the hall for a minute and asked me to hold the fort."

Driscoll reached for the unit on his desk, and Jan gestured quickly. "Please, don't chew her out. It's my fault. I shouldn't have listened."

The producer was still scowling, but his hand drew back. "Okay, so you listened. What do you want?"

Roy and George were scowling too, but Jan ignored them. And she ignored Driscoll as she turned to face the tall man standing before the desk. He was younger than she'd expected—not handsome, but with a cool, laid-back look that contrasted with the nervous frowns of the others. He eyed her steadily.

"Dr. Claiborne?" she said. "I'm Jan Harper."

He nodded, his stare softening as he returned her smile. "I've seen your photograph."

"Then you know I'm playing Mary Crane in the picture."

"Yes."

Driscoll's voice boomed. "What the hell is this, boy meets girl? Look, if you've got anything to say—"

"I do." Jan swiveled her smile, then focused again on Dr. Claiborne's face. "I need your help."

His eyes flickered momentarily. "What's the problem?"

"You."

"I'm afraid I don't follow."

"It's the picture I'm talking about. I need your cooperation. We all do."

"I've already stated my position—"

"I know. But you could change your mind."

"For what reason?"

"Because this film must be made." Jan was winging it, and as his stare challenged her, she met his question with another. "Have you read the script?"

"As a matter of fact, I haven't." The voice was firm and assured, but the stare dropped, and Jan felt confidence return. She'd caught him off guard, and now she had her cue.

"Then you should. Because it's a marvelous piece of writing."

Out of the corner of her eye she saw Driscoll and Ward watching. They wouldn't interrupt now, they'd let her run with the ball. Roy had stopped scowling too, and that was good. But she wasn't here to stroke Roy; she was playing to Dr. Claiborne.

"I'm not talking about technique," she said. "It's the concept. This isn't just another one of those horror flicks with a crazy heavy chewing the scenery. Norman Bates comes off as a human being—an ordinary man with hopes and fears and desires we all share, but caught in a compulsion he can't cope with. What he does is horrifying, but we see the reason and in the end we realize he's more of a victim than any of the others. The real heavy of the story is our own society."

164

Dr. Claiborne was smiling now. "That's quite a speech. How long did you rehearse it?"

"I didn't." Jan eyed him earnestly. "If I had, I'd give you the business about how much I want my part, how many people's jobs depend on making the picture. But there's more to it than that."

She waited a beat, then modulated her voice. The words came easily now. "You're a doctor. You worked with Norman Bates, know his problems. Haven't you ever wanted, just once, to tell people what it's really like—get them to understand and share the problem?

"Well, here's your chance. Our chance. Read the script. Tell us what's right and what's wrong, so we can tell the world. You owe that much to yourself and to your patient."

Dr. Claiborne hesitated, his eyes searching, challenging, then submitting.

"You're right, of course," he said. "As far as you go. But it's not that simple. What I've been trying to say to Mr. Driscoll and the others here is that Norman Bates may still be alive. And if so, going ahead with this project could place you all in a potentially dangerous position."

"I agree," Roy said. "Look, Jan—"

"I agree too." Jan cut him off quickly, but her smile never wavered. "But Mr. Driscoll has already decided to go ahead. And that's all the more reason we need Dr. Claiborne here with us."

She turned to face the tall man again. "Now I'll speak for myself," she said. "If you're right, if Norman Bates is still alive, I'd feel a lot safer knowing you were here."

Dr. Claiborne was silent for a moment. And when he spoke, it was not to her but to George Ward.

"I'm free until Sunday," he said. "Just what does a technical advisor do, and where do I begin?"

Eighteen

Claiborne sat across the table from Roy Ames. The commissary was filling up with the noon luncheon crowd, and their background babble made it difficult for him to catch what Ames was saying.

Not that he really wanted to. At the moment he was still listening to an interior dialogue that had begun immediately upon leaving Driscoll's office.

Why had he allowed himself to be persuaded? Was it just a matter of being caught off guard? True, the girl seemed to grasp the situation instantly, and her arguments made sense. At least she didn't discount the threat like all the others, except for Roy Ames here.

Still, that wasn't the real reason he'd agreed to stay. Perhaps the clincher was not what the girl said, but her physical presence. Claiborne remembered his reactions when he'd encountered her photograph, but actual confrontation with Jan Harper had an impact he wasn't prepared for.

He found himself voicing it to Roy Ames, and the writer nodded.

"Right. That's why Vizzini chose her. Jan's a dead ringer for Mary Crane."

"I hope not." Claiborne paused as the waitress came over and handed them their menus. "Ringer, yes. Dead, no."

"You're really convinced that Bates is alive?"

Claiborne nodded. "Isn't that your feeling?"

"Yes. But only a feeling. I can't explain why. I thought maybe you might have something more to go on—something you didn't tell them at the meeting."

"I'm not prepared to discuss it at the moment."

"Meaning you don't trust me either?"

"I don't know you." Claiborne tempered his words with a smile, gesturing toward the surrounding tables. "I don't know anyone yet."

"Your first time in a studio?"

"That's right."

"Okay, let me give you a guided tour." Ames followed Claiborne's gaze. "The people over there are part of management. Don't let the jeans fool you; they're top echelon. You're one of the team, you dress like a slob, do the I'm-just-another-working-stiff routine. But when you leave the studio you make damn sure everybody sees you're wearing a twenty-five-thousand-dollar car." He grinned. "We live in an auto-erotic society."

Claiborne smiled, knowing the reaction was

expected, but he sensed that this was not the first time Roy Ames had used the line. Now he nodded toward a group at a window table whose dark suits, white shirts, and carefully knotted neckties seemed to invalidate the writer's explanation. "What about those people over there?"

Roy Ames followed his gaze. "Visitors. Probably network execs from back east. They come out from Mad Avenue looking for new ideas—to steal. Of course, what they usually settle for is stealing old ideas."

Claiborne singled out a group of exceedingly hirsute young men across the aisle. "And those kids?"

"I'd say they're into tapes and LPs. That's where the action is today. One platinum record is worth a ton of Oscars."

Someone brushed past them and halted before an adjoining table. There was a disturbing dichotomy about his appearance; his potbellied, middle-aged body was surmounted by a bronzed and youthful face. He said something to the seated group, laughed loudly, waved, then moved on.

"Table-hopper," Roy Ames said. "If you see an actor who's laughing it up, you can bet he's unemployed. The tired-looking ones who don't talk at all are working."

Claiborne nodded and turned his attention to the menu. "What do you recommend?"

"Going somewhere else for lunch." Ames smiled. "But as long as we're stuck here, you're safe with a sandwich."

"That's odd. I expected the food would be good."

"Once upon a time it was, or so they tell me. Now

nobody seems to care." Ames put his menu down. "You know the old saying, 'You are what you eat'? If that's true, then most people must be coprophagists."

Claiborne thought about the remark as the waitress returned and took their order. Again he had the feeling that what he'd heard hadn't been improvised on the spur of the moment. Roy Ames wasn't a table-hopper, but he was definitely trying to make an impression.

"Coffee now," Ames called after the waitress when she moved away. Then he glanced at his companion. "Met anyone else on the picture?"

"Not yet. Paul Morgan's playing Norman, isn't he?"

"Supposedly. Up to now he's never played anything but Paul Morgan. Mr. *Mucho Macho*." Ames paused as his coffee arrived. "If you ask me, our culture is suffering from jock-shock."

"Then how did he get the part?"

"Ask Vizzini." Ames lifted his coffee cup. "On second thought, don't bother. Vizzini doesn't make suspense pictures anymore—just spatter-films. That's what the kids want. Plenty of special effects, and lots of punk rock during the car crashes and murder sequences. It's like the good old days in Rome—the musicians play louder when the lions eat the Christians in the arena."

More pat phrases, but they didn't answer Claiborne's question. He leaned forward. "If that's the way you feel, why did you write the script?"

"Money." Roy Ames shrugged. "No, that's not true. Or only partially. I saw something in this—a chance to reach the audience with the real thing instead of just grabbing them with gimmicks and grossout." He dumped sweetener in his coffee cup. "Maybe you'll understand when you read it."

"I'll give it a try," said Claiborne.

And that afternoon, back at the motel, he did just that.

The day had turned sultry and the air conditioner complained as the sun beat down against the west window, but Claiborne didn't notice because he wasn't really in the room.

He was inside the script, in a world two thousand miles and twenty years away.

The writing was uneven; in spite of what Roy Ames said, he hadn't entirely eliminated the elements he professed to despise. There was still plenty of shock sequences, and the emphasis was on murder rather than motivation.

But it worked. The innocent young girl and the cunning madman were stereotypes, yet somehow they carried conviction. Perhaps the girls weren't all that innocent today, but the madmen were more cunning than ever. And more numerous. There was nothing in the film that wasn't duplicated daily in the news reports. Especially out here, Claiborne reflected, remembering the Skid Row Slasher, the Hillside Strangler, the Freeway Killers, and all the other mass murderers glamorized by the media's fancy labels. But there was nothing glamorous about their condition or their activities—sick people, hung up on homicide, OD-ing on death.

Claiborne sighed as the phrases flashed. He was falling into the trap, beginning to sound like a scriptwriter himself. The thing to do was eliminate those touches from the dialogue, let the contrast between appearance and reality speak for itself.

As the sunlight subsided he switched on the lamp, took a pad from his briefcase, and started making his notes.

Now the air conditioner droned in darkness, but the lamplight above the table haloed his head as he scrawled away, losing himself in the limbo of another time, another place. Norman's world.

The rapping on the door returned him to reality.

"Yes?" He rose, moving across the room. "Who's there?"

"Tom Post."

Claiborne opened the door and the old man grinned at him. "I remembered to knock this time. You busy?"

"No." Claiborne shook his head. *Nosy old bastard— what did he want?*

"Noticed your light. Just thought I'd stop by and offer you a beer." Post nodded at the cans he clutched in his left hand. "Compliments of the house." He chuckled.

For a moment Claiborne hesitated, but the sound was a signal he'd learned not to ignore. The chuckle, the nervous laugh, wasn't an indication of amusement but of defense—an attempt to conceal the real emotion underneath. What was Tom Post hiding?

"Come in." Claiborne stepped back. "I'll see if there's a clean glass in the bathroom."

"Don't bother on my account." Post moved to a chair, put the containers on the table, and punctured the tops with a left thumb. He held out a can to Claiborne, waited until the younger man seated him-

172

self on the edge of the bed, then raised his own can. "Cheers."

"Thanks." Claiborne drank.

"Weather like this, beer hits the spot." Again the chuckle sounded. But the gray-green eyes were searching the room, finally focusing on the tabletop.

"Script?" he asked. "Thought you weren't in the industry."

"I'm not. Just looking it over for a friend."

"I see." Post tilted the beer can again. "What's the story like? Or shouldn't I ask?"

"No secret." As he spoke, Claiborne watched the wrinkled face. "Come to think of it, you may be interested. The main character is Norman Bates."

"The hell you say." Tom Post wasn't chuckling now.

Claiborne leaned forward. "I've been meaning to ask you about that remark last night. How come you know about the Bates Motel?"

"I thought everybody did. Don't you read the papers or watch the news?" Post's tone was explanatory rather than defensive. "Matter of fact, there was an item about Coronet making a film on the case." He glanced toward the table. "I take it your friend did the script."

"That's correct." Claiborne was casual. "You used to write for pictures. Care to look at it?"

To his surprise, Tom Post shook his head. "Waste of time. I don't understand movies nowadays. All those sex scenes—people in bed rolling over and over. Try doing it that way and you'll end up with a broken back. And then, when he's finished, the stud pops out from under the covers and damned if he

173

isn't wearing boxer shorts! That sure as hell isn't the way we did it in my day."

Now the chuckle sounded again. "Of course, times change. Take censorship. Maybe four-letter words are in, but other words are out. You don't believe me, try getting up in public and singing the second line of 'My Old Kentucky Home.'"

He sloshed the liquid at the bottom of his can. "Junk food, junk films. Writers have too much power nowadays."

"That's not what my friend tells me," Claiborne said.

"I don't mean pictures." Post finished off his beer. "But think about this. Some politician gets up and reads a speech. His opponent reads a rebuttal. Then a TV commentator reads a report explaining what the two men read. All of it—the speech, the rebuttal, the explanation—is the work of some anonymous writers in the back room. And we call it 'news.'

"Ten days or ten months or ten years later, another writer comes out with a book exposing everything they said as a lie. And that's called 'history.' So when you come right down to it, whether they're dealing with fact or fiction, all writers are professional liars."

He set the empty container down on the tabletop. "How about another beer?"

"No, thanks." Claiborne glanced through the window at the darkened patio beyond. "Time for me to go out and eat."

"Wish I'd thought of it sooner," Post said. "I fixed dinner early tonight. Should have asked you to join me. Must be pretty dull, eating alone when you're away from home."

"That's all right. I'm used to it."

"You're not married?"

"No." Claiborne forestalled further questions by rising and moving to the closet for his jacket.

Tom Post switched off the lamp and followed him to the door. "Plenty of restaurants around here," he said. "But you could buy a few things at that supermarket down the street and stash them away here in the refrigerator." He gestured toward the cupboard behind the unit. "You've got dishes in there, and a hot plate. Comes in handy for making breakfast."

"Thanks for the tip." Claiborne opened the door and stepped out.

Post followed, nodding his approval as the younger man closed the door and locked it. "That's the ticket," he said. "I try to keep an eye out in case anyone comes prowling around here, but these days you can't be too careful."

He started down the patio, toward the office, and Claiborne waved farewell, meanwhile inhaling the odor of night-blooming jasmine from the clump of shrubbery bordering the alleyway. Then he turned and headed for the street, where the floral scent was lost in the traffic fumes.

He breathed the stench until he entered the little steak house a block away. Here it was replaced in turn by the reek of charcoal-broil, onion rings, hash browns, and fries. But even that was preferable to the emanation from the armpits of his red-jacketed waiter. Post was right; it would be better to prepare a snack at the motel. Follow your nose.

Good enough, but what did the other sense organs convey? Post's nervous chuckle echoed in his ears. And when he closed his eyes there was a retinal recall of Tom Post watching while he locked the door of the room. *Nosy old bastard*.

Noses again, but there was more to it than that, something else lurked hidden behind the chuckling and the curiosity. Post must have a passkey; he could be in the room right now, going through Claiborne's belongings. Or the script. He'd been eager enough to learn its contents—then, when he found out, even more eager to change the subject. Why?

Come off it, Claiborne told himself. Of course there was a reason. The elderly often chuckled self-consciously to disarm possible rejection. It was a signal, a way of saying, "Look, I'm not really a serious threat, don't get angry with me for speaking to you." And many of them were inquisitive about other people's affairs merely because their own lives were empty.

It must be a dismal existence for a man still in full possession of his faculties to just sit there in a run-down motel day after day and night after night. Judging by the absence of other vehicles in the parking slots, Claiborne was presently the only tenant. No wonder Tom Post brought the beer to his room, asked questions, talked a blue streak. The old man was lonely.

Either that, or damned devious. What was that remark he made about all writers being professional liars?

Roy Ames was a writer too. Full of facile phrases. Claiborne recalled the intuitive suspicion that his

176

glib one-liners had seen service before. Like the table-hoppers, he'd trotted out his jokes seeking approval.

But for what reason? On the face of things, he must know that Claiborne was his ally; he saw eye-to-eye with him about toning down the script. Though, if so, why hadn't he fought harder, earlier on, to do the job himself? He was the one responsible for the violence in the first place.

That too could be a masking mechanism. In a sense, the Norman of the script was Roy Ames's creation. He supplied the character with his own frustrations, his own furies. And if spilling it out on paper wasn't catharsis, then it might be *cathexis*, a means of strengthening an unconscious attachment to Norman's *persona*. Which could be dangerous.

All writers are professional liars. A statement made by a writer. Which meant that it was also a lie. But everyone lied, including his own patients, whose problem was that they lied not only to him but to themselves. In a way, they were the most professional liars of all. And he was a professional truth-finder.

Truth-*seeker*, he amended. And his search wasn't always successful; Norman was a case in point.

After finishing his meal and leaving the restaurant, Claiborne moved along the boulevard. Automatically, as he thought of Norman, he caught himself glancing around for the sight of a figure that wasn't there.

The cars sped by, the vans and Broncos and Jeeps, as well as an occasional motorcycle snarling through the snarl. Youth on the prowl.

But not on the sidewalks. Claiborne squinted at

his watch; scarcely nine o'clock, and he was the sole visible pedestrian.

In spite of the gas situation, everyone drove. Walking city streets by night was too risky; even the cop on the beat made his rounds on wheels. Police were suspicious of strolling strangers, people like himself.

Passing by the darkened shopfronts, Claiborne peered at the unlit passageways between the buildings, knowing as he did so that his apprehension was absurd. Norman wasn't going to pop out from one of the passageways. Norman wasn't here. Or was he?

Damn that script! Reading it had brought everything back with a vengeance. Vengeance was the rationale.

Either that, or the whole thing was a paranoid delusion. If Norman had preceded him out here, he should have found his way to the studio by now. In the interval between psychotic episodes he was certainly capable of making plans, taking action to implement his vengeance. But everything pointed to one inescapable conclusion: Norman was dead. It was only the script that brought him to life again.

Even so, Claiborne found himself hastening toward the shopping mall looming ahead on his left. He turned into the parking area, welcoming the lights, the sounds, the presence of people.

Crossing the lot, he qualified his reaction. The presence of people wasn't all that welcomed a phenomenon, now that he observed their cars. *You are what you eat*, Roy Ames had said. Perhaps *you are what you drive* would be a more accurate observation. One can judge people by their motor-reflexes.

He noted the frantic maneuvering of vehicles

entering the lot; the way in which aggressive drivers jockeyed for position, impeding the movement of those behind as they competed for vacated spaces close to the store entrance while other motorists hurled mechanical curses at them with their horns. The banged fenders of cars already parked attested to previous encounters, and the ultimate contempt for common courtesy was evident in those that occupied positions in the *Absolutely No Parking* zone.

In the market itself, the pattern continued. Old ladies with dyed orange hair squeezed the dyed oranges at the produce counter, blithely blocking the passage with their shopping carts. Tank-topped, bare-footed beach bums crashed down the aisles, aiming their carts like weapons. Mom-and-Pop couples crowded single customers away from the displays of bargain specials, though in nearly all instances it was bulldog-jawed Mom who took the initiative while little old dried-up Pop stood meekly by. *They also serve who only pay the freight*.

Claiborne took a quart of milk from the dairy shelves, brushing against a Japanese youth in a mesh blouse. The young man hissed and shook his head, causing his earring to bob about furiously.

At the deli counter he selected a modest assortment of packaged cold cuts. Picking over the cellophane-wrapped cheese, he found a small slab, but as he reached for it, a hand snaked around from behind and snared the prize. He turned to confront a grinning girl in a bumpy T-shirt emblazoned with the classic motto: *Up Yours*.

Moving on to the next section, he halted there to pick up a dozen eggs, waiting patiently while a middle-aged housewife in curlers opened cartons to inspect their contents while lipping a cigarette.

The smoke was acrid, and Claiborne turned away. Never mind the eggs, he could do without. Right now all he wanted to do was leave. It had been a long day and he was tired—tired of people, tired of noise and lights and confusion. The smarmy strains of amplified music dulled his hearing, the overly bright fluorescence made his vision blur.

As he reached the bakery goods display, he cast an irritated glance upwards, seeking the source of the piped-in sound. But the big rounded discs hanging at intervals between walls and ceiling were not amplifiers; their shiny surfaces reflected the movements of the customers below. Spotting devices, installed to detect shoplifters. And when he looked up, the long, livid fluorescent tubes cast a glittering glare.

Claiborne turned away. As he did so, another mirror installed directly behind him caught his eye. It was angled to reflect the image of shoppers approaching the left-hand checkout counter at the front of the store, but at the moment only one man was moving through the checkout. He stared up and Claiborne saw his face.

The face of Norman Bates.

Nineteen

Thrusting his cart to one side, Claiborne raced down the aisle toward the front of the store, swerving midway to avoid a gaggle of oncoming shoppers, who scowled in annoyance as he careened past them.

Their irritation scarcely registered; it was Norman's image that impelled him to the checkout, which in thirty seconds had already attracted a line-up of carts and customers.

But Norman was gone.

Claiborne halted, eyeing the unfamiliar faces, then pushed his way through the queue to confront the gum-chewing, bovine blonde behind the counter.

"Where is he?"

The rumination ceased as the blonde looked up.

"Your last customer—he was here just a minute ago—"

She shrugged, glancing automatically toward the nearest exit. Even as she did so, he elbowed his way past the counter, striding to the door.

The parking lot was almost full now; cars were moving in and out, patrons zigzagging across the open areas. Claiborne scanned the scene, searching for a familiar figure. He moved onto the lot, trying to locate vehicles on the point of pulling out.

There were three—no, four—and still another, way down at the far right. He hurried toward it as the car backed hastily into the open lane and then moved forward. In the glare of overhead floodlights he glimpsed a woman's face behind the windshield and, beside it, the knoblike silhouette of a child's head.

Turning, he started back to the center of the lot, then jumped at the blare of a horn directly behind him. He stepped aside just in time as a dune buggy zoomed past, the roar of its motor blending with the profanity of the mustached driver, who thrust his hand out to give him the finger.

Breathing heavily, Claiborne stared out across the area beyond, knowing as he did so that it was just wasted effort now. Norman was gone.

But to where?

If he'd come here, it must mean that he was holed up someplace nearby, perhaps in one of the other motels lining the length of the boulevard.

Could they be checked out? There were dozens of places, not counting the big hotels, and Norman certainly wouldn't have registered under his own name, if in fact he was registered at all. Trying to identify every one of the single men who might have occupied motel rooms during the past three days would be a major project, even for a police task force. A project they weren't about to undertake unless Claiborne could offer them something more tangible than just his word.

Yes, I realize the man's supposed to be dead, but I saw him there in the supermarket. No, I didn't speak to him, he was up at the front of the store and I was at the back. Not directly, I saw him in one of those overhead mirrors, but I'm positive—

A lost cause. Claiborne sighed. There was nothing to do now except return to the market, retrieve his cart, and check out.

Walking back to the motel with his bag of groceries, he glanced around warily, searching the striations of light and shadow in the street. He'd seen Norman—but had Norman seen him? Had Norman followed him to the store, was he following him now?

Nothing stirred in the darkness.

Even so, he was relieved when he reached his room. The locked door yielded to the turn of the key, and when he switched on the light, the room revealed no sign of present occupancy or prior disturbance.

If Norman didn't know his whereabouts, Claiborne was secure here, at least for now. And there was always the possibility of subjective error. Noise, light, fatigue, tension—they could all add up to a simple case of mistaken identity. That was what the police would say; that was what he himself would probably say if some patient came to him with a similar story.

Under the circumstances, there was no point in

talking to Driscoll and the others. Telling them what he'd seen, or thought he'd seen, would only weaken his position unless he could offer proof. The thing to do now was exercise caution, watch and wait, and continue to emphasize the need for security. If Norman was here, he'd make his presence known soon enough.

If Norman was here.

Claiborne unpacked his groceries, put them away, shed his clothing, donned pajamas, and sank down on the bed. The air conditioner whispered to him.

Norman. Here. Planning something. Where? What?

Thank God he'd decided to stay on. At least he could keep his eyes and ears open, act as a sort of guardian angel to the others.

But even as he surrendered to sleep, a further question came.

Who would be guarding him if Norman acted?

There was no answer to that one. All he knew was that whatever happened, it would be soon.

Twenty

Roy Ames's office was in the same building as Driscoll's, but there was no resemblance between the two. The cramped cubicle with its single window was smaller than the producer's private washroom, and by no means as lavishly appointed.

When Claiborne opened the door, he found Ames already seated behind his desk, midway between the file cabinet and the single extra chair. Apparently he was accustomed to these close quarters; whatever his hangups, claustrophobia wasn't one of them.

Blinking against morning sunlight radiating from the open window, Claiborne nodded a greeting and put his copy of the script down on the desktop.

Ames glanced at him expectantly. "Well, what do you think?" he said.

Claiborne hesitated, once again debating whether or not to reveal last night's experience. No sense in taking that chance. And right now the script had priority.

"I've got some notes here," Claiborne said. "If you'd like to go over them—"

"Great."

Claiborne opened his briefcase and pulled out the yellow pages. "Hope you can read my handwriting."

Ames managed.

His eyes moved rapidly over the scrawled sheets, revealing nothing. But Claiborne had no trouble recognizing his reactions. Long ago he'd learned that mouths are often most eloquent when not speaking. Ames's mouth was no exception. At first the lips curved upward in a slight smile; then, as he read on, they tightened. And finally the upper lip curled, forming a fixed frown.

It was time to intervene. "Please remember one thing," Claiborne said. "I'm not criticizing the writing. Just content, the violence."

Ames looked up. "We use another term now. As in 'box-office gross.'"

"I'm aware of that. But I thought you were trying to avoid it."

"I did, in my first draft." Ames was on the defensive. "Most of the stuff you object to here is Vizzini's work. He did a partial rewrite and Driscoll went along with it."

"Sounds as if I'm wasting my time," Claiborne said. "As technical advisor, I thought I was the one to suggest changes."

"Technical, yes. Suggest, yes. But Vizzini has the

clout—script approval, casting, the works. I told you how he insisted on Jan just because she was a lookalike for Mary Crane."

"That's another thing," Claiborne said. "Did you notice my comments on her scenes?"

"I noticed." Ames's voice was tight, and Claiborne cut in quickly.

"It just seems to me that her character comes across as a bit too simple, too one-dimensional—"

"Okay, so it shows." Ames shrugged. "If you must know, I wrote it that way on purpose. Jan's not ready for anything heavy, even though she thinks so, and I want to keep her from screwing up. She comes on pretty strong, but when you know her better, you'll see there's something else behind it."

"I hope to," Claiborne said. "Matter of fact, I ran into her on the lot just now. She invited me to have dinner tonight."

Ames didn't reply, but the sudden set of his silent lips spoke for him.

And so did Claiborne's inner voice. *Talk about screwing up—what'd you have to tell him that for? It's obvious he's emotionally involved with the girl. You need an ally and now you've got a jealous rival.*

He smiled quickly, indicating casual dismissal of the statement. "But that's not important. We've got to—what do they say out here?—lick the script. If you're willing to revise along the lines I've indicated—"

"Indicated?" Ames's antagonism was open now. "All that stuff about displacement, latent content, reaction-formation—it reads like a medical report!"

"Sorry. What I was trying to do—"

"Don't draw diagrams. You're playing doctor, aren't you?" Ames shook his head. "Psychs are like economists, meteorologists, seismologists—just a bunch of guessers with gadgets. Someday all you shrinks will be replaced by computers."

"Suits me." Claiborne kept his cool. "But that's not going to help us now. I'll go along with the way you've handled Jan's role. The big job is to eliminate some of the violence."

"No way. I told you Vizzini wants it in."

Claiborne shrugged. "Then we'll have to change the emphasis."

"What's that supposed to mean?"

"The real problem with this kind of film isn't violence itself—it's the *attitude* toward violence. That's where the danger lies today, in the way antisocial behavior is exploited as the final solution to everything. Heroes, antiheroes, or villains, all winning out by taking the law into their own hands. We can keep Norman's behavior just as it is, without dulling the knife-edge or mopping up the blood. But let's not justify it."

Ames was listening now, and Claiborne pressed on quickly. "Let's tell the truth for once. Make it clear that murder solves nothing; it's not heroic, and Norman Bates is no one to envy or emulate. You actually won't have much rewriting to do if you keep this in mind. All it takes is a slight shift of emphasis to show him as a driven, tormented man whose compulsive behavior brings misery instead of satisfaction."

"And that's your big solution?" Roy Ames grimaced. "Turn the clock back fifty years to tell the audience 'Crime does not pay'?"

"Maybe it's time to do just that. There was a hell of a lot less homicide fifty years ago, and what there was went on mainly among professional criminals. Now it's Amateur Night—student terrorists, kids on the street, all competing for status by slaughter. Because our films, our television, our books and plays tell them that violence is rewarding."

"Haven't you ever heard of 'the me generation'? This is what sells today."

"Not exclusively. Damn it, I'm not a religious man, but I know the Bible is still a top best-seller. And it spells out its message loud and clear: 'The wages of sin is death.'"

Ames stared at him for a long moment. It was no longer the stare of a jealous suitor; his concern now was for every writer's first love—the work at hand. "I get it. What you're really pitching is what old Cecil B. De Mille did to get around the censors. Put in the orgies, but make sure you show the consequences. And you're right about changes. All that needs work are the scenes showing Norman's reactions. Less gloating, more grief." He paused. "Level with me. Did he actually feel that way?"

Claiborne nodded slowly. "In all my experience, I've never seen a more unhappy man."

Roy Ames sighed and picked up the script again. "Might as well get to work. I should have pages sometime tomorrow, unless I run into problems."

"If you do, give me a call." Claiborne moved to the door. "Now I'll get out of your way."

He left the office, walked down the hall. For the first time since last night he felt a resurgence of hope. At least part of his task was done; the script would be improved and he'd managed to retain Roy Ames's allegiance.

But not Norman's.

That was the problem. If he could just sit down and talk, reason with him, explain that the script was being changed, assure him there was nothing to fear or resent. Maybe—just maybe—it still might work before anything happened.

Only he had to find him first.

Where?

Needles hid in haystacks. Searching for them was a waste of time. The easiest way to draw a needle out was with a magnet.

Claiborne moved onto the studio street, and it was there that realization came.

This was the magnet. The studio itself—the magnet that had drawn Norman here.

No need to worry about a manhunt, private or public. Norman would come to the studio. If he hadn't taken action before, it might merely mean that he'd just arrived. But he was on the scene now, and if he got onto the lot—

Claiborne glanced along the street in the direction of the main gate. The guard stood beside it, monitoring the cars as they drove up. There were other entrances, of course; he'd checked them out and knew that all were similarly protected.

Which meant nothing. Norman wouldn't attempt to pass through a gate.

Claiborne turned and headed toward the rear of the lot, glancing at the studio wall to his left as he did so. The wall was a solid mass of masonry, high and thick. But thickness was irrelevant. Norman wasn't going to tunnel his way through the wall. And height itself was no guarantee of protection. Anyone with a rope or a ladder could scale one of these walls unobserved in darkness. The lot was patrolled at night as well as by day, but once he was atop the wall, it would be a simple matter to wait until the coast was clear and drop down inside to seek shelter somewhere in the studio.

Now Claiborne moved past a concrete cluster of offices, set-storage sheds, the studio garage, wardrobe, and makeup departments. Many of these structures had outside stairways leading up to projection rooms and editing booths. Angled against the sides of the buildings were trucks, trailers, campers, and semis; beyond them loomed the vast sound stages with their tangle of overhead catwalks and equipment bins.

Turning right toward the rear of the lot, he came upon an empty, unpatrolled, deserted domain of standing exterior sets: a western street with a bar, livery stable, feed store, hotel, dance hall, bank, and sheriff's office. Behind it was a small-town square bordered by the friendly facades of white houses nestling amid lawns and shrubbery, a high-steepled church, a bandstand in a wooded park. Beyond lay a big-city street with its shops and theaters and tenements; past that, still another half-dozen smaller enclaves of foreign settings.

There were a million hiding places here, and no security force could possibly cover them all completely. Once over the wall, Norman need only keep moving from place to place, stay out of sight. And it could have happened; for all Claiborne knew, he may have spent the night sleeping in Andy Hardy's bed. He could be on the lot now.

If the studio was a magnet, it was also a haystack in its own right, offering far more concealment than the world outside. A needle would be safe here, but even more dangerous to others. Needles are sharp, they have eyes—

And so have I, Claiborne told himself. *Watch and wait*. This was no time to spread panic, not without something substantial to support his suppositions, not until he was sure of his ground.

He turned and walked back, coming abreast of the sound stages. Number Seven, on his left, was open, its huge sliding doors secured in the slotted wall. On impulse, he approached and peered inside. A half-circle of sunlight revealed concrete flooring laced with snakelike coils of cable, but the vast area above and beyond was steeped in shadow.

Claiborne moved past the doorway, trying to adjust his vision to the inner gloom. He'd never seen these surroundings except in films *about* films, and then only as a background to accompany action. But there was no action here, only the solitude and the silence.

Stepping forward, he eyed the dim outline of the rounded roof high above the walkways. Somehow he hadn't realized the immensity of the stage; block-long and bleak, it was like an old-style zeppelin hangar or the interior of a cathedral reared to some strange god of darkness.

The darkness wasn't complete. Beyond the barricade of lath-and-plaster wall backgrounds encased in wooden supports, he caught a glimpse of dim light— a bare bulb dangling on a cord from an iron grid overhead. The area it lit was obscured by other walls mounted and joined together at right angles on three sides.

Claiborne approached it, passing a row of portable dressing rooms at his right. Their doors were closed, and no trace of illumination issued from beneath them.

A million hiding places.

He started over to the nearest one, then slackened his pace before the wooden steps leading up to the door.

Suppose he was right? Suppose that by some crazy coincidence he'd actually find himself coming upon Norman, crouching there in the dark behind the door—crouching and waiting?

Claiborne hesitated, deep in internal debate. *What are you waiting for? Damn it, that's why you're here, isn't it? To find him?*

He mounted the steps slowly. *Don't worry. If he is in there, he's frightened. As frightened as you are.*

Again he paused. He *was* frightened, admit it; his tightened muscles offered tense testimony. There was a prickling across his scalp, a trickling beneath his armpits.

That was a normal reaction to fear, and he could accept it. But would Norman's reaction be normal? When Norman was afraid, he lashed out. If he had a weapon—

You've faced that problem before. Occupational hazard, it comes with the territory. Only it won't happen. He isn't here, can't be here, not with a million hiding places to choose from.

Claiborne reached for the door.

And heard the sound.

It was quite faint; even here, in the cavernous echo chamber of the sound stage, there was scarcely more than a hint of it. A rustling sound followed by a creak.

But it didn't come from behind the door. The source was the lighted area beyond.

He turned away, descending the steps before the dressing room. Now there was silence, broken only by the soft scraping of his own footsteps over concrete as he started forward. Even this was stilled as he slowed his pace, moving in quiet caution, feeling the fear, straining to detect a repetition of the rustling and the creaking.

Nothing.

He came to the open area at the right of the three-sided set where the lightbulb dangled. There he halted, peering forward.

No one moved beneath the light. The set was deserted.

Slowly he started past the walls enclosing him on both sides, into the rectangular room set beyond. Then, as he entered, something changed. Looking down, he saw carpeting beneath his feet. Red and faded carpeting, the kind one finds only in old houses where old people ignore the passage of time.

And he was in such a house now, standing still in a room where time stood still.

Claiborne glanced at the old-fashioned dresser and vanity, their tops littered with mementoes of long-ago yesterdays. A gilt clock, Dresden figurines, a pincushion, an ornate hand mirror, glass-stoppered bottles of scent. These objects, and a glimpse of the garments hanging from a rack in an open closet, told him he was in a woman's bedroom, even before he saw the bed itself.

The bed stood in the far corner at the right, past the high-backed rocker facing the window in the shadows to the left. He stepped forward, surveying the contours of the four-poster, admiring the hand-embroidered bedspread. But as he neared it, he noted that the spread had been tucked in carelessly, so that a portion of the double pillow was visible at the top. On impulse he reached down and pulled the covers back, revealing grayish sheets dotted with brown flecks. And the telltale indentation of recent occupancy—the deep indentation that could only have been made by someone resting here a long time.

Someone.

Some thing.

Claiborne knew where he was now. He'd never seen it, never been there before, but he'd heard and read enough to recognize what it must be.

The bedroom of Norman's mother.

It was here, of course, that the mummified body of Mrs. Bates, preserved by Norman's crude attempts at taxidermy, had lain untouched and unsuspected for all those years while Norman preserved the illusion that she was still alive—a crazed invalid, confined to her room. But it was Norman himself who had been crazed, who had assumed her *persona* when he killed. Wearing her clothing, talking in her voice, here in this room.

No, not this room. It's only a set.

Claiborne confirmed the reality by contact, pulling the bedspread up again to hide the indented outline.

But his scalp crawled as he did so, and he couldn't hide the thought crawling beneath it.

What had it been like for Norman, living in the real house, sitting in the real bedroom night after night, mumbling to a mummy? *Mummy, Mommy*—

Then he heard the sound again, the creaking and the rustling.

He turned as the shadows stirred.

The creaking came from the high-backed rocker facing the window.

And the rustling came from the dress as the old woman rose from the chair and glided toward him.

She came out of the shadows with her gray hair gleaming, mouth contorted in a ghastly rictus. Her arms rose, her hands scrabbled upward, the wig came off.

Claiborne stared at the grinning face—a face he'd seen so many times on the screen.

The face of Paul Morgan.

Twenty-One

Claiborne sat at the bar in the Tail o' the Cock, still nursing a beer as Morgan ordered his second drink.

Wearing skintight jeans, the V-neck of his shirt spread to reveal the gold locket nestling against a hairy chest, Morgan bore no resemblance to the hunched old lady on the darkened set of the sound stage.

"Sorry about that," he was saying. "I didn't mean to shake you up."

"Forget it. You don't have to keep apologizing." Claiborne shifted on his bar stool. "Actually, I had no business being there in the first place."

"Neither did I." Morgan reached for his glass as the bartender set it down before him. "It was Vizzini's idea."

"The director?"

"I'm not used to this kind of jazz. He wants me to really sell those scenes in drag. Not just wearing the dress and wig—it's the walk, the gestures, the whole bit. I figured doing it on the set would help me get used to the feel, dig?"

Claiborne smiled ruefully. "Well, you certainly sold me."

Morgan raised his glass and drank, obviously pleased by the verdict.

Claiborne wondered just how pleased Morgan would be if he knew about his unspoken reservations. Morgan was indeed convincing when disguised as the old woman, but playing Norman would be an entirely different matter. Without makeup, he was imprisoned in his own image, instantly identifiable.

As if to prove the point, a girl rose from a group of three seated in one of the nearby booths and came over to the bar. Petitely pretty, she had shiny auburn hair and brown eyes that were accentuated by the outfit she was wearing; white slacks and open blouse emphasized both the baby fat and the plump, budding breasts. She was probably a tourist and undoubtedly not a day over sixteen.

Ignoring Claiborne, she moved up alongside his companion. "Excuse me," she said. "Are you Paul Morgan?"

The actor put down his glass and turned, flashing his familiar grin. "What do you think?" he said.

The girl's eyes dropped before his gaze and her hand came up clutching a small book, bound in imitation leather, and a ballpoint pen. The hand trembled almost imperceptibly, but the tremor in her voice was quite evident. "If you don't mind—could I have your autograph?"

Morgan's gaze zeroed in on the front of her blouse. "You can have anything I've got," he said. She flushed and his grin softened. "Come on, honey, don't be nervous."

She relaxed, reassured by his change of expression.

"Where you from?" he murmured.

"Toledo. My girlfriends and me, we're out here on a tour." She smiled shyly, glancing back at the booth. "They dared me to come over. I hope you don't mind."

"No problem." He reached for the book, opening it to a blank page, then took the pen from her hand. "What's your name?"

"Jackie. Jackie Sherbourne."

"Want to spell it for me?"

She did so, and he scribbled across the page in a bold, florid script, winking at her as he wrote. "There, that ought to do it." Closing the book, he handed it back to her along with the pen.

"Thank you," she said.

"My pleasure."

The girl went away and Morgan turned to reach for his glass again. Claiborne watched the girl as she and her companions moved, chattering, to the exit.

Morgan swallowed his drink. "Anything wrong?"

Claiborne shrugged in denial. But the gesture was meaningless, because he'd seen what Morgan had written in the autograph book. *To Jackie Sherbourne, who gives good head.*

A shabby trick, and for a moment Claiborne was tempted to call him on it. He promised himself that he would, later, when the time came. But not yet. Now he needed allies. The script—

"Stinks, if you ask me." Morgan was talking about it. "Don't think I'm too dumb to know what Ames is up to, throwing all those scenes to the girl, building up her part. But she can't hack it. Why the hell Driscoll signed her I'll never know, he must have been out of his tree."

"I get the impression the director is responsible for casting the role," Claiborne said. "After all, she does look like Mary Crane. He's trying for realism."

"Then where do I come in, playing a gay?"

"Not a gay, a transvestite."

"But Norman thinks he's his own mother—"

"His fugue doesn't necessarily involve homosexuality, except on the subliminal level."

"Then what the hell does it involve?" Morgan frowned. "Skip the two-dollar words, give it to me straight. What was Norman Bates really like?"

Claiborne shrugged. "Very much like you or me," he said. "If we were stripped of identity, reduced to a numbered case history, confined to a room that's really a cell, subject to orders, surrounded by sickness and aberration—"

"I know about all that." Paul Morgan spoke softly. "I've been in a flake-factory."

Noting the involuntary flicker of surprise in Claiborne's eyes, he continued quickly, "Don't get me wrong, I wasn't whacko. Voluntary commitment, a couple of years ago—stayed for a month, just to dry out." Morgan picked up his glass and downed the ice-diluted residue. "Didn't work."

His tone was sardonic, but there was no trace of

the attitude in his face as he leaned forward. "Neither did I," he said. "You want the truth, I didn't work for damn near a year and a half. That's one hell of a long time in this business, and once the word is out, you can't even get arrested."

"But Vizzini wanted you for this part."

"He didn't want me—just the name. And he got it dirt cheap. That's the only reason Driscoll went along with the deal. He told me so to my face, the scumbag bastard."

Morgan's hand tightened around his empty glass. "Son of a bitch keeps riding me, thinks he can give me the needle, but he's got a surprise coming. If he'd been alone with me on the set this morning instead of you—"

Conscious of Claiborne's stare, the actor broke off with an abrupt laugh. "Forget it," he said. "Have another drink."

Claiborne slid off the bar stool, shaking his head. "I'd better get back to the motel." He hesitated. "Sure you're all right?"

Morgan nodded. "Just had to blow out my exhaust. But it's okay now. I goddam know I can cut the part, so there's nothing to sweat about." He summoned the all-purpose grin. "Remember, I'm Paul Morgan."

Driving away, Claiborne remembered. The disturbing vision of Paul Morgan in drag on the set— the casual cruelty of Paul Morgan with the autograph-seeker—the bitterness and anger of Paul Morgan at the bar. And it wasn't until he reached the motel that he asked himself the question:

What is Paul Morgan really like?

Twenty-two

It was almost seven when Jan opened the oven door to check on the roast.

She frowned. *Still not done.* Closing the door, she turned the oven up to four hundred. *Give it another fifteen minutes while I do the salad. With luck, maybe he'll be late. He doesn't know these hills.*

But as she tossed the lettuce she caught herself listening for sounds of a car approaching outside. All she heard was the endless repetition of a nightbird's two notes, defiantly defining its territory. And inside, Connie's slamming things around in the territory of her own bedroom, getting ready to go out for the evening. *Here's hoping she's gone before he arrives.*

Jan drowned the thought in a mixture of oil and vinegar. She poured it over the salad, and then it was time to take another look at the roast, turn off the oven, give it a final basting, and let it brown a bit more—

Domesticity, you can have it. Strictly for the birds. Suddenly she was aware that the nightbird's call had ceased. And she'd never even heard the car drive up, but now the door chimes sounded, followed almost immediately by the buzz of voices. *That bitch Connie answered the door herself. I told her—*

Too late now. Jan untied her apron, flung it over the back of a chair, and freed her hands to smooth her hair. Why hadn't she had the sense to hang some kind of mirror here in the kitchen, just a little one for emergencies like this?

And it was an emergency, anytime she'd let herself get stuck in the kitchen with this cozy little dinner-for-two routine—

Hastily she grabbed a tissue from the open box on the counter and patted her face and forehead. At least she wouldn't make her entrance with a shiny nose. Once she lit the candles on the dining room table, it wouldn't matter so much. Dining by candle-light, a nice intimate touch, work the conversation around slowly over a few drinks, find out just what he and Roy came up with when they huddled this morning. Damn it, this was all Roy's fault—him and his weird notions about shutting down the picture. If he'd done a selling job on Claiborne, it was up to her to un-sell him, fast. Or slowly—with the candles, the drinks, the salad, the roast, and whatever else seemed necessary.

Moving across the kitchen, she heard the voice-buzz fade, then the final punctuation of the front door slamming. Connie must have left; sure enough, her clunker was rattling away as it backed out of the carport.

Jan paused at the kitchen doorway to give her hair a final pat, then started forward. *Okay, kid, you're on. Break a leg.*

Funny about showbiz: everybody in the profession has stage fright, even the biggest. She remembered the stories she'd heard about Al Jolson on Broadway, how Jolie used to run the dressing-room water faucets full force before his performances, drowning out the sound of applause for the act preceding him. It didn't matter whether you were doing live theater, films, or television. There was always that terrible moment before you went on—the glands pumping flop-sweat, the stomach turning into a netful of butterflies. But when the curtain rose, the director yelled, "Roll 'em!" or the monitor blinked red—that was when everything changed. That was when *you* changed, took over, delivered. There's no business like show business; it's the greatest orgasm in the world.

Jan was enjoying the foreplay now, welcoming her guest and lighting the candles, pouring the ready-made martinis from the pitcher on the bar.

What she hadn't anticipated was enjoying Dr. Claiborne himself.

She remembered finding him attractive, and she'd always been a sucker for men with deep voices, the virility thing. But most of the actors she knew had similar qualities. What made Claiborne different was that he didn't ego-trip. He had that calm, reassuring approach—if it was his bedside manner, it might be worth finding out about—and didn't talk about himself.

Over drinks, he complimented her in a way she hadn't expected—not on her appearance but on the looks of the apartment, the table-setting, the candles. And during dinner he even ran a number on Connie.

"Your friend is an actress too?"

Jan nodded.

"Hard to believe. She seems so reserved. What sort of roles does she play—character parts?"

"Meaning you don't think she's pretty."

"I didn't say that."

"But you're right, in a way. She is a character and she does parts. Mostly hands and feet."

Claiborne eyed her across the candle flame. "I don't follow."

"Connie's always working. You must have seen her a hundred times in TV commercials or theatrical features, but you wouldn't recognize her because they never show her face. They use her for inserts— tight closeups—doubling for stars whose hands or feet aren't right. There's a lot of that going on out here. Some people just dub vocals or loop lines of dialogue, but the big call is for bodies. A casting director can find whatever he needs from checking pictures in a catalogue—legs, thighs, breasts, anything he wants."

"Sounds like picking out cut-up chicken parts at the supermarket." Claiborne smiled, then sobered. "No wonder she's shy. There must be a tremendous feeling of inadequacy and resentment, knowing that others take the bows while she's doomed to anonymity."

"True."

"At least that's not your problem," Claiborne said. "Obviously you don't need doubling or dubbing, and you don't have to worry about rejection."

"How do I take that?" Jan smiled. "Is it flattery or just analysis?"

He pushed his plate aside, reaching for his coffee cup. "Which would you prefer?"

"I get enough stroking in this business—everybody does. But you have to make it big before you can afford analysis. Or need it."

Claiborne leaned back in his chair. "Maybe so. Then again, if more people understood their own motivations at the start, they might not end up in therapy."

"You offering me a freebie?"

"Hardly that. I couldn't even take a stab at it until I knew more about you."

"Ask."

"All right. First, a generalization. Seems to me most actresses come from either of two backgrounds. One is the broken home—father died, divorced, or just drifted away when the child was young, and the mother took over. Aggressive, ambitious, using her daughter as a puppet, forcing her into the limelight, but always keeping a tight hold on the strings. Sound familiar?"

"Right on," Jan murmured.

"The second group evolves from a slightly different situation. Again no father, but the mother is missing too—dead, perhaps, or sometimes psychotic. The girl is orphaned. Finding no security in a foster home, she often rushes into an early marriage, but that solves nothing. So she seeks out men in power who use her, just as she uses them to further her career."

"Like Marilyn Monroe." Jan nodded. "I know that kind too."

"Good enough," Claiborne said. "But now we come to the question. Which type are you?"

"Can't you guess?"

He met her smile and returned it. "From what I've observed, you belong in the second category."

"Now wait a minute! If you think I'm one of those crazy, mixed-up, pill-popping, suicidal—"

Claiborne shook his head. "Of course not. That comes later. And my whole point is, it needn't come at all if you understand the problem."

"How'd we ever get into this?" Jan forced her laugh, knowing it was her fault for letting things get out of hand. Time to stop with the ad-libs, just stick to the script she'd mentally prepared. *The script—*

"Enough of my problems," she said. "How'd you make out with Roy this morning?"

"Pretty well, I think. He seems to agree with most of the changes I suggested."

"What kind of changes?"

"It's mainly a matter of how to handle Norman's characterization. That's what he's working on right now."

"How about my scenes?"

"I don't imagine they'll be affected very much. Perhaps you'll lose a few lines here and there."

"Why?"

"If Norman's attitude is changed, naturally your reaction changes too. A few dialogue cuts would emphasize that."

208

"Dialogue cuts?" Jan stiffened. "What is it in this business? Nobody tells a producer how to produce or a director how to direct, but everybody and his brother thinks he's a writer."

Something inside her said, *Cool it, you're out of line.* But if he was screwing up her part—

And meanwhile he was sitting there with that professional smile of his, telling her not to worry. Who did he think he was, giving her advice? The words seemed to tumble forth. "How long have you been out here—two, three days? Since when did you become an expert?"

"I'm not." *God, he looked smug. And that deep voice of his, that phony medical manner.* "It's just a question of logic. Changing Norman's attitude means changing the way you respond to his input."

"I don't need a doctor's diagnosis. What's your idea of good input—a suppository?"

That broke him up, but she wasn't playing for laughs. She was playing for keeps. Damn it, she wasn't playing at all, this was too important. "Let me tell you something, buster—"

"You already have." He wasn't laughing now. "I know what you're saying. You're protecting your part."

"It's not just a part, it's my whole future, can't you see that?"

"Nobody can see the future. The only people who want to are the ones who can't stand to look at the past." He nodded. "And in your case, with the background you told me about—"

"I'm not a case, I'm an actress! And what the hell do you know about my background anyway?"

"I'd like to hear."

209

"Sure you would! That's how you shrinks get your rocks off, isn't it? Listening to all those soap-opera stories about teenies from broken homes getting beat up and raped, running away and balling everybody who comes along just to get a break." She stared at him, watching his reaction. "Well, I've got news for you. That fancy theory about actresses is a load of crap.

"You want to know where I come from? Right here in North Hollywood, that's where. My folks are still alive, out in Northridge. They never got divorced, never even had a real quarrel that I know of, and it was my own idea to go into drama classes after I graduated from Van Nuys High. For the last five years I've been making it on my own.

"That doesn't mean it isn't rough sometimes—this is a rough business, you fight for everything you get, and maybe it's even rougher when you don't have one of those stage mothers or some barracuda agent or producer to open doors for you. Sure, I fool around a little, but that's how you play the game; it doesn't mean I'm some kind of a prostitute—"

"Hollywood's the prostitute," Claiborne said.

Jan checked herself, frowning. "How's that?"

"Don't you see? It's the syndrome of entertainment. Film itself prostitutes to audiences. The very way in which it advertises is pandering—come rape me, get your kicks, I'm here to rent myself for your enjoyment in the dark, I invite you to unleash your wildest fantasies of lust, murder, revenge. I lure you to identify with sadists, sociopaths, the polymorphically perverse, tempt you with dreams of destruction." He smiled apologetically. "Don't get me wrong. I'm not

210

putting down entertainment. We all need catharsis, a temporary escape into make-believe. That's what the audience gets, and when the show is over it's just a matter of walking out and returning to reality.

"But if you're one of those who created the make-believe, you stay behind, living with fantasies night and day. That's the danger, because you have no alternatives. In the end you lose contact, lose the ability to cope with reality. And when it touches your life, it can destroy you."

"Who the hell are you to tell me how to run my life?" Jan rose quickly. "Maybe it's not the greatest thing in the world, maybe I'm selfish and stupid and I'll fall on my face. But I know what I'm doing. You want to dig alternatives, go talk to Kay."

"Kay?"

"My kid sister. She's the one who's got everything going for her—a damned sight smarter than I am, and a lot prettier too—or was, until she turned sixteen. That was when she got into that real-life scene you're so big on. Real life, right there in her belly where some stud put it. At seventeen she was a mother, at eighteen she was doing dope and living in a camper with her boyfriend and the baby. Then the guy got busted and they took the kid away and put it in an orphanage. She split, and God only knows where she is now. My folks blew their minds trying to find her, but no use. Maybe she'll luck out and meet some shrink who'll tell her not to worry, that what she did was better than throwing her life away on a career."

Claiborne pushed his chair away from the table. "Stop fooling yourself. You talk as if those were your only choices. But there's a wide area between those two extremes, and most of us manage to compromise and make a life there."

Jan turned on him, eyes flashing. "What about you? Didn't you do the same thing—spend years studying, slaving away, giving up everything just to get where you are today?"

"That's just it." Claiborne spoke softly. "I'm telling you this because I went the route. And where I am today is in limbo. Nowhere at all. No home, no family, no personal life. Being a workaholic isn't living. By now it's too late for me to change, but you still have a choice. Don't throw it away."

Jan listened, her anger ebbing. Maybe he wasn't a phony, maybe he really believed what he was saying. Poor bastard, living in a hospital and busting his butt over the problems of a lot of crazies, just one long downer twenty-four hours a day. The thought flashed suddenly—*I wonder how long it's been since he's had a woman.*

And with the thought came the warmth building within her, a warmth she couldn't quite explain. It wasn't a sex thing, it wasn't just sympathy either, but more like a mixture of both, and somehow that made it even stronger. Without realizing it, she found herself moving toward him, her hands reaching out, and then—

The chimes rang.

She turned, frowning, and moved to the front door. *Now who—*

Roy Ames.

And at a time like this. So he was jealous; since when did that give him the right to crash?

"What do you want?" she said.

He brushed past her into the room. "I tried to call, but your line was busy."

Jan's frown deepened. "This phone hasn't rung all evening."

Roy glanced toward the end table. "So I notice."

She followed his gaze. "Connie made a call earlier, before she went out. She must have left the receiver off the hook."

"Right." He nodded at Claiborne. "You're the one I wanted to reach. Let's get going."

Claiborne rose. "Where?"

"Coronet. Driscoll phoned me at home. Come on, we'll take my car."

"What's the rush?"

Roy turned and headed for the door. "Somebody set fire to the studio."

Twenty-three

Roy drove swiftly, hunching toward the left to make room for Jan and Claiborne on the seat beside him.

Cornering hillside curves, speeding across the boulevard below, he listened for the sound of sirens. But there was nothing to hear and—as they wheeled into the entrance—nothing to see. The studio beyond loomed flame-free in the night.

"False alarm?" Claiborne murmured.

"Can't be," Roy said. "Driscoll called me himself."

And Driscoll himself was at the gate, standing beside a guard.

They pulled up just past the entrance as he hurried over to them, scowling at Roy and gesturing toward his passengers.

"Where the hell did they come from?" he said.

"Dr. Claiborne was having dinner with Jan," Roy told him. "Under the circumstances, I thought he ought to know—"

"Screw the circumstances!" He turned to Roy's companions. "Okay, you're here. But remember one thing. Keep your mouths shut, both of you." He started off, not waiting for a reply. "Come on."

"Aren't you going to tell us what happened?" Claiborne asked.

"You'll see. There's been an accident."

Halfway down the studio street, Roy realized their destination. One of the sound stages at the left was open, and parked before the entrance he saw the shiny red hatchback used by Frank Madero, head of the studio fire patrol.

Inside, Stage Seven blazed with light. Driscoll led them past a row of dressing rooms to the set beyond.

Roy recognized it as they entered; the decor was immediately identifiable. This was the bedroom of Norman's mother, just as he'd described it in his script. Or almost so.

Two men were waiting there: stocky, mustached Madero and old Chuck Grossinger, one of the night-duty security guards, talking together over in the corner next to the four-poster bed.

Roy blinked in the brightness; at first glance the set seemed untouched. But there was a pungent odor in the air—the smell of burnt cloth.

Then he noticed the bedspread—the charred ends, the scorch marks across the pillow cases, which extended beyond the headboard to darken the wall of the set behind it.

"Caught it just in time," Grossinger was saying.

"The door was open just a crack when I come by, and I seen the light, kind of flickering from inside. Then I smelled the smoke. I run in and here was the bed on fire, so I grabbed the extinguisher off the wall—"

"And damned near got yourself barbecued." Frank Madero shook his head. "Thing like this happens, you're supposed to call me."

"Hell, the whole place could go up before you guys got the equipment out of the garage. If that gasoline had exploded—"

"Gasoline?" Driscoll was scowling again as he moved toward Madero, who stooped down on the far side of the four-poster, below Roy's range of vision.

"Found this under the bed just now," he said. And held up a five-gallon drum.

Driscoll reached for the can and shook it. "This hasn't even been opened."

"Cap's loose," Madero told him. "Somebody was all set to use it, but he got interrupted."

"How do you know?" Driscoll bent forward, peering under the four-poster. "Look, there's paint cans here too, and brushes. Lazy bastards stow this stuff away when they knock off work, instead of taking it back to the stockroom. Maybe one of them caught himself a nap, dozed off with a cigarette in his mouth. The bed starts to burn, he panics and splits."

Madero shook his head. "Take my word for it, this is a torch job. We'd better call—"

"Hold it." Driscoll turned to the guard. "You talked to Talbot yet?"

Roy recognized the name; Talbot was head of studio security.

Grossinger shifted uneasily under Driscoll's stare.

"I didn't have a chance. You know where he lives, clear out in Thousand Oaks. I figured by the time he got down here—"

"Never mind what you figured. Anybody else on the night shift know about this?"

"No. Jimmy's on the gate, Fritz and Manhoff are covering the back lot."

Driscoll faced Madero. "What about your people?"

"Perry and Cozzens are on duty, but they were upstairs sleeping when Grossinger called in. He told me no sweat, the fire was out and anyway it looked like an accident, so I just hopped in the car and ran over here alone."

"So nobody else knows what happened here except us."

"And the guy who did the job." Frank Madero gestured toward the gasoline drum in Driscoll's hand. "I know what you're driving at, but this is arson—"

Driscoll stepped back, shaking his head. "You're wrong. It was an accident."

Madero's face reddened. "Since when are you giving orders around here?"

"Since Barney Weingarten left for Europe," Driscoll said. "Ruben took off for New York, and that leaves me minding the store. Why the hell do you think I was still here at the office tonight when you called? I've got enough headaches without somebody trying to tell me how to run my job."

Madero's voice rose. "Maybe so. But if you try a coverup, we're going to be in big trouble—"

"Shut up and listen! You want trouble, go running to the cops. Write up your reports, both of you, just the way you told it to me. And when Weingarten comes back and finds out how loose security was tonight—when he hears about those clowns on fire-duty sleeping through a blaze that could have burned down the whole goddam studio—I guarantee you'll both be out on your canastas."

"You'll never get away with this." Madero's voice was no longer strident; he was asking for reassurance.

"Trust me." Driscoll faced Roy, Jan, and Claiborne. "All I want from you is to button up. Anyone wants to know why you're here tonight, it's a production meeting."

Grossinger moved forward. "Aren't you forgetting something? The evidence—"

"What evidence?" Marty Driscoll tapped the side of the gasoline drum. "This I'll toss personally." He glanced over at the four-poster. "You and Madero strip that bedspread and get rid of it. Tomorrow I'll tell Hoskins the design was too busy, he should get me something in another pattern." The producer glanced up. "Find something that will take those smudges off the wall. Turn on the air conditioning and get this smell out of here."

Madero shrugged. "Okay, but if anything goes wrong—"

"It won't, if you keep your nose clean." Driscoll smiled. "Just do what I said and tomorrow you're home free." He started to move off the set. "Okay, that's it. I'll check with you first thing in the morning."

Roy trailed his companions out onto the darkened studio street, frosted by silvery slivers of moonlight. Jan and Claiborne hadn't spoken, but he knew what they were thinking: *Coverup. Accessories after the fact.*

He quickened his stride to catch up with Jan; her eyes seemed almost glazed, and moonrays emphasized her pallor. It was too late to see Claiborne's face, because he'd already moved forward beside Driscoll.

"I've got to talk to you," he said.

"Go ahead."

"Privately."

The producer shook his head. "Look, we're all in this together. You got anything to say, let's hear it."

As Roy and Jan approached, Claiborne fixed his gaze on what Driscoll was holding in his hand.

"That gasoline drum," he murmured. "I saw one last Sunday, when Norman burned the van."

"Oh Jesus, not again!" Driscoll's balding forehead wrinkled in protest. "You going to tell me Norman started this fire?"

"I warned you he'd try something," Claiborne said. "Who else has a better motive?" He nodded toward the can. "As for method—"

"Coincidence. Anytime somebody wants to pull a stunt like this, gasoline's the first thing he thinks of."

"Then you admit there was an arsonist."

"I admit no such damn thing! It could still be the way I said it was, just an accident. If you're trying to throw a scare into me, forget it."

"I wish I could." Now Roy saw Claiborne's face, the perspiration beading his forehead. "That's why I kept my mouth shut, because I didn't want to frighten anyone and I wasn't one hundred percent sure. But after tonight there can't be any doubt. Norman's here."

"The hell you say." Driscoll brandished the gasoline can. This proves nothing."

"But I saw him."

"What—?"

"I saw him," Claiborne repeated softly. "Last night."

Nobody spoke. Roy watched Claiborne; they were all watching him now, standing there as moonlight faded into shadow, waiting for him to continue.

The perfect setting, Roy told himself. *Tell us a story, Daddy. Tell us about the bogeyman, coming to get us in the dark.*

Only Claiborne wasn't anybody's Daddy, and he wasn't talking about something glimpsed in darkness. Roy listened intently as the words and phrases echoed in his ears. *The supermarket on Ventura. Crowds of shoppers. Bright lights. The mirror. Saw him standing there as clearly as I see you now. Ran out—got away—*

"Then how can you be sure?" Driscoll said. "Maybe you made a mistake."

"The only mistake I made was in not telling you sooner. If you'd taken my advice and shut down, this wouldn't have happened."

"Nothing happened." Driscoll shifted the can under his arm and its contents sloshed. "Nothing's going to happen."

"But he'll try again—"

"Don't worry. From now on, we're beefing up security. No more sack time for anyone on duty, no goofing off. I still think you're wrong, but if not, we'll be ready for the bastard."

Roy stepped forward. "Why take that risk? Couldn't

221

you at least postpone the start-date and give the police a chance to find him?"

Claiborne nodded, smiling his gratitude for Roy's support, but Driscoll spoke quickly.

"Too late. Madero and Grossinger are already cleaning up the evidence. And how do we explain why nobody called in first thing when we found out about the fire?" He shook his head. "No police."

"But a postponement—"

"I'll sleep on it."

Driscoll turned and started away.

"Meaning he won't shut down," Roy murmured. He glanced at Claiborne. "You're positive it was Norman you saw?"

"Absolutely."

Jan's eyes were troubled. "That supermarket on Ventura," she said. "The one I'm thinking of is only three blocks away."

"He won't show himself around there," Claiborne told her. "Not if he recognized me last night. But if he's found a hiding place around here—"

Roy glanced down in surprise as Jan edged up beside him, her hand reaching out to grasp his own. When he looked up he saw the face of an actress, eyes mirroring composure, mouth miming calm control. But the truth was in the touch of her fingers tightening around his hand. This was a frightened girl.

She'd turned to him for reassurance and protection, but there was none to give. They were all vulnerable now.

"Come on," he said. "Let's get out of here."

Twenty-four

The knife blade was six inches long and one inch wide, double-edged and razor-sharp.

Santo Vizzini stood in shadow, gripping the hilt, his gaze fixed on the pointed tip as he raised it toward the light.

He froze, startled, as Claiborne entered the room.

"Mr. Vizzini—"

"Yes?"

"I'm Dr. Claiborne. Your office told me you were over here. Hope I'm not interrupting."

"On the contrary, you're just in time." Vizzini placed the knife on the tabletop under the light, then extended his hand. "A great pleasure," he said. "I have been wanting to meet you ever since they told me of your arrival."

Claiborne caught the scent of after-shave—no, stronger, it must be perfume or cologne—masking the smell of stale perspiration and another odor he couldn't identify. The director turned and glanced at the knife once more. "Too thin," he murmured. "Don't you agree?" And now the light flooded his features as he frowned down at the narrow blade.

Claiborne didn't look at the knife. He was staring at Vizzini.

"Don't you agree?" the director repeated. "We need something wider—"

"Yes." Claiborne nodded, forcing his eyes toward the knife instead of the face before him.

"This prop department!" Vizzini sighed. "An abomination. I tell them what I want, and they send me switchblades!" He rolled his eyes. "I say no, this is not for Norman Bates, and they say why not, everybody uses switchblades today." He sighed again. "Incredible!"

Again he smiled, and again Claiborne avoided his gaze.

"I am glad you're here," Vizzini was saying. "It is a good omen. We will select the proper instrument together."

Vizzini started over to a rack at the rear of the room. Moving after him into the shadowed area, Claiborne became fully aware of his surroundings for the first time.

You'll find the weaponry stockpile down at the far end, to the left, the prop clerk had told him. And so he did, but now he realized that description was an understatement.

This room was a miniature armory. Mounted against

224

the right wall was a double rack holding implements of ancient warfare—spears, pikes, halberds, lances, assegais, clubs, knobkerries, battle-axes, and maces—each item tagged and numbered for identification.

On the opposite wall, the rifle stands stood row on row. Harquebuses, flintlocks, Winchesters, Mausers, Enfields, Garands, and more modern firearms ranged in order. Beyond them were bins crammed with longbows, crossbows, quivers of arrows for primitive Indian and sophisticated oriental archery. In glass cases overhead he saw handguns, dueling pistols, pepperboxes, Colts, Lugers, service revolvers, police models, and Saturday-night specials.

But it was the rear wall that attracted Vizzini and now claimed Claiborne's attention. Here, even in the shadows, there was a glittering. The glint of burnished steel half-unsheathed from mounted scabbards—Roman broadswords, serrated Aztec blades, cutlasses, scimitars, yataghans, rapiers, the longswords of Vikings, and the sabers of Napoleonic cavalry.

Vizzini ignored the display; he was inspecting the cluttered contents of the shelves above. "Look how they store these things! Sheer madness." He shrugged. "But we will try to find something." Reaching up, he fumbled gingerly through an assortment of tagged daggers, poniards, dirks, and stilettos, his fingers curling around a thick handle as he pulled it free. Now he glanced down at the foot-long, single-edged blade, which protruded from the guard and terminated in a curling tip.

"What is this?"

"Looks like a bowie knife," Claiborne said. "The kind they used on the frontier back in pioneer days."

"But not now, eh?" Vizzini replaced the weapon with obvious reluctance. "A pity. It would be most impressive."

His hand strayed along the shelf, then halted. Once more he reached forward, drawing out an eight-inch, double-edged knife with a broad shaft and plain handle. He held it against the light from the other end of the room, nodding appreciatively at the blade shimmering against the shadows.

"A butcher knife. This is what he will use."

"Will—?"

"In the film." Vizzini smiled. "The right size, the right length, and it will photograph beautifully. I will have them make up some duplicates."

He turned away, tapping the steel surface. "A fortunate discovery. After all, the knife is the real star of our picture, don't you agree?"

Claiborne avoided the smiling stare. "In a way—"

"Not that the script isn't important," Vizzini said. "I read the revised pages Ames brought in this morning."

"That's what I wanted to find out about. And meet you, of course," Claiborne added hastily. "What do you think?"

"There are some good things. I like the way he handles Norman's reactions; it gives more depth to the character. But those cuts in the murder scenes— this is wrong for us."

"I'll take responsibility for that," Claiborne told him. "It was my suggestion to eliminate some of the overt violence."

"For what reason?" Vizzini wasn't smiling now. "After all, we are only telling a story."

"People tend to believe what they see."

"Of course! But our story is about murder, and that is what I must show them—what you call the gory details, to make it seem real."

"Violence isn't the only reality."

"Oh, no?" Vizzini gestured toward the walls. "Look around you. These weapons here—they are like a history of mankind. First the club, then the bow, the cold steel, the firearms. All that is missing are the nuclear weapons of today. The progress of civilization, eh?"

"But you're talking about war—"

"I have the right." Vizzini stared at the knife. "When Sicily was invaded in World War II, I was still a child. But I saw it all, the looting, the tortures and the killings. That is long over and done with, but the violence has never stopped—in Biafra, Bangladesh, the Gulag Archipelago, the prisons of Papa Doc, the 'tiger cages' of Vietnam. We live today in a world of Turkish prisons, Latin American dungeons, Irish bombings, PLO terrorists, Iranian atrocities, Cambodian genocide. A world where kids kill their parents, rape their teachers, murder strangers on the streets, trample each other to death at rock concerts, even smash their own idols the way John Lennon was destroyed. Violence is normal now."

"So is kindness and understanding."

Vizzini shook his head, and on the wall behind him the weapons glared and glinted. "Kindness is a luxury afforded only in times of prosperity. The world isn't prosperous anymore, and we will see worse. There will be more people like Norman Bates, the son of a bitch. His mother was a bitch and he is a child of our times." The director gripped the knife

227

handle tightly. "This I believe and this is what my film must say."

Again, Claiborne looked away. He didn't want to see Vizzini's face, but he had to speak.

"Some of us still hold the belief that there's good in the world."

"Perhaps so. But to believe in good, you must also acknowledge evil." Vizzini started toward the doorway at the far end, still holding the knife. "There is a part of the Devil in every man. And I will show him to you."

He moved out of the room as Claiborne stood silent. *Paranoia. A sickness, a disease, very possibly a danger.* But it wasn't the diagnosis that disturbed him; after all, he'd seen it many times before.

The real shock was the sight of Vizzini's face. He had seen that before too.

Because Santo Vizzini looked exactly like Norman Bates.

Twenty-five

As a writer, Roy tried to avoid cliches. But when Claiborne entered his office, he found himself using one.

"What's wrong? You look like you've seen a ghost."

Claiborne seated himself across the desk. "I've just had a meeting with Vizzini."

"And he doesn't like the changes." Roy nodded. "What did he do, give you his pitch about violence?"

"Yes, but—"

"Forget it. He's been handing out that line for years now, every time he does a talk show or a film seminar. I know, because a friend of mine wrote it for him. For two hundred dollars." Roy grinned. "Never got paid, either."

"It's not that." Claiborne still seemed dazed. "Why didn't you tell me?"

"Tell you what?"

"That Vizzini looks like Norman Bates."

"You're putting me on." Roy's grin faded. "We have photographs—"

"From years ago. He looks the way Norman looks *now.*"

Roy stared at him and the wheels began to turn. "Then he could be the one you saw the other night in the market?"

"Possibly." Claiborne paused. "What do you know about him?"

"Only what I've read, things I've heard. He started out in Italy, playing heavies in spaghetti westerns. When horror flicks caught on, he switched over and started directing. Went to France, made a couple of things there. *Loup-garou,* the one about the werewolf, was his first biggie. That gave him the mix."

"Mix?"

"Sex and violence." Roy shrugged. "They loved it at the film festivals."

"You weren't impressed?"

"Nobody asked me. The art-house crowd liked what they saw on the screen, and the accountants liked the figures they saw on the books. He came over here on a three-picture deal, and the rest is history."

"Got anything on his personal background?"

"He's always kept a low profile. Of course, you hear a lot of rumors."

"What sort of rumors?"

"The usual. He's been married and divorced five

230

times, he's as gay as old Paree, he swings both ways, he's hooked on drugs and can't get it up at all. Take your choice."

"You have no opinion?"

"Only about his work. I think he's a real kinko. The kind who'd update Jack the Ripper and have him do his jobs with an electric carving knife.

"Vizzini's really got a thing about mass murderers. I suppose you know he's the one who brought this project to Driscoll in the first place. That was before they called me in, but I heard his original idea was to play Norman himself."

"I didn't know." Claiborne shook his head. "Of course, there's the resemblance—"

"Driscoll must have talked him out of it, told him they needed a name, and signed Paul Morgan. But Vizzini's coaching him personally. He's even picked out the wigs and the dresses."

"And the knife," Claiborne said. "That's what he was doing when I saw him just now. He seems to know just what kind of weapon Norman used."

Roy took a deep breath. "No wonder you were shook up. If he really identifies with Norman—"

Claiborne rose. "I think we ought to have a chat with Mr. Driscoll."

But Anita Kedzie had other ideas.

She was shaking her head almost the moment they entered Driscoll's outer office.

"Sorry, he's not in," she told them. "I can't say whether he'll be back this afternoon or not—"

"Good girl."

Miss Kedzie looked up as Marty Driscoll opened

231

the door behind her and nodded at his visitors. "Congratulations," he said. "I like the pages."

Roy glanced at Claiborne. "Vizzini doesn't."

"I know." Driscoll didn't seem upset. "Want to talk about it?" He waved them forward.

"Mr. Driscoll." Anita Kedzie captured his attention as he turned to follow. "On your call to New York—"

"Don't worry." The producer consulted his watch. "It's after seven there now, he's probably gone to dinner. If he checks in, he'll ring me at home tonight."

Closing the door on her frown, Driscoll seated himself behind his desk to face Roy and Claiborne. "Glad you stopped by. I was going to get in touch with you anyway, after Vizzini sounded off to me." He smiled at Roy. "Gave you a hard time?"

"I'm the one he spoke to," Claiborne said. "It seems he objects to the way the murder scenes are toned down."

"Well, I don't." Driscoll's smile broadened to include them both. "Remember one thing. Vizzini's feeling a lot of pressure right now. We're all under the gun with that start-date coming up."

"That's what I wanted to discuss," Claiborne told him.

"Go ahead."

As the psychiatrist repeated the story of his encounter, Roy watched Driscoll's reactions.

He seemed to be listening patiently enough, sitting immobile behind the big desk. It wasn't until Claiborne brought up Vizzini's resemblance to Norman Bates that he interrupted.

"I don't see it," he said.

"But Vizzini does. He even wanted to play the part."

"George Ward will love you for that." Driscoll chuckled. "It's his gag—he planted the item in the trades."

"I'm serious. This man is—"

"A signature director." Driscoll hunched forward. "Without him we come up with zip. Paul Morgan may still sell tickets out in the sticks, or at least that's what we're hoping, but he isn't bankable. Jan is nothing. Vizzini's what they're buying, he's the key to the whole thing."

"Even if he's mentally unbalanced?"

"All directors are a little flaky. Don't let it bother you."

"But it does bother me." Claiborne frowned. "Last night, when you heard about the fire, you called Roy. Why didn't you try to get hold of Vizzini?"

"Matter of fact I did." Driscoll hesitated. "I left a message with his answering service."

"Meaning he was out." Claiborne's frown deepened. "Did he tell you where he was? Did he ever call back at all?"

"Christ on a bicycle!" Driscoll thumped his hand down on the desktop. "You think Vizzini set fire to sabotage his own picture?"

"Somebody did."

Driscoll's heavy eyebrows rose. "Look, Doc. What I said to those jokers last night about not telling anybody about what happened—that was a shuck, I wanted to be sure they'd keep their own mouths shut. Just between us, I had Talbot in the office at seven o'clock this morning."

"Your security chief?"

"Right. He got the whole story. And the gasoline can. It had my prints all over, and Madero's, but when he checked it out he came up with another set. We know who stowed that can under the bed and it sure as hell wasn't Vizzini."

Roy leaned forward. "How can you be certain?"

"We've got a print filed on every employee in the studio. And Talbot made a match. The other set on the can belongs to Lloyd Parsons, one of the set dressers. We saw him this noon, and after Talbot leaned on him, he talked."

"About the fire?"

Driscoll smiled triumphantly. "Remember what I told you last night? Well, that's almost the way it happened. Parsons worked Stage Seven yesterday afternoon with a crew—not on the bedroom set but one farther over. They're finishing up a bathroom for the shower sequence. The job ran late, and come quitting time, he stayed behind to collect the gear. Way he tells it, the gasoline can wasn't even supposed to be there; they'd requisitioned shellac to use on the wall tiles, but somebody made a mistake.

"Anyhow, he got ready to lug this stuff back to supplies, but he couldn't locate a handcart. What he should have done was fetch one from maintenance, but he was either too tired or too damned lazy. So he shoved everything under the bed on the set next door. Then he decided to stretch out for a minute and have himself a cigarette—they don't let the crew smoke on the job."

"But all he had to do was go outside," Claiborne said.

"That's what we told him, but he gave us a lot of

234

doubletalk about being beat. You ask me, he's on grass—they all are, particularly the younger ones—and he didn't want to get caught out on the street. Of course, he wouldn't admit it, but it sure as hell explains why he dozed off. When the fire started he woke up scared and ran, just like I figured. Lucky for him he didn't burn to death."

"Do you believe his story?" Roy said.

"If he was lying, why come up with something like that when he knew we could press charges?"

"Will you?"

"And get in a hassle with the insurance people? That'd be all we'd need right now." Driscoll pushed his chair back from the desk. "Naturally I didn't tell him that. He kept begging me not to bring him up before the union and I said okay, on one condition—I wanted him off the lot. I don't know what excuse he gave them—ill health, death in the family—but he punched out this afternoon. Don't worry, it won't happen again."

Roy waited for Claiborne to protest, but he merely nodded.

He was still silent after they left the office and filed out into the hazy late-afternoon sunshine of the studio street. And it was Roy who finally spoke.

"So what do you think? Was he telling the truth?"

"If you're asking about the workman, I don't know. But I'm not sure about Driscoll."

"Is there some way we could find out?"

Claiborne stared toward the setting sun. "There damned well better be," he said.

Twenty-six

At twilight the fog came into the hills.

It came softly, like a serpent, encircling clumps of cypress and the shrubbery below. Coiling silently through the streets, its gray maw devoured darkness and swallowed the stars.

Jan watched through the window as she spoke into the phone.

"I don't understand," she said. "Messenger service delivered the new pages here an hour ago. And now you tell me—"

"Never mind the pages. We won't be making any changes in the script," said Santo Vizzini. "There has been a mistake."

"Mistake?"

"It's not important. I will explain tomorrow when you rehearse."

"What time?"

"Probably late afternoon, after I finish with Paul Morgan. Wait for my call."

"All right. But are you sure—"

Jan broke off, conscious that the line was dead. Vizzini had hung up and there was only a buzzing.

As she replaced the receiver the buzzing faded, but now there was another sound—softer, and from a different source.

Someone was crying.

Jan went to the window. The fog billowed against the pane, shrouding the hillside beyond. Here, neither shape nor shadow stirred, but the crying continued, faint and forlorn.

A child, lost in the fog?

She opened the front door, peering out. The light at the corner was barely visible, and there was no sound here, only a chill stillness.

Damn Vizzini—it was his fault, getting her all shook up over nothing. That was what *he* said: nothing. Then why had he called? Disregard the changes, he told her. But the changes were mimeoed at the studio, which meant someone had okayed them, or else why send them up by special messenger? Too much was happening—that business about the fire and what Claiborne had said about seeing Norman Bates—no wonder she was flipping out, hearing things.

And while she was at it, damn Connie too. Why couldn't she stay home nights at least once in a while, instead of leaving her all alone like this? Right now, Jan felt the need of someone's presence, anyone's. Maybe if she called Roy—

As she closed and locked the front door, she heard the phone ringing.

Telepathy?

No, because it wasn't Roy. Lifting the receiver, she found herself talking to Adam Claiborne.

"Sorry to bother you," he said. "I just thought I'd check and see if you got the new pages."

"Yes, I have them."

"Well, what do you think?"

She told him about Vizzini's call.

"You mean he's not going to use the changes?" Claiborne sounded disturbed, and that disturbed her, too.

"What's going on?" she asked. "Won't anybody level with me?"

Claiborne didn't reply for a moment. Then, "It's rather involved—"

"So am I," Jan told him. "Completely involved." She stared into the grey world beyond the window. "Look, if you're not busy, why don't you come by for a drink?"

Again he hestiated, and it was Jan who broke the silence. "Please. I've got to know."

"I'll be right over."

And that was that.

But not entirely. Because when she hung up and started down the hall into the kitchen, Jan heard the crying again.

It seemed louder here, and as she moved forward the sound held a note of urgency that impelled her to the back door.

Opening it, she saw the kitten.

The tiny yellow bundle of fur rested on the doorstep, staring up at her with topaz eyes. She picked it up; almost weightless, the kitten snuggled against her arm and the mewing modulated into a purr of pleasure.

"Where'd you come from, kitty? Are you lost?"

"*Rao*."

The smoky green eyes regarded her gravely, but now she sensed a shudder rippling across the moist flanks.

"Poor baby, you're all wet—"

Jan closed the door and carried the kitten over to the sink. Taking a dishtowel from the rack, she rubbed it gently over the damp curlicues of fur. Gradually the shivering subsided.

"There, that's better." She let the towel drop to the sink top. "Are you hungry?"

"*Rao*."

"Okay, let's see what we can do about that."

Jan put the kitten down on the linoleum. It rested there motionless, but the little green eyes followed her movements as she opened the refrigerator and brought out a carton of milk. Taking a saucer from the cupboard, Jan filled it full and placed it on the floor beside her waiting guest.

And then her other guest arrived.

At the sound of the chimes she hurried through the hall to the living room, but this time she switched on the outside light and peered through the peephole to identify her caller. Then she swung the door open, admitting a wave of clammy dampness and Adam Claiborne.

"You made good time," she said.

240

"The motel's just down the hill, on Ventura." He glanced toward the window. "But I almost got lost— couldn't even make out the street signs. No wonder you don't want to be alone up here."

"I'm not alone," Jan told him. "I have a visitor."

She led him into the kitchen and they halted in the doorway. The kitten crouched beside the saucer, its pink tongue lapping lazily at the last drops of milk.

Claiborne smiled. "Friend of yours?"

"I hope so. She turned up at the back door a few minutes ago."

"She?" Claiborne stared down at the fluffy figure. "How can you be sure of its sex?"

"Feminine intuition." Jan went over and scooped the kitten up into her arms. "All right, baby, you've had your drink. Now it's our turn."

"*Rao.*"

It nestled contentedly against her as she led Claiborne back into the living room, and when she started to put it down, the tiny claws curled into the folds of her sweater. Jan tried to disengage its hold, but the kitten clung fast.

"Come on, give me a break," she murmured.

"Never mind." Claiborne went over to the bar. "I'll do the honors. Scotch and rocks?"

"Super."

Jan settled on the sofa while he fixed their drinks, stroking the kitten as it purred. Her fingers found the warm flesh beneath the wisps of fur and she marveled at the softness of its skin. Under the thin texture one could actually *feel* the purr vibrating through the inner organs. How fragile it was!

241

Almost instinctively her free hand went to her own throat, touching the pulse beating there. As it throbbed beneath her fingertips, she marveled anew. *Why, we're all like that. So vulnerable. This fraction of an inch covering our flesh is our only protection. And if it were to burst, or be cut, here at the artery—*

"Penny."

She looked up as Claiborne held a glass out to her. "What?"

"For your thoughts."

"Oh." She reached for her drink and shrugged. "Nothing."

"Make it a nickel. I keep forgetting about inflation." He lowered himself beside her on the sofa. The kitten blinked and disengaged its claws. Scampering down onto the rug, it curled up at her feet.

Claiborne turned to Jan. "That gesture you made just now—what were you thinking about?"

"Mary Crane."

She didn't consciously intend to say it, and until the words came out she hadn't even realized it was true.

"What about her?"

"Not her. Me." Jan nodded self-consciously, avoiding his intent gaze. "It's one of those professional things, I suppose. As you get familiar with a role, you start to identify with the character."

"Don't."

She met his eyes, and he wasn't smiling now. "But I should, really, if I'm going to play the part."

"Don't."

Jan raised her glass and drank, but as the scotch

242

went down, resentment rose. Damn it, he'd seemed so nice when he came in that she'd almost forgotten his hangup about the picture. But this time, she promised herself, she wasn't going to lose her temper.

"Please." She kept her voice and expression under control. "We've been through this number before. Just because I told you Vizzini isn't going to make those changes—"

"There's more to it than that," Claiborne said. "Something happened this afternoon."

She sat back, sipping her drink as he began to talk. About meeting Vizzini, and how he looked like Norman Bates. About seeing Roy and going to Driscoll, hearing his explanation of the fire and his own reservations about Vizzini.

Jan listened in silence until he finished. "Is that all?" she asked.

Claiborne's eyebrows arched. "Isn't it enough?"

She lowered her glass. "Maybe it's too much."

"Look, if you don't believe me, ask Roy Ames."

"Just what am I supposed to believe? First you tell me Norman is alive, now you say he's dead and Vizzini started the fire."

"I'm not sure about Norman, and I've no hard proof of Vizzini's responsibility. But one thing's certain. He does identify with Norman Bates, and that's why I warned you about identifying with Mary Crane."

Jan reached down to pet the kitten as it rubbed against her ankle. "I identify with kitty here, too. And with all sorts of people, all sorts of things. Maybe because I'm an actress—"

"Most of us tend to identify, to a degree."

243

"Most of us?" Jan straightened. "But not shrinks, I suppose. They're above such weaknesses."

"*Rao.*" The kitten nodded in seeming approval.

But Claiborne frowned. "Stop beating me over the head with a label," he said. "Shrinks aren't above or below anything. It's just that experience tells us complete identification with anyone, whether it's Jesus Christ or Adolf Hitler, is dangerous. We can still empathize, though, and relate—"

Jan's eyes challenged. "And just who do you relate to?"

"Everyone." Claiborne shrugged. "At least, I try to. Norman, of course—I share his resentment of confinement and restraint. I understand Marty Driscoll's drive for success because there's a little of that in me too. I can see Roy Ames's position as a writer trying to tell it like it is; I wanted to tell the truth about Norman in a book."

As she listened, Jan found herself recalling the other evening here with Claiborne, and her own sudden unexpected surge of feeling. Seeing him now, she felt the same reaction starting to build; it wasn't what he was saying, but the sound of his voice as he said it. This wasn't professional put-on, he really wanted her to understand, just as she wanted to reassure him that she did. It was all she could do to restrain herself from reaching out in response, reaching out physically—

She checked the impulse quickly. Words were safer. "Paul Morgan?" she said.

Claiborne nodded. "I don't like what he does—the petty cruelty, the autograffiti thing. But I can share his insecurity, the doubts about one's self-image. And

244

the same with Vizzini. Perhaps even more so. I know what it's like to be an orphan."

"You?"

His voice was soft. "Yes. I don't know who my parents were, or my real name. The only difference is that I didn't run away from the orphanage." He paused. "When you told me about your kid sister, it hit home. For all I know, my mother was in the same bind, and your sister's baby and I are twins."

Claiborne looked up at her with a smile. "Are you beginning to see what I mean? You don't have to completely identify in order to relate; if you just look deeply enough, you'll find something of yourself in everyone.

Jan nodded. "That's exactly how I feel about Mary Crane. Only it's closer, somehow, because there's the physical resemblance too. Sometimes I can't help thinking that if I play the part right, it could almost be like bringing her back to life again—"

"Even if it means ending your own?"

He leaned toward Jan, taking her hand. His voice deepened. "I know how much this means to you. But it's only a role, just remember that. Mary Crane is dead and you're alive. What happens to you is what's important now."

She met his gaze, and his eyes told her more than his words. *He cares. He really does care.* She could feel the warmth and pressure of his fingers, the throb of his pulse matching hers. He was turning her on and that was good, because it turned off the thoughts. Even though she'd kept her cool, the fear was there and she didn't want to think about it. Maybe he was right and she was wrong, but what did it matter?

245

What mattered was here and now, the touching and the throbbing. That was what she wanted, that was what she needed, because it was real.

Jan moved into his arms, eyes closing, mouth seeking and opening against his own, and now their bodies were touching and throbbing together, soft fingertips grazing hard nipples, hips arching as hands went to her waist—

And thrust her away.

She opened her eyes. "What's wrong?"

"Jan, listen to me." His voice was gentle. "I know what you're trying to do, but it won't help. Your safety is what matters, not just the threat to your career. Buying me off like this won't solve anything."

She rose quickly. Startled, the kitten sprang to its feet, stubby tail curling.

"Buying you off? Why, you smug bastard—"

"I'm sorry." He was rising, facing her. "I didn't mean it that way. You know I want you. But not like this, on these terms—"

The impact of her hand against his cheek halted him. "Terms? You're the one who's making terms. But not anymore. Just get the hell out. Out of here, out of my life!"

Jan turned, striding to the front door, and flung it wide. The kitten was mewing in fright somewhere on the floor below, but she couldn't see it.

"Don't be a fool," Claiborne said. "You've got to realize—"

The sound of his voice blurred; everything blurred as he came toward her across the room. Sensing that he wanted to touch her, she edged back.

"No—get out!"

His hand fell and he moved past her. Then she

slammed the door and leaned against it, shaking. It was only when she heard his car start up and pull away that the blurring sensation ebbed and she could see and hear clearly again.

But now there was nothing to hear, not even the frightened mewing. And as she stared around the living room, there was nothing to see.

The kitten was gone.

Twenty-seven

Two hours and two scotches later, Jan was still wide awake in her bed.

Alone, damn him!

She plumped the pillows, then settled back again. *While you're at it, you might as well damn yourself.*

It was her doing. She was responsible for everything; losing her temper, losing Claiborne, even scaring the kitten out into the fog. Hell hath no fury like a woman scorned.

Only he hadn't scorned her. All he'd done was tell the truth. She did want him, but that wasn't her only reason for turning him on; doing so was also a way of turning him off about the picture. *Crazy Lady*—a good title to describe herself. She must have been crazy not to see that he was really anxious to protect her.

But from what? Hints and guesses didn't add up to proof. Was there something more, something he hadn't told her?

Maybe Roy would know.

Switching on the bedlamp, Jan reached for the phone atop the nightstand. She dialed Roy's number, then listened.

No answer.

And no answer to her question.

She replaced the receiver, turned off the light, pulled the covers back up around her shoulders. Now, oddly enough, she felt relieved that her call hadn't been completed. Roy would probably just have said the same things, tried to talk her out of doing *Crazy Lady*. Maybe she was crazy after all, but not *that* crazy. Unless he and Claiborne came up with something besides conversation, nobody was going to make her back down. Not after all she'd gone through. *Five years. Face it, you're not getting any younger. This is the heavy trip, so hang in there. You don't want to end up a nothing, like Connie. Poor Connie . . .*

Poor Connie was having a ball.

Or was the ball having her?

It didn't matter, really. Either way, she was balling. Or about to be balled, as soon as that smartass cameraman stopped fiddling with the focus on her crotch. Probably got his funsies peeking at her, but she was dying here under the lights.

Dying, but living.

Because for once nobody was ignoring her. There were seven others in Leo's rec room, and every one of them was concentrating on Connie, or some part of Connie. The clown with the hand-held camera had staked out his claim between her legs, the body-makeup girl was rubbing pink goo on her munchies, the klutz handling the lights flooded her face, framed by the black pillowcase. The boom man positioned the mike above her head, the sound man squatting behind his controls was concerned with her voice level, and Leo himself—the producer, director, and production designer responsible for erecting this set in his own pad—was eyeballing her approvingly. The sixth person, if you could call that hairy, naked ape a person, was also responsible for some erecting of his own. And when the others finished, he'd begin.

Okay, so maybe it wasn't exactly rose-garden time, holed up in a Boyle Heights bungalow to moonlight a porno flick. But who cared?

I care, that's who. Me, Connie. Because for once they're looking at me.

They were looking at her now, and the audience would be looking at her up on the screen. Not just her hands or feet or ankles, but all of her. So what if the audience was just a bunch of dirty old men with hats on their laps; at least she'd be *seen*. And nobody was complaining about the size of her boobs or trying to keep her face out of the shots. For this kind of film they could make do with a Japanese sex-doll or even a model of Godzilla, but Leo had picked her personally because he recognized talent when he saw it.

Connie lay back. They were about to go now. The cameraman nodded at Leo, he waved to the sound engineer, and the ape got ready to haul his banana into the shot on cue.

"All set, everybody?" Leo said.

Connie winked at him. Leo was no Marty Driscoll, but it didn't matter. What mattered was that she was playing the lead in her first feature film.

The clown who handled the lights stepped forward with his clapper board—a term she hoped was merely a figure of speech. "Scene one, take two," he told the camera.

"Speed!" Leo said.

Connie smiled.

"Action!"

Connie spread her legs.

To hell with Driscoll. She was a star . . .

Marty Driscoll couldn't see a star.

Usually the big glass sliding doors leading onto the patio gave him a magnificent view of the Valley below and the sky above, but tonight nothing was visible outside the den except a solid wall of gray.

The fog comes on little cat feet—

And so did the quotation. Driscoll grimaced, wondering just what reaction he'd get if he came up with the line in the presence of co-workers at the studio. Not to wonder, really; he was already quite certain of their response.

Literacy dated you. In an era obsessed with youth, most producers graduated directly from acne to autonomy, and the older group lied about their ages even more than the performers did.

When Marty Driscoll had reached this realization, his body had already betrayed him. It was too late for hair dye or hairpieces, and any obvious attempt to emulate postadolescent lifestyles would be futile. The din of a disco dance floor couldn't drown out his wheezing, and no corset could conceal his flab.

The only ploy remaining was the one he'd adopted: play it smart by playing dumb. Come on strong, come on crude and loud and vulgar, give them a stereo version of a stereotype—the no-taste, no-talent tyrant. Forget about the degrees from Princeton; they're not interested in your B.A., what counts is your b.s. And while you're at it, forget about those early low-budget features, the idealistic efforts born of a desire for quality, only to die at the box office.

The formula worked. That's why Driscoll was sitting here now in the den of the big house on Mulholland where—except for a few foggy nights like this one—he could look down on the studio below. And that, he supposed, had been his ultimate gratification, to look down on the studio in every sense of the phrase. Look down on its vacuity, its vanities and venalities, even though he himself shared in them, *mea culpa*.

Driscoll shrugged as he considered the success of his deception. As far as the studio people were concerned, he wouldn't know *mea culpa* from Mia Farrow.

For that matter, his own wife hadn't learned the secret; none of them had. To Deborah he was just a big fat slob with a big fat bank account. She'd taken the kids down to the Springs for the week just to get away from the slob, but she called every day to pay her continuing respects to the bank account.

Suppose she found out there was no bank account?

And that this house and the one in the Springs were creaking beneath the weight of heavy second mortgages plus interest penalties for overdue payments?

Irrelevant questions. She wasn't going to find out, not if his luck held. Luck—that was the random factor.

Bad luck with the last three films. He should have sold them to the Pentagon; with bombs like those, they could destroy the Soviet Union. It was after the release of the third that the mortgaging began.

Then, good luck again, when Vizzini brought him the development deal on *Crazy Lady*. And it had all been smooth sailing until this week, when New York heard of Norman Bates's escape and the murders.

They want to pull out, Ruben told him. *They think the news turns your story into ancient history.* Somehow he'd managed to sweet-talk Ruben out of an immediate cancellation, citing George Ward's conviction that the publicity would be a help rather than a handicap. But the best he got was a reprieve until Ruben and the money people came in for tomorrow's meeting. That was when the final decision had to be made.

And Claiborne was an unexpected complication. Until now, he'd been able to handle Roy Ames and his qualms of conscience, but Claiborne was really rocking the boat. Day by day their objections were undermining morale; day by day the interest rates mounted and the prospect of his receiving a healthy producer's fee on the picture's start-date sank.

This afternoon had been the worst. Labeling Santo Vizzini as mentally unstable hardly qualified as a late news bulletin, but that didn't prove him guilty of arson. One thing was certain: he hadn't started the fire.

Driscoll paused at his desk long enough to light a cigar, then wished he hadn't. The flaring match was a painful reminder.

Rereading the production-insurance contract the other day, he'd discovered the disaster clause. Everyone would be paid off in full in the event of demonstrable accident, the death or serious injury of stipulated principal performers, destruction of facilities due to water or fire damage—

Good luck again. Why risk further problems or gamble on persuading New York to let the picture proceed? He could get his money now—not just the upfront fee but the whole sum, guaranteed, more than enough to bail him out. And nobody could fault him for an act of God. He'd have another project in the works long before he ran short of cash again.

It had all seemed so simple once he worked out the details. Luck held when he carried the gasoline can onto the set unobserved. His mistake had been to ignite the bedspread before spreading the gasoline around; the flicker of flame had alerted the guard, and there was just enough time to shove the can under the bed and get out through the side door.

Good luck had borne him back to his office without being discovered, but bad luck had aborted the fire. And all he could do now was hope that Claiborne bought his story about the set dresser. In a day or so the shrink would leave, and by then the meeting with Ruben and the New York people would be over. It was going to take some doing to convince them that George Ward was right about the publicity helping *Crazy Lady*; he'd really have to make a pitch tomorrow. But rough, gruff Marty Driscoll, that hard-nosed slob, would hardball it through. He had no choice now.

He paced before the glass doors, staring out into the night. The fog blurred the lights, but they'd shine again tomorrow, bright and clear. Better get some rest so that he'd be bright and clear too, come meeting time.

One more day, that was all he needed. One more day to get the final okay. And then to hell with them all: the neurotic writer, the loudmouthed shrink, the stupid girl, that crazy director, and his over-the-hill star.

Don't worry, he told himself. *You can handle them. But it won't be a picnic . . .*

Twenty-eight

"This really is a picnic," Paul Morgan said. He gestured toward the nude males crowding behind him at the dressing table's three-paneled mirror. "I mean, look at all those buns and weenies!"

Robert Redford giggled. "Speak for yourself, dearie. Whenever I see naked bodies, it just reminds me that God didn't know very much about anatomy."

"Let's not be blasphemous." John Travolta peered at his image intently, teasing his eyelashes. "Why are you always putting down religion?"

"Because my grandmother was raped by the Mormon Tabernacle Choir."

"Are you sure it wasn't your grandfather?"

Everybody let out a shriek except Clint Eastwood. He glanced up from the chair in the corner, where he sat waxing his legs. "You're a fine one to talk—you and your group-gropes!"

Sylvester Stallone elbowed his way to the mirror, pursing his mouth as he applied lipstick. "Personally, I detest the action at orgies. It's like opening a dozen beautifully wrapped Christmas packages and finding them all empty."

"But isn't that what we're doing here?" Robert Redford asked. "We're peddling illusions, not just the bare necessities—"

Clint Eastwood rose. "It's getting late. You'd better stuff your bare necessities into your jeans and get downstairs before Queenie throws a snit fit."

Burt Reynolds tossed his powder puff into a tray on the dressing-room table. "Oh my God, I forgot! That party of Iranians is coming in again tonight—"

"Not again!" John Travolta made a face. "Iranians suck."

"Doesn't everybody?" asked Paul Morgan.

There was a hoot, and Clint Eastwood moved up beside him, nodding appreciatively. "That's telling them, hon. Don't pay attention to what they say. I know it's your first time here, but there's nothing to get uptight about. Just remember, Queenie's here to protect you."

Paul nodded, reaching for his Jordaches and peek-a-boo blouse. The others were dressing frantically now, jostling in front of the mirror panels and making last-minute inspections. He was grateful for their self-preoccupation and equally grateful for Eastwood's reminder.

Because it *was* his first time and he *was* edgy. He thought of Queenie's blonde wig, the beaded gown, the artificial breasts, and wondered why he never bothered to shave off his beard. Now he visualized the scene downstairs—bit fat Queenie playing madam in his grotesque outfit, surrounded by all those gorgeous studs. No wonder customers came into Queenie's parlor from all over the world to be serviced by just about every top male star in the business.

As Robert Redford had said, they were peddling illusions, and perhaps Queenie's beard was a not-too-subtle reminder that what came down here was fantasy.

Everybody knew the studs weren't actually stars, but only lookalikes—gay guys, playing macho. But most of them took their work very seriously, copying voices, mannerisms, and *schticks*. With the prices Queenie charged, his clientele wasn't about to make it with ordinary beefcake.

Well, some of them would be getting *filet mignon* tonight, and more than illusion.

Paul sat at the mirror pretending to work on his eyebrows when the others trooped out, their chatter echoing down the hallway as they headed for the stairs. Nothing remained of their past presence here except for a peculiar scent compounded of powder, perfume, and jock-sweat.

Thank God *that* part was over! Talk about illusions—he'd managed to fool them completely. None of them had guessed he was for real, not even Queenie himself, when he'd stripped down for the interview. It almost cracked him up when he'd heard those words of grudging approval.

"You're a little old to do Morgan, but the delivery isn't bad. And once the word gets out that you're

259

hung like a horse, you ought to get quite a play. Some of my regulars are into quantity, not quality."

So why was he sitting here now with the shakes? Queenie had assured him there'd be no trouble. "No bondage, S-and-M or leather freaks, no tearoom acrobats. This is strictly a straight gay house."

But I'm not gay. That's the problem.

Sure, there'd been exceptions, like that time on location in Morocco with that little Arab go-fer—what was his name, Abud, Abdul?—and the Jap kid, the gardener, that afternoon when he was so smashed. But you couldn't count such things, and if it weren't for Vizzini, he wouldn't even have remembered crap like that. Jesus, there was a real kinko for you, Vizzini, giving him the business. Telling him he had to psych himself into the role.

"Let's hear it again from the top. And this time forget the balls. I don't want Paul Morgan, I want Norman Bates. You know what I mean?"

Paul knew exactly what he meant. Play gay. Wearing the dress and the wig had helped, but not enough.

What had Queenie said? *You're a little old to do Morgan.* And that was the nitty-gritty. If he wanted to stay alive in the industry, it was time to segue into character parts, like Newman and Peck, time to make the switch.

Switch.

He raised a hand to smooth his hair, hoping the gesture would brush the word away, but it hung there in midair between his face and the mirror, blurring his image. All he could see was the trembling of his fingers.

Maybe he should have taken a few more belts to calm himself down before coming here. Or maybe he shouldn't have come at all. It was belting drinks that gave him the crazy notion in the first place, made it seem like a smart move. Okay, so Claiborne told him Norman wasn't gay, just a transvestite. But what did that dumb shrink know about the Method?

All these years he'd steered clear of that Actor's Studio jazz, but he needed it now if he was going to stop jiving and really play the character. He had to do more than just work in drag if he wanted to get the feel of the part. Even if it meant that in a few minutes some stranger, some garlic-breathed old oil-peddler, would be getting it off feeling *his* parts. Maybe it wasn't too late to bug out—

He forced himself to stare into the mirror again and this time the image was clear. He didn't see Vizzini, or Queenie, or the lousy teenagers who thought he was over the hill. What he saw was Paul Morgan.

So quit rattling the cage; crashing this scene was his own idea. And there was no sense in splitting now. Vizzini was right, he had to play for real because this was his last chance at the brass ring. That's why he was—

"Here, now!"

He looked up as Queenie peered around the side of the dressing-room doorway, his bearded lips framing a pout.

"What's keeping you, sugar? We're jammed downstairs, simply Jump City—"

Paul pushed back his chair and rose. "Okay, I'm coming."

"Later." Queenie tittered. "I've spread the word to some of my specials and they're just frantic to meet a new face."

Paul trailed Queenie's waddling bulk down the hall, hearing the babble rising from the stairwell. Shrill voices, shrill laughter. Jesus, what was the matter with him—he'd known a lot of gays in the industry over the years, and most of them were decent dudes. But you wouldn't find that kind here, camping it up in a male whorehouse.

Suddenly the shakes came back. He wanted to turn, turn and run, but he couldn't because a hand was squeezing him. A huge, invisible hand, pushing him forward, pushing him down. Vizzini's hand...

Rose out of the fog and popped a 'lude into his mouth. Then it descended, lost in the mist that swirled about him like thick steam.

For a moment Vizzini had a vision of dead, boiled bodies and peeled, fleshless faces bobbing amid the bubbles of a hot-tub.

Imbecile. No hot-tub here. Wherever *here* might be. *Here* was lost in the fog and so was he. Fog, not steam. Cold, not hot. Prowling the hills, walking ten feet above the ground, he knew he should have stayed clean, should have stayed home, put down the thoughts that came with the fog and the night. But the thoughts had driven him to the pills and the pills had driven him from the house.

No, not thoughts. The memories, that's what he was trying to run away from, the memories of the dead.

Mama mia—

Yes, *Mama mia*, that day when the soldiers came to the village and she took his hand and they ran to the town square where they used to sit at the long picnic tables on Sunday afternoons while the band played Verdi. Only today the bandstand's shell was cracked like an egg from the bullets and there was no music, only the shrieks and the thud of boots on cobblestone as the soldiers came spreading out across the square. They had gotten into the wine and now they were getting into the women, and when Mama saw them she tried to turn back but it was too late because they saw her too. She had just enough time to grab him by the collar and push him under one of the tables and then they caught her; there must have been five or six of them, maybe more, or maybe the others came later.

He couldn't be sure because he was crouching under the table, listening to himself crying and the soldiers laughing and Mama screaming.

Then came the creaking and a louder sound—*bam, bam, bam*—shook the table above his head. The table was pounding and his head was pounding too. No more laughing, no more screaming, just the pounding. And the moans. *Mama mia*, moaning, and the boots scuffling in a line that stretched back away from the table, then moved up slowly, one pair at a time, to replace the ones that had stood closest just before. The boots were dirty, caked with mud and slime, and the fifth pair—or was it the fifteenth? —was speckled with spatters of red.

He knew what it was, but he had to look. Better to look at the boots than to hear the moaning and the grunting and the gasping that was worse than the pounding in his head.

That was where it was, that was where it always would be, the pills couldn't cut the sound, the fog couldn't deaden it. *Bam, bam, bam.*

Finally it stopped, all but the echo that never stopped. They were laughing again, moving away, and he crawled out from under the table, stood and stared. Five years old and the first naked woman he ever saw was his own mother. They'd ripped her dress off and torn her underthings and he saw her under thing with the blood oozing and there was blood trickling from the bruises all over her body and face and from her mouth as it opened and she whispered, "Santo."

The word was a big pink bubble bursting between her lips and that was his legacy, the last memory he had before he fainted. Maybe she died then or perhaps that came later; he never knew because when he woke up he was in the hospital ward at Catania. No one could or would tell him how he got there or what had happened at Vizzini and he never returned to the town that had given him his surname.

Vizzini—that was what they called him at the orphanage because he didn't remember his real family name. For a long while he didn't remember much of anything, and the good sisters scolded him for being a dunce and neglectful of his lessons.

But he did remember the pink bubble. *Santo.* Why did those doe-eyed Sicilian mothers insist on burdening their sons with such appellations—Angelo, Salvatore, Santo?

What's in a name?

When he ran away to Palermo at thirteen, an Angelo took him in and trained him as a thief. The man was his first real teacher, educating him in the ways of the streets, but surely he would never be mistaken for an angel.

Later, in Napoli, there was Salvatore, who did indeed act as his savior when the *carabinieri* made the bust and broke up their little operation. But Salvatore hadn't saved him from getting hooked on the products he peddled.

And Santo himself was no saint. What saint could survive what he had in Roma, Milano, Marseilles? What saint could have made that first snuff-film in the days when even nudity was still a scandal?

Vizzini stumbled up the steep grade, breathing hard; the fog was so dense that he couldn't see light from the streetlamps or hillside houses, let alone read the signposts. Where was he now?

Then all at once the pavement firmed under his feet and he knew. He was on top. The top of the world. The climbing was over, he had arrived, the past vanishing behind him in the fog. There was one more capsule in his pocket; he swallowed it dry, not remembering what it was and not caring.

No point in remembering. Forget what *Mama mia* revealed to him on the table, forget the good sisters who had the same thing concealed beneath their robes; all black bristles and bloody too, every month when *la maledizione* visited them. Forget the pig in the snuff-film and what happened to her when the knife entered. *Cut,* he'd said, and that was what the knife did, but she'd deserved it, she was a *putana* and deserved to die.

How she had laughed before the knife came! Laughed and groaned and gurgled, enjoying it. They all enjoyed it, even the good sisters would have given anything to feel the *bam, bam, bam*. Of course, they'd scream and carry on at first, just as Mama had with the soldiers.

Could she have enjoyed it too?

What was the difference between a groan of pain and a groan of pleasure? How could a five-year-old boy know, how could he be sure *now?* Only one thing was certain: they all had things, and things didn't reason, merely responded. Black, bristly, bloody things, secret things with secret cravings for more, more, more. *Mama mia*, when he was conceived, rolling in a hedgerow with some nameless *paisan*. And Norman Bates's mother—

Vizzini ran a forefinger over the sweat-beaded surface of his upper lip, tracing the outline of his missing mustache. *He* could have played Norman, should have, because he understood him.

Instead it would be Paul Morgan, who understood nothing, not even his own latent homosexuality. But Norman wasn't homosexual, there was nothing about the crimes to indicate it. Nobody really knew Norman, not even that stupid doctor. Nobody knew except him, Santo Vizzini.

They didn't know he'd researched the case, visited Fairvale last year, seen the ruins of the house and the motel, taken photographs. Being there was an excitement, an excitement he had hidden and preserved and would put on film for all to see and share.

Crazy Lady. It would be a triumph because it

would be real, almost as real as the snuff-film. The documentary flavor, that was what counted.

Driscoll didn't understand; the only thing he knew was money. To him, the bank statement was important, but to the creative artist, the film itself was all that mattered. The statement of reality, in a world where women hide the dirty secret under their skirts. It took a man like himself, a man like Norman, to reveal that secret, expose the evil and punish it.

That was what Norman had done with Mary Crane, and that was what he'd do with Jan.

Vizzini blinked, groping his way through the fog. He was disoriented. Too many pills, too much fog swirling inside himself. He was here for a reason, if only he could remember. What had he been thinking about?

Jan. She looked like Mary Crane, and that was why he'd chosen her over all the objections. Now he must teach her how to *be* Mary Crane, that thief, that *putana,* flaunting herself and her secret at poor Norman. He must strip away all those silly acting-school mannerisms, strip her bare of everything but the flesh itself, until she was Mary Crane, standing in the shower.

Suddenly the fog cleared away and he could see her, he could see Jan naked, writhing in climax—the final climax that was death.

And suddenly he could see something else, something that drugs and fog had hidden away all these years, something he'd forgotten completely. The little five-year-old boy rising up from under the table and staring at *Mama Mia*'s secret. The little boy who fainted, not from fright, but to blot out the realization that he had an erection.

Just as he did now.

Now, after a lifetime of thinking he was impotent, like Norman Bates. But it wasn't true. Norman was a man, he must have played the man with Mary Crane. And he himself was a man, this proved he could perform, would perform the role. With Jan...

She moaned, enjoying Roy's performance. It was good, so good, and he was good. Even better now, because as she looked up at him his face changed and all at once it was Adam Claiborne on top of her, just the way she'd wanted him earlier this evening. Only his features kept blurring and then it was Paul Morgan, doing her. She closed her eyes, telling him to stop, but when she opened them again, Jan realized something terrible was happening. Paul's face had disappeared and now she was making it with Santo Vizzini; he panted with effort, and drops of perfume trickled from his armpits. She reached up, clawing, and her nails shredded Vizzini's face. What was on top of her now had no face, none that she could see, only a blur. Yet she knew, something inside of her knew exactly who it was.

Norman Bates.

He was the one, he'd been doing it all along, the other faces were just masks. But *his* face was real and she wanted to see it clearly, *had* to see it clearly.

Then came the scream and she awakened, her eyes really opening now to stare into the darkness of the bedroom.

Again the scream, and the frantic pounding on the door.

Jan thrust the covers away, switched on the lamp, slid her feet into the slippers beside the bed. Grabbing her robe from the chair, she ran through the hallway.

"Let me in—"

Connie's voice, from behind the front door.

And when the door opened, Connie stood shivering in the fog, shivering and crying.

"For God's sake, honey, what's the matter?"

"I just came home." Wailing, her tear-stained face contorted like a child's.

Jan nodded. "Where's your key?"

"In my purse—can't find it—he was there—"

"He?"

Connie gestured toward the fog-choked street. "Someone—a man—standing under the trees when I got out of the car. I thought he was coming after me—"

Jan peered past the trembling girl. "I can't see anyone."

"He must have run when I screamed. But he was there—I saw him—"

Tightening the robe around her waist, Jan started down the walk.

Connie turned quickly. "No—don't go!"

But Jan was already moving toward the trees. And it was there, beneath them, that she stooped and picked up the little blonde kitten.

The kitten made no resistance and it didn't move. Because its throat had been cut.

Twenty-nine

Claiborne had overslept, but he didn't feel rested.

There was too much on his mind, there were too many things to consider. He shaved and dressed, sorting out the events of the past twenty-four hours. The encounter with Vizzini, the meeting with Driscoll, the episode with Jan.

Episode? It was far more than that. If only he could have gotten through to her, made her realize her safety was important because she was important to him. But he hadn't, so the danger remained. And this was Saturday already; time was running out.

He hurried to the phone and put through a call to Steiner at the hospital.

"*In* the hospital," Clara told him. "That's right, they took him over to County General on Thursday night. Bronchial pneumonia. You know we've had those terrible rains here all week—"

Claiborne asked questions and got answers. No, Dr. Steiner wasn't in intensive care, but there'd be no calls or visitors, at least not for a few days. And as far as she knew, there'd been no word yet from the coroner's office. Sheriff Engstrom was keeping after him for a report, he said Monday at the latest. "And by then you'll be back, thank God. We're having a rough time here—"

He thanked her and hung up. *Rough time*, she said. Things were rough all over.

But there was no point in self-pity, or self-recrimination either. It was enough to admit that so far he'd accomplished nothing. Steiner had been right; he was a doctor, not a detective. And he'd fallen into the most common pitfall of his profession; he'd become so interested in the people that he'd failed to give priority to the immediate problem. A detective knew that sticking to the problem was the only way to come up with solutions.

Claiborne sat on the side of the bed, reviewing options and priorities. Then he picked up the phone again.

He made two calls.

After the second one he went into the bathroom and put his head under the cold water tap. It was the unreasoning gesture of a man with a hangover, but the stinging shock of the spray helped, even though he had to change his shirt and comb his hair again.

After making sure the key was in his pocket, he left the room and started down the patio walk, glancing at his watch. *Past noon already*. He hadn't had breakfast yet, but there was no time for that, not after what he'd heard—

"Hello."

Tom Post was standing in the office doorway, tendering a seamed smile of greeting. "Care for a cup of coffee?"

Claiborne started to shake his head, but the appeal of the invitation was reinforced by the odor of the offer itself.

"Thanks. I can't be too long, got an appointment—"

"No problem. It's ready."

Post led him into the office and opened the door at the rear. "In here," he said. "Might as well be comfortable while we're at it."

The room beyond the doorway was comfortable enough, or had been at one time, when the parlor furnishings were new. But now the upholstery was faded and the drapery dimmed with dust; only the framed photographs on the walls seemed bright and ageless in the lamplight.

As the old man busied himself before the urn on the corner table, Claiborne turned his attention to the pictures. Like the ones on the wall of the outer office, they appeared to be studio publicity portraits, but none of them sparked recognition.

Tom Post came over and handed him his cup. "Cream and sugar?"

"Black is fine, thank you."

And it was. Claiborne hadn't consciously realized how much he needed something; hot coffee was even better than cold water at this moment.

"Another scorcher," Post said. "But the fog'll be rolling in again tonight. Usually does, this time of year." He glanced up at the faces on the wall. "See anyone you know?"

"I'm afraid not."

"Doesn't surprise me. Before your time." A bony finger jabbed in the direction of an elderly man's smiling countenance. "That's Sol Morris. He was the head of Coronet Studios back in the twenties, when they were over on the other side of the hill."

The younger man nodded and Post moved along the wall, like a tour guide in a museum. But then this *was* a museum, Claiborne realized; the faded furnishings and dusty decor were appropriate in a place where all clocks had stopped long ago.

"Theodore Harker," said Post, looking up at the portrait of a hawk-faced man dressed in black. "Big director, like Dave Griffith in his day. The one next to him is Kurt Lozoff. I worked with him too, some said he was even better than Von. But nobody remembers now. Nobody cares."

He turned away, and for a moment Claiborne thought the movement was meant to mask emotion. Instead, Post reached up into the darkened corner of the room and switched on a light attached to the portrait hanging there in single splendor.

Splendor. That was the word, the only word, for the incandescence of the face flaming forth—not a photograph, but a portrait in oils. The girl was young and very beautiful. There was something vaguely familiar about her face; somewhere he'd seen those eyes and that smile before.

"Dawn Powers." The old man smiled. "That's where I got the name for this place. The Dawn Motel."

"I think I've seen pictures of her," Claiborne said. "Was she an actress?"

"Yes, but only in silents. She could have gone on, she could have been the biggest of them all." Tom Post's voice sank to a soft murmur and Claiborne glanced at him.

"You were in love with her?"

"I still am."

"What happened?"

The old man shrugged. "Retired. Married outside the business. Died years ago." He switched off the light, then faced Claiborne from the dark corner. "They're all gone now. I'll be going soon myself and maybe it's just as well."

"Don't be in such a hurry. You've still got your health."

"And when I lose it?" Post shook his head. "I've seen those nursing homes. Do you know what it's like to have everything you own in the world on a one-foot shelf next to your bed? People who had a whole houseful of possessions, reduced now to a plastic comb, a cracked mirror, a drinking glass, a sun-faded Polaroid snapshot of grandchildren who haven't visited them in three years. And that's not the worst. The real loss is dignity, privacy, self-respect. And hope.

"That's the future, and we're all afraid of it. Sure, they keep you calmed down by doping you up—the final ripoff, taking away your emotions. Tell me, Doc, which is better—sedated smiles or tranquilized tears?"

"It's not just a medical problem," Claiborne said. "If the world is falling apart, we've got to look at our culture pattern and value judgments to find an answer."

"Don't worry, we've got plenty of answers." Tom Post nodded. "A new one comes along every year. Isometrics. Organic foods. Zen. Biofeedback. Encounter sessions, Transcendental Meditation, jogging." He smiled. "So where are all the perfect specimens?"

"I wish I knew." Claiborne put his empty cup down on the coffee table. "But right now I've got to get going—"

"Sorry. Didn't mean to bend your ear that way."

"Don't apologize. What you said makes a lot of sense. No, really, I mean it."

"Thanks." Post chuckled. "Some people think the only thing of value that comes out of an old man's mouth is his false teeth."

As Claiborne started for the door, his host followed. "Forgot to ask you," he said. "That picture you're interested in—*Crazy Lady*. How's it working out?"

"That's a long story."

"Like to hear it." Post held the door open as Claiborne moved out onto the patio. "Look, if you're free around six, why don't you come by and have dinner here with me? I'm not the greatest chef in the world, but I promise not to poison you."

"Sounds great," Claiborne said. "I ought to be back sometime later this afternoon. Okay if I let you know then?"

"I'll be here." The cotton-haired man chuckled as Claiborne crossed to his car. "Good luck."

As Claiborne drove off, the echo of the nervous chuckle seemed to follow him, and once more he found himself wondering about Tom Post. Was loneliness the sole reason for his hospitality and his curiosity?

From what he'd just said, it was obvious that the old man was bitter as well as lonely. Sitting there brooding in the dark, night after night, trying to recapture the past, resurrect the dead.

But that's what Norman did. Norman had a motel too.

Claiborne frowned the thought away, or tried to. The parallel was too farfetched; Post didn't seem to be fixated on his mother, and he certainly wasn't hiding her body. All he had was the portrait of the girl he'd loved, a dead girl—

A dead girl with something about her eyes and smile that Claiborne recognized. Not from other pictures of Dawn Powers, but in another photograph, a newspaper shot. The face was different, but the eyes and smile belonged to Mary Crane.

Nonsense. How many basic facial types were there— thirty-seven? There must be thousands of girls who shared a similar resemblance. Take Jan Harper, now—

He shook his head. *You could have taken her, last night. Why not? You wanted her.*

Claiborne sighed. Yes, but did he want her as much as Tom Post wanted his Dawn, enough to spend his life with her in reality, or even in memory? He honestly didn't know the answer. And maybe it would have to be just memory, if Jan couldn't forgive him for his rejection. *Or if something happened to her—*

He thought about the calls he'd made. For the first time he was armed with more than a hunch or an educated guess. Now he had the weapon he needed, and he intended to use it.

If he could find Marty Driscoll.

But when he drove onto the lot and headed for the Administration Building, he discovered that Driscoll's office was closed and locked; not even Miss Kedzie worked on Saturday afternoons. He should have remembered to call here too. Perhaps he could locate Roy Ames.

He walked down the hall, past closed doors, then quickened his pace as he neared Ames's cubicle and found it open.

Open and vacant.

Did that mean Ames was still somewhere on the lot? Could be—at least it was worth a try.

Back on the deserted street, he started off in the direction of Stage Seven. Wasn't Jan supposed to be rehearsing with Vizzini today? If so, Ames might have decided to sit in on the session. And yes, somebody was there, because the big sliding door stood open.

The darkness beyond the doorway was cool, and he moved into it gratefully, glancing ahead for signs of light and life. But the sound stage was soundless, and the only light came from a distant corner, past the bedroom set where the fire had broken out.

It was here that he saw the bathroom and shower stall of Number Six in the Bates Motel.

He'd never been there himself, of course; the place had burned down years before Norman became his patient. But it was plainly recognizable from Norman's description. Correction—*vividly* recognizable, with its tiled walls, porcelain fixtures, shiny faucets, and heavy shower curtain.

The scene of the crime.

For a moment he found himself visualizing that

scene: the walls spattered with crimson, the water gushing forth to churn in a pink froth over the naked figure lying sprawled and slashed at the base of the stall. And the other figure standing over it—

But the bathroom was just a three-sided film set, and the figure standing there was Roy Ames.

Ames turned. "What are you doing here?"

"Looking for you," Claiborne said. "I called last night. Where were you?"

"Here."

The writer nodded. "That's right. I always figured security was a farce, but I wanted to prove it. Anybody could climb over the walls. Maybe the fog helped me get away with it, but now I know how easily it can be done. Thank God, Jan canceled rehearsal today."

"Canceled?"

"I talked to her this morning. She's still too shook up after last night."

There was no hint of accusation in Ames's voice, but Claiborne found himself avoiding his gaze. *He really does love her,* he told himself. *Damn it, why do I keep blundering into other people's lives?*

He glanced up defensively. "We had an argument," he said. "But I don't think I upset her that much—"

"You didn't." Ames told him about the kitten, and Claiborne listened, his eyes narrowing. *Cutting the kitten's throat.* Suddenly he remembered Vizzini and the knives. *But why—?*

"Now do you see why she's so uptight?" Ames said.

"Yes."

"What do you think?"

"Let me work it out."

"Is that all you've got to say?"

"No." Claiborne shook his head. "Now it's your turn to listen."

"Keep talking."

"I made some calls this noon. First I phoned the security office here, trying to get hold of the man in charge."

"You're talking about Talbot."

"Right. He wasn't in, but they gave me his home number and I called him there."

"Any particular reason?"

"I asked about his meeting with Driscoll yesterday, after the fire, and the fingerprints he found on the gasoline can."

"Did you learn anything new?"

"Several things." Claiborne nodded, stony-faced. "Talbot didn't examine that can. He never even came to the studio. He's been in Vegas since Thursday, just got back this morning."

"Then what about the set dresser?"

"Lloyd Parsons?" Claiborne spoke slowly. "There's nobody by that name working here at the studio. As far as Talbot knows, there never has been."

"So Driscoll did lie." Ames frowned. "You think he's covering for Vizzini?"

"Perhaps." Something was forming now, the pieces were coming together.

"But it sounds crazy—"

"So does that business with the kitten," Claiborne said. "Maybe it ties in. The blonde girl, a kitten with yellow fur. It could be Jan's surrogate. That man in

280

the fog—suppose he came after Jan, but Connie's arrival scared him off. So he killed the kitten instead."

"Why?"

"Think for a moment." Claiborne's voice deepened. "The synonym for kitten is *pussy*. That's why it was killed, because that's what the killer really wanted to do. He stabbed her pussy."

"Jesus! You really believe Vizzini would do a thing like that?"

"I don't know." Claiborne shrugged. "But Norman would."

"What are you going to do?"

"The first thing is to talk to Driscoll. Do you have his home phone number?"

"Yes, in my office."

"Then we'll call from there. This time he can't wiggle out of it. Either he stops the picture or we go to the police."

In the shadows beyond the set, a figure stirred.

Thirty

Police.

Santo Vizzini felt the anger rise within him. It filled his throat, he could taste it on his tongue as he swallowed hard, knowing he must keep silent. Silence had saved him when he came onto the stage and heard the voices, and it would save him now.

He melted back into the darkness behind the side wall of the set as Ames and Claiborne stepped out, moving to the opening at the far end and out onto the studio street beyond.

Then he started after them, halting inside the open doorway to watch as they walked toward the Administration Building. When they disappeared inside, he was free to follow.

The street was empty, and as he entered the

building he found the halls deserted. That was good, and now fortune favored him further. The door of Ames's cubicle was open at the end of the hall, and the office next to it was unlocked.

Vizzini pushed the door open quietly, then positioned himself next to the wall.

Ames was already making the call; his muffled voice sounded at intervals. "No, not on the phone. Look, I'm not going to argue. If you don't want to hear it, we'll do our talking to the police."

That word again. The anger was strong and bitter now.

"You're damned right I'm serious! It's up to you— we're giving you one last chance."

Anger had a scent, too; no perfume was powerful enough to disguise it.

"What time? You sure you can't make it earlier? Okay, we'll be there."

Ames hung up, and in a moment Claiborne's voice sounded through the wall.

"What did he say?"

"He's taking a meeting in an hour—Ruben, Barney Weingarten, some of the people from the New York office. He'll see us tonight at eight."

"You're sure he'll keep the appointment?"

"He'd better. I think I scared him enough so there'll be no tricks."

"All right. I've got a date to have dinner with the fellow who runs the motel where I'm staying. If you'll give me the address and directions, I'll meet you there."

Vizzini huddled behind the doorway as the two

men came out of the office. They were still talking as they walked down the hall.

"That's easy. He's just up the hill on the other side of Ventura. You can take Vineland, then—"

Then they were gone, but the echoes lingered.

Meeting. Eight o'clock. No tricks.

Vizzini's jaw muscles tightened. There's been too many tricks already. Jan, canceling rehearsal. Now the business with Driscoll. This time they'd do it, cancel the picture, cheat him out of everything. He couldn't stop them, too late for that, he was powerless, impotent.

Impotent.

But not with Jan.

Not if he could come up with a trick of his own.

Thirty-one

"It's getting foggy again." Connie turned away from the window. "Are you sure you'll be all right?"

"Stop worrying." Jan picked up her leatherette-bound copy of the script from the table. "I told you what Vizzini said. Paul Morgan's rehearsing with me. And they've tightened security."

"I don't understand you." Connie shook her head. "All afternoon you keep saying you're through, no more taking chances, it isn't worth it. But the minute he calls, you start peeing all over yourself, can't wait to rush down there. Couldn't you at least have told him to hold it until tomorrow morning?"

"We'll be rehearsing then too." Jan reached for her purse and started toward the door. "Don't you see? This means the picture's going ahead on schedule."

Connie opened the door for her, then peered out into the gathering fog. "Come on, I'll walk you to the car."

"But it's right here—" Jan broke off, smiling. "Thanks, hon, I appreciate it."

"Don't mind me." Connie watched Jan slide behind the wheel and switch on the ignition, and raised her voice over its roar. "Just promise you'll be careful."

"You too."

Connie nodded. "Don't worry, I'm staying put with the doors locked until you get back. And if anything happens—"

"Nothing's going to happen." Jan released the brake and backed the car down the driveway. She waved as Connie went inside and closed the door. Then she shifted into low and started down the hill.

The fog was thickening, but Jan drove cautiously and there was no traffic to impede her progress. Most of the hillside residents seemed to be staying home tonight; families entertaining company, kids staying up to watch television. Passing an open garage, she glanced into the lighted interior and saw a potbellied man in a T-shirt, slicing up chunks of firewood with a power saw; a can of beer rested on the bench beside him, and a Rorschach-spotted Dalmatian sat watching as he worked. From behind a window next door came the blare of stereo; somewhat to her surprise, she recognized the final bars of a Strauss tone-poem, *Tod und Verklarung*.

I don't understand you, Connie had said.

What was there to understand? Of course she'd been frightened—who wouldn't be, with some nut running around killing kittens? But that was last night and nothing had happened since, no sign of anything wrong. Things like that went on all the time nowadays, no shortage of sickies around, and yes, you did need to be careful. Only you had to draw the line between caution and overreaction; you couldn't live your life behind locked doors.

That was what Connie and Roy and Adam Claiborne didn't seem to understand. She wasn't going to end up behind one of those locked doors in Saturday-night suburbia. A young matron doing the nervous-hostess routine for the new neighbors from across the street; a harassed housewife warning the kids that the set had to go off promptly at nine-thirty—*don't forget you're going to Sunday school tomorrow morning;* a middle-aged woman darning socks while her old man puttered around the garage with his power tools; a gray-haired widow sitting alone and listening to the stereo. *Tod und Verklarung.* That was no way to spend your life, waiting for death and transfiguration.

There were other roles to play, and she meant to play them. It was just a question of getting her act together, and that's what she was doing now. *Be a foxy lady.*

Vizzini might be a horny bastard, but he wasn't a fool; now that the film was going ahead, he'd changed his tune. He had too much riding on this picture himself, and he wouldn't louse up his chances just to make a pass at her. Calling a rehearsal with Morgan proved he meant business.

And he hadn't lied about security. When Jan drove up to the studio entrance, she saw not one but two men on the gate. The younger guard checked her sticker carefully before lifting the crossbar and waving her forward. As she parked and walked down the street toward Stage Seven, she passed Chuck Grossinger making his rounds, and noted that he carried a revolver in his shoulder holster.

It gave her a comforting feeling; there wasn't going to be any trouble now. Not tonight, or ever. Let the good times roll—she was up on her lines, ready for what was to come.

Through the fog, she saw that the big sliding doors of the sound stage were closed. In the smaller side doorway ahead, Santo Vizzini stood smiling at her. As she approached, he glanced at his watch.

"Right on time," he said. "It is a good omen, don't you agree?"

Jan nodded. She intended to be agreeable, but she'd be careful too. Careful and in control. No sense acting like a scared kitten—

Forget the kitten, she told herself. *That's all over with now.*

Vizzini stepped aside and waved her onto the stage.

Then he closed the door.

Thirty-two

Claiborne sat in the car, waiting.

Here on the hilltop, the fog was a solid mass. As he stared out across the semicircular driveway, he could scarcely distinguish the outlines of the sprawling structure beyond its borders.

He glanced at his watch. *Five after eight*. Where was Roy Ames?

Claiborne rolled the window down, listening for the sound of a car approaching, but nothing stirred in the silent street below. After a moment he found himself shivering and he reached out to roll the window back up again.

The thin glass pane provided a barrier against dampness and darkness, but it couldn't shut out the thought of what the fog might hold. And the thought was colder than fog, darker than night. The thought of Norman prowling, Norman with a knife. He could sense his presence, feel him out there, waiting.

Don't let your imagination run away with you.

Good advice, but what did it mean? What is imagination, and just how does one distinguish it from thought? And isn't it just as valid an approach to reality as sensing or feeling? *You're the authority, let's have some answers.*

But he had no answers. After all these years he couldn't even define his terms, distinguish between allusion, illusion, and delusion.

Cogito, ergo sum. I think, therefore I am—*what?* A rational being? But man isn't rational; that much his experience had taught him. Man lives by instinct and intuition, and he was no exception. All that his training had done was to give him an esoteric vocabulary. He couldn't heal himself because he didn't know himself. Consciousness is all one possesses, and it's a fleeting phenomenon; we lose it in sleep, alter it with narcotics, distort it through emotional reaction, surrender it completely when stronger forces within ourselves take over. Consciousness is like a pane of window glass—a flimsy protection erected against the fog beyond. But the fog is there always, there and waiting.

Forget theory, forget logic. Try to see what's hidden in the fog. Claiborne sighed, visualizing last night's murky mist and the figures it concealed. The kitten cowering under the trees, the man with the knife. Norman, thwarted in his attempt to reach Jan, thrusting his weapon into the kitten instead. And why not? *All cats are gray in the dark*—

Something thudded against the windowpane. He

turned, peering through the glass as a hand drew back to reveal the face behind it.

"Hey, wake up!" said Roy Ames.

Claiborne opened the door and slid out. "I wasn't asleep," he said. And at the same time he told himself this proved his point. How easy it was to lose awareness; Ames had driven up and he hadn't heard him coming. Anyone could have sneaked up on him in the fog, even Norman—

He erased the thought, eyeing his watch. "Eight-ten," he murmured. "You're late."

"Sorry about that," Ames said.

The night air was clammy; Claiborne turned away and started up the walk to the front door. "Doesn't matter. Let's get inside—the least he can do is offer us a drink."

Ames followed, coming up beside him as he pressed the buzzer and listened to the silvery sound of door chimes echoing from within.

For a moment they stood in the shadows of the darkened stoop. Again, Ames thumbed the buzzer. The chimes echoed obediently, but there was no other response.

"What is this?" Ames muttered. "You think he stood us up?"

"I doubt it." Claiborne glanced toward the slatted blinds that covered a side window. "There's a light inside."

Ames balled his fist and thumped on the door. It moved under the impact, opening inward.

"Unlocked," he said. "Come on."

Beyond the door, a spacious two-story entryway faced a white-railed staircase that curved upward against the far wall. Entrances on both sides of the hall blazed with light from rooms beyond.

Roy Ames cupped his hands against his mouth. "Anybody home?"

No reply. But the silence wasn't total; from the right-hand doorway came a murmur of music.

"Doesn't hear us," Claiborne said. "Probably watching television."

The two men moved to the opening, descending the carpeted steps in the den beyond. But the den had no denizen; on the wall screen, figures flickered and sound surged forth as a symphony orchestra began the final movement of *The Pines of Rome*.

"Somebody was here." Claiborne nodded at the chairs grouped around the coffee table in the center of the room, and the clutter of glasses and ashtrays atop it.

"Well, they're gone now." Ames glanced past the fog-blurred glass doors and toward a small doorway on the far side of the room. "Maybe he's in the john—"

But when they crossed over to enter the hall beyond, the bathroom at the left was open and unoccupied. So was the big bedroom opposite it.

Ames peered inside, inspecting the gaudy decor. "How about those mirrors? Place looks like a funhouse."

Claiborne nodded. Maybe it was a funhouse, but the music rising from the den was inappropriate for such a setting. The ghosts of Roman legions advanced along the Appian Way, their tread a distant thunder in the night.

He was ready to turn back, but Ames started down the hall in the other direction, attracted by a lance of

294

light issuing from the room at the far end. He halted as Claiborne moved up beside him, and together they stared into the kitchen beyond.

Like the other rooms, it was oversized and overly ornate. The caprice of some decorator had dictated the use of an oaken motif from flooring to overhead beams. Wall stove, cupboards, cabinets, enclosed sink, and built-in refrigerator and freezer were encased in dark oak paneling, which absorbed the dim illumination from overhead. In sharp contrast, the array of knives and cutlery hanging from the long rack at the center of the room radiated a dazzling intensity of light.

Blinking at the glittering blades, Claiborne was reminded of the weaponry in the studio prop department. But these knives weren't props, and neither was the massive solid oak block beneath them.

It was an old-fashioned butcher's block, big enough to support a quarter of beef, and the cleaver imbedded upright at the far edge seemed more than adequate to do the job. But the job had already been done.

The round blob of bloody meat resting on the butcher's block was the head of Marty Driscoll.

Thirty-three

Santo Vizzini walked Jan to the camper at the far end of the stage, just outside the bath-and-shower-stall set. He mounted the step and opened the door, disclosing the lighted interior.

"Your dressing room," he said.

Jan peered inside, her face brightening at the sight of the full-size theatrical mirror, the vanity, the couch and armchair, the carpet on the floor.

"Neat."

Vizzini nodded. It had been wise to provide her with these niceties, let her know she was getting the full treatment.

Jan's smile faded. "Where's Morgan?"

"Paul should be here any moment now. Why don't

you step inside and make yourself comfortable? I'll go see if he's arrived."

Jan moved past him into the camper, carrying her purse and leatherette-bound script. As she entered, she saw the three red roses rising from a bud vase atop the vanity.

"Flowers!"

"You like them?" Vizzini shrugged. "A star should always have fresh flowers in her dressing room."

He moved off, not waiting for a reply, knowing she'd closed the door, and started across the shadowed stage.

Everything was working out. There would be no picture now, but it no longer mattered. What mattered was to make the dream come true. Wasn't that what a director did? Turn fantasy into reality with a wave of his magic wand? Up to now it had only happened on the screen, because the wand held no magic for him. Not until she came—the sorceress. Silly, stupid sorceress with the face of a dead girl and the body of a live woman. Not Mary Crane, not Mama, not anyone he'd ever known, except in dreams when the power entered his wand and he entered the sorceress. And always the awakening, before it happened.

But it was going to happen now. He thought of how Jan stood there in the doorway of the dressing room, the light outlining the cradle-curve of her hips beneath the sheer skirt. The skirt would go up, the wand would go up, it was going up now, *Mama mia*—

He opened the side door, staring into the fog, making sure the guard was gone, just as he'd arranged. *We will be rehearsing—I would appreciate it if we are not disturbed.* Nobody suspected, nobody would suspect, not even Mama.

Santo is always a good boy, she said. She was saying it now, he could hear her, he could see her face there in the swirling fog, so he shut the door. Shut her out, shut them all out, they mustn't see him now, mustn't see his wand. The wand of power.

Power. Power from the pills, they did it—made you hear things, see things that weren't there. But the power was real.

He'd started again this afternoon—the amytal—and now he couldn't remember how many he'd taken. He could remember very little except the plan. Calling Jan.

Then everything speeded up, like the camera undercranking, and he was here. Now normal speed again, twenty-four frames per second. So she didn't notice anything wrong, he'd played the scene perfectly. Actor, director, producer, completely in control.

But there were too many pills in the camera. That was why he'd seen Mama's face, heard her voice in the fog. Trick photography, special effects.

Next scene. Santo Vizzini turns, walks back through the darkened sound stage. Walks. Glides. Floats.

Camera out of control again. First too fast. Now too slow. Slow motion. *Everything. In. Slow. Motion.*

Change lenses. New focus. Distortion. Walls bend, catwalk swinging down, *look out!* Crazy camera. Crazy pills. *Mama mia, not me, I'm not crazy.*

No, he wasn't crazy, because he had the power. The secret power stirring in his loins. *The wand of power, the secret weapon, stabbing into the warm, yielding flesh—*

Ready now, Santo Vizzini moved up to the dressing-room door.

Thirty-four

Roy Ames watched as Claiborne knelt beside the corpse on the floor behind the butcher's block.

It had all happened so quickly—first the glimpse of the severed head and the bulging eyes, then the sight of the decapitated body. Claiborne was a doctor, he'd seen death before, and he conducted his examination with professional detachment. This, Roy could understand, but not his own reaction. Instead of fear and revulsion, there was only a numbness. Even his voice was unnaturally calm.

"There's not much blood," he said.

Claiborne looked up, nodding. "No signs of bodily incision." Rising, he bent over the block. As he reached down, Roy turned away, but listened intently.

"Massive occipital and parietal lesions," Claiborne said. "He must have been struck from behind with the flat of the cleaver. Dead before he hit the floor. Then the head could be detached with a minimum of arterial or venous exudation—"

Roy understood what he was saying. Once the heart stops pumping, blood won't spurt from a wound. He'd researched when he wrote the script, because it was a story point. That was why nobody suspected Norman; without bloodstains on his clothing, he didn't even suspect himself. Blood on his hands, of course, but that could come just from touching the body. And it was easily washed away.

On impulse he found himself moving to the sink, staring down at the white porcelain basin. Only it wasn't white, it was pinkish, and the wet rills fringing the drain were dark and red. *Blood will tell—*

"What's wrong?"

Claiborne was standing beside him. Roy pointed at the drain. Claiborne nodded; he understood. *Norman was alive, he'd killed Driscoll here, and now—*

Now Roy found his voice. "The reason I was late, I tried reaching Jan at the apartment before I came here. Connie told me she'd just left to rehearse with Vizzini."

"At the studio?" Claiborne's fingers dug into Roy's arm. "How long ago?"

"Half an hour. She'd be there by now. Do you think Norman would—"

"Why didn't you tell me before?" Claiborne's hand fell away and he turned, striding across the room. "Call the police, get them over here. And call the studio—ask security to contact Jan and Vizzini. I'll be there in five minutes."

"Wait—"

But by the time Roy got back down the hall, the front door had slammed and he could hear the motor throbbing from the driveway outside the house, over the symphonic sound of the orchestral broadcast.

Switching off the television, he glanced around and located the telephone on a desk in the corner beside the doorway. He hastened toward it. Then, just as his hand moved out, the phone rang.

Roy lifted the receiver.

"Hello." A man's voice, muffled by the hum of a poor connection. "Mr. Driscoll?"

"No." Roy spoke quickly. "Get off the line. Emergency—I've got to call the police—"

"This is the police."

"What?"

"Milt Engstrom, county sheriff here in Fairvale. Who'm I talking to?"

Roy identified himself. Then, "Please, I told you it's an emergency. Mr. Driscoll has been killed—"

"Homicide? How'd it happen?"

"I can't talk now—"

"Then maybe you better listen." Sheriff Engstrom didn't wait for a reply. "I've been trying to get hold of Claiborne all evening. Dr. Steiner gave me Driscoll's number, figuring maybe I could reach him here. But you can give him the message. Tell him we've got Bo Keeler."

"Who?"

"Bo Keeler. He's the hitchhiker the nun picked up in her van last Sunday. According to his story, she attacked him with a tire iron. There was a struggle, he got it away from the nun and killed her in self-defense. Then he set fire to the van and made a run for it. Hid out in a friend's house until he couldn't stand it—came in last night and made a voluntary confession. Idea of killing a nun kept eating on him. Only it wasn't a nun."

"I don't understand."

"Neither did we, until this afternoon. Coroner identified the body from dental records. You tell Claiborne he was wrong. It wasn't the hitchhiker and it wasn't the nun. It was Norman Bates."

Roy felt the phone slipping through his fingers. Everything was slipping away now. *If Norman is dead, then Vizzini must have killed Driscoll.*

And he was with Jan—*now.*

Thirty-five

Jan closed the script as Vizzini opened the door.

"Ready," he said.

She rose. "Is Paul here?"

"He's on the way. We can get started without him." The director moved up from the single step and into the camper. "I'll play Norman."

Jan held the script out, but Vizzini shook his head. "Not necessary. He has no lines in the shower scene. Neither do you."

"We're doing the shower scene first?"

"Of course. It is the key to everything, don't you agree? We will block out the action together."

"What about cues?"

"I will tell you what I want. It is all very clear." He smiled. "But first you must strip."

"Now wait a minute—"

"Please. It is important to visualize your movements the way they will appear on camera." Vizzini was still smiling as he closed the door behind him.

Jan shook her head. "Forget it. I'm not taking my clothes off."

"No false modesty." The smile was frozen. "I have seen naked women before. And this is not the first time you have undressed at a man's request."

"What's that got to do with it?"

"Everything." The frozen smile was mirthless, and as Vizzini moved into the light, she saw the tiny pinpoint pupils of his eyes. Little cat-eyes, like the kitten's.

He started toward her and she could smell the reek of his perfume, mingled with another odor, sickly sweet. *He's on something. I should have known.*

"You are a woman," he said. "I am a man. It is only natural—"

For a moment she wanted to laugh. A voice inside echoed a mocking question— *Who writes your dialogue?*

But he was reaching out, pressing her against the vanity, arms encircling her as slit-eyes stared, mouth opening to slash away the smile, breath-stench flooding forth. Jan turned her head to avoid his lips, then realized that wasn't his intention. The hands against her back were clawing at the folds of the blouse.

She felt the cloth shred, felt his fingers fumbling the clasp of her bra, tugging it open so that the bra fell.

Jan screamed and jabbed at his eyes with her nails;

306

averting his head, he caught her wrist, twisting it as he pulled her toward him.

Suddenly he released his grip and her arm dropped, numb. She tried to move back then, but his right hand slapped her face and his left rose to grasp the front of her blouse and tear it away, feeling her bared breasts. Dazed, Jan watched his fingers splaying toward her nipples.

As he cupped and squeezed her breasts, his head dipped down and forward and she reached behind herself, her fingers sliding across the vanity top until they encountered the crystal stem of the bud vase. She gripped it tightly, raised it high, and smashed the vase against the side of Vizzini's head.

Roses fell in a red shower, and a red bloom blossomed below his temple. He cried out, lurching back.

Jan ran past him to the door, and tugged at the knob. The door swung open and she hurtled out—then down. She'd forgotten the single step, but it was too late to think of that now; all thought was submerged in the torrent of pain racing from her right foot up to her thigh.

Was her ankle broken or merely sprained? It didn't matter, she had to get up. Sobbing, Jan started to raise herself from the floor, then fell forward as Vizzini's knee smashed against the small of her back.

This time the pain was so excruciating that she almost fainted. Forcing her eyes open, she fought against the encroaching darkness, but she couldn't fight the encroachment of his hands. Strong hands, yanking her skirt away, ripping her panties down and off. And then, as she gasped and panted, Vizzini's fingers tightened in her hair, jerking her head back. She felt herself turning, sprawled face upward on the cold dampness of the concrete floor.

Jan stared up, fighting for breath as he bent over her. Blood streamed down his left cheek, but he was smiling again; his teeth were yellow and there were yellow highlights in the flecks of saliva at the corners of his twisted mouth.

"Get up!" he said.

"I can't—my ankle—"

Still smiling, he slapped her again, then reached down and grasped her shoulders, pulling her erect. The pain pouring from her ankle made her moan, and the sound seemed to excite him as much as her nakedness.

"*Putana!*" His hand dug into the gooseflesh of her upper arm. "Walk—"

Jan tried to break free, but he captured her wrists, then shoved her forward. Wincing, she stumbled out of the dark and into the lighted area beyond. The light of the set—the bath and the shower. He was pulling her toward the curtained stall. Little drops of red fell from his bleeding face to mark their progress across the tile flooring.

"Inside," he said. "I want you inside."

"No," she whimpered. And realized she was doing just that—whimpering, like an animal. And now she knew what he wanted, what he'd intended all along. He was going to jump her there in the shower stall, take her like an animal, helpless and beaten—

Not helpless—

She sucked air into her lungs, strength into her arms, then twisted free. As her hands loosened, she

308

raised them swiftly, clubbing her fists together and smashing at his bloody temple.

Vizzini made a sound deep in his throat, then staggered back, clawing at the shower curtain behind him to keep from falling. Panting, he recovered his balance; for a moment he stood motionless as their eyes met.

Then, without warning, his hands darted forth.

Jan turned, but it was too late. Before she could move further, his nails bit into her shoulders.

And fell away.

She looked back, then halted. Vizzini still stood with his back to the shower, his face contorted in a grimace.

"Mama mia—"

His voice trailed off into a gurgle and he toppled forward to the floor, revealing the redness spurting and spreading from between his shoulder blades.

Then, as the shower curtain ripped back, Jan saw the occupant of the stall lunging forward, knife in hand.

The blade swooped out at her throat.

She had only time to scream before the shot echoed and the knife stabbed down to strike the floor, still clutched in the hand of Adam Claiborne.

Thirty-six

Dr. Steiner wasn't afraid.

There was nothing to fear, because Claiborne was harmless now. They'd dug the bullet out and the wrist was healing nicely, but he would never hold a knife in his right hand again.

For that matter, he might never leave this room. It had been a hassle—even without a trial, there were all those extradition hearings and court orders—but in the end, permission came through and Steiner brought him home.

Home. Steiner sighed, glancing around the room. Home was a cubicle with a few sticks of plastic furniture, a bed bolted to the floor, a lightbulb behind a mesh screen. Home was a barred window.

But at least the surroundings were familiar, if

Claiborne was aware of them. At times he seemed capable of awareness, and even though he never spoke, he appeared to recognize Steiner and welcome his presence.

Claiborne was smiling now, looking up from the bed as Steiner entered, but then he was always smiling. The smile was a barrier he'd erected to shut out the world and shut the secrets in.

Dr. Steiner nodded at him. "Hello, Adam," he said.

No answer—only the smile and the silence.

Steiner pulled a chair over beside the bed and seated himself, knowing even before he started that nothing would bring the barrier down. Still he had to try, he owed him that much.

"I think it's time we talked about what happened," he said.

Claiborne's expression didn't change, but his eyes seemed clear; perhaps he'd understand.

Then Steiner spoke, choosing his words carefully, remembering that the relationship had altered—no longer doctor-to-doctor, but doctor-to-patient. Even so, he did his best to tell the truth.

And the truth, as he saw it, was that after all these years together, Claiborne had come to identify himself unconsciously with Norman Bates. Both of them were motherless and alone, both confined, each in his own way, by institutional restraint.

Claiborne smiled.

"But there's more to it than identification," Steiner said. "After a time you began to feel that your fate, your future, was bound up in your patient—restoring his reason, writing a book about the case. Sanity would set him free, and the success of the book would give you the opportunity to get out of here on your own. And when Norman escaped, it meant you had failed, failed him and yourself. He was gone, leaving you a prisoner in his place.

"It must have started then, with the conviction that the only way you could escape now was to identify with Norman, share the triumph of his freedom. Yes, I know you went after him, but I think you were secretly hoping he'd get away for good. Then, when you found the body in the van and realized who it must be, hope vanished. You blacked out.

"Norman couldn't let his mother die, so he *became* her. You couldn't let Norman die, so you became him. And in the same way, during amnesic episodes when the alternate personality took over."

Claiborne stared at him with the smile of the Mona Lisa, the silence of the sphinx.

"That's what happened when you saw the body in the van. As Norman, you went on to Fairvale and killed the Loomises." Steiner paused. "When the coroner's verdict finally came in, they searched your car and found the stolen money from the cash register hidden under the floorboards. Do you remember putting it there?"

Claiborne was silent, his smile fixed.

"After hiding the money in your car down the street, you snapped out of fugue and returned to the store. Am I correct?"

No reply, only the set smile.

"The clipping you found prompted your trip to Hollywood. As Claiborne, you had rational reasons for trying to stop the film through argument and persuasion. But as Norman, you were ready to kill to stop it.

"Most of the time in Hollywood you maintained control—but Norman was there too. Reacting to Jan's resemblance to Mary Crane, seeing the sets that recreated the scene of the crime.

"I talked to the people out there—Roy Ames, Jan, and the girl who shared her apartment. Some of the things they told me helped in reconstructing what happened. The rest is guesswork. For example, that face you saw in the supermarket mirror. It could have been Vizzini, it could have been hallucination. You were losing control rapidly after that, and when you quarreled with Jan, it was Norman who came back to kill the kitten. Of course, that was only a prelude."

Claiborne's smile never wavered.

"Time was running out for Norman, and so was all semblance of rational behavior. He had to destroy the film project, even if it meant destroying everyone connected with it.

"You broke your dinner engagement with Tom Post because Norman took over. Norman went to Driscoll's house and murdered him. When Ames arrived, he found you there and waiting, but after you heard about Jan and Vizzini, it was Norman who rushed to the studio—not to warn them but to climb the wall, take a knife from the prop department, and hide, ready to attack. If Ames and the police hadn't arrived when they did—"

Steiner broke off, glancing at Claiborne, but there was no reaction, only the silence and the smile.

Sighing, he rose and moved to the door. "We'll talk again," he said.

Even as he spoke, he realized the futility of his promise. He'd failed Claiborne, failed to reach the violence within him, the violence guarded by silence and hidden behind a smile.

There were too many of those smiles surrounding him now—not just here in the asylum, but outside in the streets. Smiles that concealed but couldn't cure the secret sickness. Violence was a virus, a disease becoming epidemic everywhere in the world, and maybe there was no cure. All he could do was keep trying.

"See you later," he said.

Claiborne smiled.

Thirty-seven

Claiborne wasn't listening to Steiner.

And when Steiner left, he listened only to himself. To Adam Claiborne. Adam, the first man. Claiborne, born of clay. God created him.

God created all things, including Norman Bates; we are all God's children.

Am I my brother's keeper?

I was *his* keeper.

We are all brothers. God said that. God said many things that we must heed.

Vengeance is mine, saith the Lord. Claiborne may die, but Norman lives. God will protect him, for he is God's instrument against evil.

Norman Bates will never die . . .

SHOCKINGLY FRIGHTENING!

__AUDREY ROSE
by Frank DeFelitta   *(B36-380, $3.75)*
The Templetons have a near-perfect life and a lovely
daughter, until a stranger enters their lives and claims that
their daughter, Ivy, possesses the soul of his own daughter,
Audrey Rose, who had been killed at the exact moment
that Ivy was born. And suddenly their lives are shattered by
event after terrifying event.

__THE AMITYVILLE HORROR II
by John G. Jones   *(B30-029, $3.50)*
The terror continues... When the Lutz family left the house
in Amityville, New York, the terror did not end. Through the
next four years wherever they went, the inescapable Evil
followed them. Now the victims of the most publicized
house-haunting of the century have agreed to reveal the
harrowing details of their continuing ordeal.

__THE KEEPSAKE
by Paul Huson   *(B90-790, $2.95)*
It was only a souvenir of Ireland—a small stone that bore, if
you looked very closely, the suggestion of a human face.
She couldn't know that only the power of St. Patrick had
kept its evil in check through the centuries...that in her
own home, when the lights were out, it could become a
gateway for an unimaginable malevolence with a thirst for
blood and for her unborn child.

SURPRISE YOURSELF

__**THE IMAGE**
by Charlotte Paul   *(F95-145, $2.75)*
The gift of sight came to Karen Thorndyke as the bequest of
an unknown man. His camera, willed to the Eye Bank,
enabled the beautiful young artist to see and paint again.
But with that bit of transparent tissue came an insight into
horror. With her new view of life came a vision of death.

__**CRY FOR THE DEMON**
by Julia Grice   *(F95-497, $2.75)*
Where the lava flows and sharks hunt, Ann Southold has
found a retreat on the island of Maui. Here the painful
memory of her husband dims, her guilts and fears are
assuaged, and she meets a dark man who calls to her—a
man who wants her more than any man has ever wanted her
before. Out of the deep, a terror no woman can resist...
CRY FOR THE DEMON

__**VISIONS OF TERROR**
by William Katz   *(F91-347, $2.50)*
Broken glass, a car crash, an explosion...these are part of
Annie McKay's dream world. Ever since the illness that
almost blinded her, the seven-year-old has had nightmares
—and they all come true. So when Annie dreams of her
own murder, her mother is forced to take action—alone,
because not only does she know who the murderer is—but
she is beginning to understand the truth of her daughter's
VISIONS OF TERROR.